# LOVE'S GRIM JEST

Two men loomed larger than life in Nellie's consciousness.

One was Adam Truff, the man whom she desperately desired. She would do anything for him, offering him her body, her honor, her every possession. Yet this strong and handsome man only smiled at her pleas—and told her that he would never be hers.

The other was Thad Phenwick, heir to the family name and fortune, home after years of sailing the seas and experiencing all that the world had to teach a young man. He asked Nellie to be his wife, promised her all that she had ever dreamed of having—yet she shrank from final surrender to him.

In love with one man . . . loved by another . . . Nellie was a divided young woman, faced by a choice that could bring her long-sought happiness or long-dreaded damnation. . . .

#21
KATHERYN KIMBROUGH'S
Saga of the Phenwick Women
# NELLIE,
## THE OBVIOUS

POPULAR LIBRARY • NEW YORK

Published by Popular Library, a unit of CBS
Publications, the Consumer Publishing Division
of CBS Inc.

April, 1978

Copyright © 1978 by Kymko Associates

ISBN: 0-445-04202-8

*Dedicated To*
*Mildred and Joe Parnham*

# CAST OF CHARACTERS

JOHN COLLIER — A well-meaning, industrious man who has established his own furniture business. A loveable man.

KATE PHENWICK COLLIER — His lovely wife.

NELLIE COLLIER — His eldest child. As a young beauty she discovers her psychic ability.

Elizabeth Collier — His second daughter.

George Collier — His third child, eldest son.

Rupert Collier — His youngest child.

ADAM TRUFF — The dear and trusted friend of the Phenwick family.

DR. CHARLES MUMFORD — A young doctor of Greenfield, a member of an old family in the town, he is stalwart and conscientious.

Nana Carlyle — Housekeeper to the Colliers.

Alvin Paxton — Driver and general handyman for the Colliers.

Horace Boggs — Foreman at Collier furniture factory.

Kit Snyder — A well-seasoned seaman.

NANCY PHENWICK — The matriarch of the Phenwick family in Boston. A lovely lady who has raised four fine sons.

THADIUS PHENWICK — Her eldest son. An adventurer of sorts, Thad has returned to Boston to settle.

| | |
|---|---|
| JOHN PHENWICK | Her second son. He is an attorney. |
| PAUL PHENWICK | Her third son, recently departed for California. |
| DANIEL LOUIS PHENWICK | Her youngest son, with the makings of becoming a playboy. |
| SUSANNAH PHENWICK CORNHILL | A long-time concert pianist, Susannah thus far is the most professionally successful Phenwick woman. She is in her seventies. |
| STUART PHENWICK | The undisputed male head of the Phenwick family in Boston. |
| RUTH PHENWICK | His beautiful second wife. |
| DANNY PHENWICK | His son by his first wife, Marcia. |
| ANN MARIE PHENWICK | His daughter by Marcia. |
| Peter Polly Donald | The children of Stuart and Ruth. |
| MILLIJOY PHENWICK | Stuart's sister-in-law, widow of Gordon. She is the most extravagant, and perhaps the wealthiest, of all the Phenwick women. |
| TOMMY PHENWICK | Her son by Gordon. |
| Amos Carrier | Millijoy's butler. |
| LEON (LEO) PHENWICK | Previously known as Michael Black, during the time he had amnesia, Leo presently goes by his own name as eldest son of Joshua Phenwick of London. Leo is Stuart's first cousin. |
| ANN PHENWICK | Leo's charming and lovely wife. |

| | |
|---|---|
| Otis | Leo's stableman. |
| Eugene | Leo's clerk. |
| SAM DODSWORTH | A felon who is serving a prison term. |
| Clancy O'Malley Stanley Dubrowski | Workers at Collier furniture factory. |
| Toby, Mandy, Red | Dogs. |

## THE PHENWICKS

**\*AUGUSTA**

Founder of the family, married to Barrywell, then to Joshua Phenwick. The three children by Barrywell were murdered by their father; DANIEL CHARLES was the only son of her marriage to Joshua. She later adopted EDWARD and JANE MUNSK, whom she raised as PHENWICKS. Augusta maintains an eerie hold over the surviving members of her family.

**DANIEL**

Augusta's only son who lived to adulthood. Father of Elias (by Kate Mumford); married to \*Margaret O'Plaggerty; father of Alexander, Peter, and \*Rachel.

**Elias**

Married to \*Patricia Kelburn; father of \*Rebecca.

**\*Rebecca**

First married to Johnny Ornby; second marriage to Robert Cathcart; mother of Kate Phenwick.

**\*Kate**

Married to John Collier. Mother of \*Nellie, Elizabeth, George, and Rupert.

**\*Nellie**

Married to Thadius Phenwick.

**Alexander**

Married to \*Susannah Phenwick; adopted two children: Marcia and Gregory Wing.

**\*Marcia**

Married to Stuart Phenwick; mother of Daniel Charles II, and Ann Marie.

**Gregory**

Married to \*Ilene Dumphy. Father of \*Isabelle and Elena (twins), Alexandria, and Albert.

**Peter**

First married to Helen Barnfather; father of Augustus, Joanne, Prentise, and Joshua. Second marriage to \*Nancy Cox; father of Thadius, John, Paul, and Daniel Louis.

\*Denotes Phenwick women about whom books were written.

AUGUSTA (con't)
DANIEL (con't)
Peter (con't)

| | |
|---|---|
| **Augustus** | Married to Lillian Webb; father of Stuart and Gordon. |
| **Stuart** | Married to *Marcia Phenwick; father of Daniel Charles II, and Ann Marie. Second wife, *Ruth; children: Peter, Polly, Donald. |
| **Gordon** | The strange dual-natured son. Briefly married to *Millijoy Gray, father of Thomas. |
| ***Joanne** | Only daughter of Peter. Unmarried actress. |
| **Prentise** | Married to *Harriet Pettijohn; father of James, Frances, Louis, Martha, Patrick, Sam, and Tom. |
| **Joshua** | Married to *Olivia Pritchard; head of Medallion Enterprises in London; father of *Ophelia, Arnold (Leo), Ruth, Carrie, Elizabeth, and David. |
| **Thadius** | Eldest son of Peter and Nancy. Married to *Nellie Collier. |
| **John** | The lawyer son. |
| **Paul** | Married Lottie Wells. Father of John Adam. |
| **Daniel Louis** | Youngest son of Peter and Nancy. |
| ***Rachel** | Daniel's only daughter. Died in her teens. |
| **EDWARD (Munsk)** | Adopted son of Augusta; married to *Patricia Kelburn; father of David and *Susannah. (Actual son of John and Lydia Munsk.) |
| **David** | Edward's only son, killed War of 1812. |
| ***Susannah** | Edward's daughter; married to Alexander (Lex) Phenwick; foster mother of *Marcia and Gregory. (See under Peter's children.) |

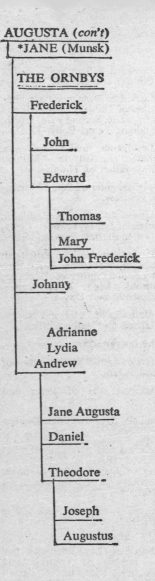

# AUGUSTA (con't)

**\*JANE (Munsk)** — Adopted daughter of Augusta; married to Jeffrey Ornby; sons: Frederick, Johnny, and Andrew (Actual daughter of John and Lydia Munsk.)

## THE ORNBYS

**Frederick** — Jane's eldest son; married to Henrietta Ellsworth; sons: John and Edward.

**John** — Married Dorothy Wren; children: Millicent, Crandall, and Virginia.

**Edward** — Married Sarah Hadley; children: Thomas, Mary, and John Frederick.

**Thomas** — Married Zelda Casey. No children.

**Mary** — Died in teens.

**John Frederick** — Married Sally Battell; children: \*Ann Rose and Frederick.

**Johnny** — Father of Adrianne and Lydia by his first wife; second marriage to \*Rebecca Phenwick. No children.

**Adrianne** — Murdered in England.

**Lydia** — Unmarried.

**Andrew** — Married to Livinia Hendricks; father of Jane Augusta, Daniel, Theodore, Angela, Bertha, and Jeffrey.

**Jane Augusta** — Married to Eustace Clark, no children.

**Daniel** — An attorney. Wife: Mellissa Kesler; children: James, Henry, Thomas, and Sarah.

**Theodore** — (Dr. Ted.) Wife: Louise Lacy; children: Joseph, Augustus, Collin, Mary Rose, and Ruth.

**Joseph** — A physician. Wife: Sheila Dumphy.

**Augustus** — A physician. Wife: Nell Willet; children: Charles and \*Louise.

# Prologue

Obvious! Some things are obvious from the start. Or, if you think in terms of the continuity of the individual spirit, some things are obvious long before the start of a particular lifetime on earth.

At any rate, what I started to say is that it was obvious that Nellie Collier was destined to become a Phenwick woman. On the day she was born, I found myself hovering at Phenwick House in Greenfield, Maine. Periodically through her early childhood, I would return to witness her progress. And the more I saw of little Nellie, the more obvious became her destiny.

I have found over the countless years that most of those women chosen to follow in my lineage and become heiress to the title of Phenwick woman have had unusual encounters, devastating experiences which, in the long run, have strengthened them and have made them more universally aware of their heritage. Life in physical form is a learning place, a school, as it were, where certain lessons must be dealt with and learned.

During the reconstruction period after the Civil War, the cities of the United States began an expanding growth. More and more immigrants were coming to the country's shores, and towns once small were developing into cities. Even the little community of Greenfield was enlarging, the population growing.

Yet a strange consciousness was beginning to creep through the villages, the towns, the cities. A negative vibration of low frequency pulsated throughout the districts as greed and the results of greed became increasingly apparent. When such conditions move through a group consciousness, negative effects begin manifesting in a variety of different ways. Predominant among such adverse conditions is disease, of both the body and the mind.

Epidemics have been known from the sunrise of man. They are a natural result of the perverse consciousness that is prevailing at the time. When such mass destroyers of physical man take their toll, it is not without reason. And I suspect it is part of an overall plan in which the balance of nature is kept.

I mention this only because it seemed that the early years of Nellie Collier, eldest daughter of John and Kate Phenwick Collier, were torn by the whims of Providence.

I could see what was coming. The best I could do was to stand by and give Nellie whatever assistance I could from this side, for I was determined that she would become a triumphant Phenwick woman. It is so difficult at times to observe, yet to be so physically helpless.

# PART I

# Chapter One

Obviously the child was having a nightmare.

"Moth-er!" Nellie shrieked as she tossed restlessly in her bed in the second floor bedroom of Phenwick House. "Moth-er!" Beads of perspiration matted strands of fine golden hair to her forehead. She sat up. Her twelve-year-old body was still that of a child. Lavender-blue eyes stared with terror as they tried to penetrate the blackened room. No moon. Clouds. Thin frost on the window panes. "Moth-er!"

Soft and lovely, even in a drowsy awakening state, Kate Phenwick Collier lifted her head from the goose-down pillow. Had she heard a sound that had aroused her? She listened to the thick stillness of the early morning air. Closed windows shut out the rustlings of nature and the creatures that prowled in the night. A faint draft of wind played on the sill of a window that was not tightly closed. In the far distance the ever-present drone of the tide filtered into her consciousness. The gentle purring of her husband's heavy sleep-breathing assured her that she was not alone.

"Moth-er!"

Quickly Kate put her feet to the floor and eased them into a pair of waiting slippers. One of her children was calling. At that distance, she was not quite certain which it was. The two youngest children, George and Rupert,

15

shared a room at the rear of the house. If one awakened, usually the other did too, within a few minutes. Nellie, the eldest, and Elizabeth, the second child, each had her own room. Elizabeth was a sound sleeper and rarely complained of disturbed sleep. Nellie, on the other hand, was different. She possessed an active, creative imagination and a precognitive sense that was sometimes uncanny, particularly when she made prophetic statements that actually came true.

Deductively, Kate decided she must first go to Nellie. She did not bother with a robe, nor did she take time to light a candle. However, by the time she reached the door, a match was struck at the bed and she turned back to see John putting it to a candle.

"What is it, Katie?" her husband asked, sitting up in bed.

"One of the children is calling me."

"Only a bad dream, I suspect."

"Still, bad dreams need comforting, my darling," Kate replied, and slipped from the room.

John Collier's love for Kate had grown over the years, although at the time of their marriage he had believed it was impossible for him to love her any more than he did at that moment. She was everything to him, his motive, his incentive, almost the complete driving force of his existence. And he had a deep, encompassing love for their children. If he showed a partiality to Nellie, he reasoned it was simply because she was the eldest, the first-born, and he had known her longer. His devotion to Elizabeth was second only to Nell, and he was equally proud of George and Rupert—but they were still little boys and full of whatever that thing is that makes a difference between boys and girls.

"Oh, Mother! Mother!" Nellie sobbed, as Kate entered her room.

"What is it, darling?" The mother went to the bed, sat and embraced the child. "A bad dream?"

"It was terrible, Mother! Absolutely terrible!"

"Can you tell me about it? Cousin Joseph says that it's best to talk out bad dreams, to get them out into the open so that you can examine them for what they are," Kate stated as she held her face to her daughter's cheek.

Nellie tried to see her mother's features in the darkness. Only the faint candle glow came from across the hall. "I can't tell you about it, Mother. I simply can't."

"Was it all bad?" Kate questioned as she caressed the child.

"Mostly all of it," Nellie replied. She stifled a sob. "Yet, toward the end of it, I had a strange awareness that I was walking down by the seashore and I encountered a beautiful lady. She just seemed to float out of the ocean and came toward me. I recall a very pretty smile. Then she handed me some flowers, all done up in a little bouquet."

"Flowers?"

"I believe they were violets. No, I'm certain they were violets," Nellie said. "Then she pointed to the cemetery."

"Augusta," Kate whispered. "Violets."

"Then she pointed me toward the cemetery," Nellie continued. "I didn't want to go, but before I knew it, I was there. I tried to run away, but I couldn't. Oh, Mother, hold me, hold me!"

John Collier arrived at Nellie's room, candle in hand. He held it high. "Is my little Nell all right?"

"Oh, Daddy! Daddy!" Nellie released her hold on Kate and held her arms toward her father.

Kate smoothed the child's brow and pushed hair back from her face. Then she rose, kissed Nellie tenderly, and made room for John to take her place.

"Another bad dream, my precious?" John asked.

Kate sneezed.

"You'd better go back to bed, Katie," her husband suggested. "There's no need of you catching a chill. I'll tend to Nellie."

"Yes, John." Obediently Kate scuffed back to her own bed. She knew that John had a remarkable rapport with his eldest daughter.

For several minutes Nellie allowed herself to be tightly held in her father's embrace until the thumps of their hearts seemed to be beating in unison.

"Will you tell me about your dream, sweet Nell?"

"It was obviously a nightmare, Daddy. I don't recall all of it, not the details. I just know the horrible feeling I had as it was happening. Then, after I was at the seashore and met the lady who gave me the violets, I found myself in the cemetery—the one just the other side of the drive from the house. I saw four gravestones that seemed to have a dim gray light around them. I didn't want to look at the names, but I couldn't help myself."

"What were the names?"

"My mother's, my sister's, and both of my brothers'." Nellie whimpered as she spoke.

"I don't believe that means they are going to die right away," John said comfortingly. "I think there must be some kind of symbolism in what you dreamed. Perhaps you had an argument with your brothers or your sister, and Mother intervened. You must have thought you were in the right and that you were unjustly punished. That sort of thing will cause that kind of dream."

"I haven't had an argument with anyone. I love Elizabeth, George, and Rupert—and certainly I love my mother as deeply as anyone can love anyone," Nellie protested. "I'm frightened, Daddy. I know there is some kind of mysterious meaning to that dream."

John held her tightly again, his head pressed firmly against hers. "You must try to go back to sleep, Nellie. It's only three-thirty in the morning. There's school tomorrow, and you'll find yourself falling asleep at your desk." He kissed her forehead.

"Don't leave me yet, Daddy, please," Nellie coaxed. "Hold me and talk a little longer."

"Talk? About what? Your dream?"

"No." Nellie kissed him. "Tell me about you and your work."

"You know all about me, my little one," John commented. "And you know the furniture factory is coming along nicely. I hired three more men on Monday and I've got enough orders ahead to keep everyone busy for at least the rest of this year."

"Three new men?"

"Two of them are Polish immigrants who happened to come out this way from Portland," John said. "Frankly, I suspect that they applied for work with Crandall Ornby at Medallion and he sent them out. They speak very broken English, but they're good carpenters—I should say craftsmen. The third is a relative of the Mumfords. He's not the worker the other two are, but he puts forth a passable effort."

Nellie had taken an active interest in her father's business from the time she was eight years old. Mature for her age, she gave the impression of being a little adult instead the child she actually was. "One day, I believe you will be selling furniture in other places than Greenfield and Portland," she said.

"We already have customers who come from Bangor and Augusta," John stated proudly. "And last time I was in Portland, I met a man from Bar Harbor, who is doing business with Mike—well, Leon Phenwick." He laughed. "Mike suggested that I go to Boston and speak with Cousin Stuart about expanding business operations into that area."

"Oh, Daddy, I think that would be wonderful!" exclaimed Nellie. "Collier Furniture can become a big operation like Medallion is."

"Not quite that big, my precious," John returned, chuckling. "Not hardly. Medallion has beome a giant, what with operations in Boston, Portland, and London. And I understand that Jim Phenwick is attempting to revitalize the company in Savannah—with the help of Stuart, of course. No, I will be content with a factory here in Greenfield and exporting goods to other parts of the country."

"When will you go to Boston?"

"I hadn't really given that any concrete thought, Nell. Not until after the spring thaw—if then. It's all just in the thinking stages. And I'm not so certain I really am ready to expand my business."

"Yes, you are, Daddy. I know you are."

"How do you know?"

The quivering candlelight danced impishly over Nellie's pretty face. Her eyes glistened with a residue of tears. "I just know. I've seen a big mill right here in Greenfield. I know you're going to be very successful. And I'm going to help you."

John squeezed his daughter tightly. "You know, I've been told that your mother and I are soul mates. But I do believe you and I must have an extraordinarily strong tie to each other."

"So do I. I don't think it's a mistake at all that I'm your daughter." She kissed him. "Daddy, when you go to Boston, may I go along with you?"

"Go to Boston with me?" John asked. "Why?"

"Because there's someone I have to meet there."

"Who is that?"

"I don't know. I just know that I must," Nellie replied. "It's something I just know." She brightened. "Besides, I'm curious to meet all of the Phenwicks who live there. After all, I am the great-great-great-granddaughter of the notorious Augusta Phenwick, aren't I?"

"Did you count that up on your fingers?" John teased.

"I did years ago," Nellie returned. "Now I know it by heart."

"Very well, in that case, you certainly will accompany

me to Boston." John hugged and kissed her again, then rose and stood beside the bed, still holding her hand. "You may not be sleepy, precious, but I'm tired and need at least two more hours of sleep. Shall I leave the candle?"

"No. I'm not afraid of the dark," Nellie replied. "And I'm certain to fall back to sleep before too long. Good night again, Daddy."

Sitting up in bed, Nellie watched as her father left the room, taking the light with him. Remembered pictures from the nightmare she had had flashed into her mind; but she did her best to shut them out. Still, she knew her dream of the four gravestones was not a good omen.

Kate was staring into the darkness as John took the candle to the bed. She had been having curious thoughts. A premonition had come over her that had caused her to become inverse and reflective.

"Are you asleep, my darling?" John asked, as he climbed beneath the covers beside her, then reached over to blow out the candle.

"No. I'm still quite wide awake," Kate replied. "The children crying in the night always disturbs me. I'm always so relieved when I learn that all that was bothering them was a bad dream—and that they're not sick."

"Nellie is quite well."

"Oh, I know that, John. I know that." Kate sighed. "Sometimes I wonder—" She caught herself.

"Wonder *what*, Katie?" John turned toward her.

"Oh, nothing, I suppose."

"But it was something, or you wouldn't have mentioned it."

Kate thought a moment. "John, hold me. Please hold me."

"What it is, Katie? you're trembling."

Bravely she breathed deeply and found the words to go with the thoughts in her mind. "I'm not afraid of dying."

21

"Of dying?"

"The thought of death keeps returning to me," Kate confessed. "In a way, I imagine, I'm rather looking forward to the experience that it will be. You know that I fully believe in a continuation of life after death. That isn't the problem. But I do worry about the children—and *you*, of course, my dearest."

"Why should you have thoughts concerning death? You're still a very young woman, Katie."

"Oh, they're just silly thoughts, I suppose," Kate said. "I shouldn't have said anything about them."

"I should think it would be abnormal if you didn't give some consideration to the notion of death," John comforted. "Everyone does, I should suppose. The thought enters my mind every so often. I give it momentary attention then shove it back somewhere into the recesses. Now I want you to put such ideas from your pretty head and get some sleep." He kissed her.

"John?" Kate said nearly five minutes later.

John yawned and sounded groggy. "Yes?"

"Nellie is destined to become a Phenwick woman, isn't she?"

"How's that?"

"Nellie—her dream about receiving violets from Augusta. Oh, I know she will become a Phenwick woman. I don't know how, but I'm certain she will. It's really quite obvious to me that that will happen."

John made an incoherent sound and began to breathe heavily.

"Yes, so very obvious to me," Kate whispered to herself. "I only pray I will be around to share her happiness. Nellie Phenwick. Oh, that sounds very nice indeed." Her thoughts changed. "But I wonder if I will witness Nellie's happiness—at least, from this side."

# Chapter Two

Nellie was obviously determined to accompany her father to Boston. From the time the first crocuses appeared—yellow, white and lavender—the girl began making plans. Already she was an accomplished seamstress, and she made herself four new dresses for the trip. Kate was proud of her eldest daughter's handiwork and did what she could to help.

By the second week of April, John was convinced the trip would be of great importance to his business. Horace Boggs, the factory foreman, was given instructions and was put in charge of seeing that the work got out. John had generated excitement over the forthcoming trip and appeared eager to travel again to Boston. He had been well accepted among the Phenwicks, especially by Stuart, who was the undisputed head of the clan. Nancy Phenwick was also partial to John Collier. And from time to time, Millijoy Phenwick had taken curious interest in him. But Millijoy took a curious interest in most men who exuded charm and physical good looks. John was never unkind to Millijoy, but he made every effort to avoid being alone with her.

On the morning of departure, John called middle-aged Nana Carlyle aside to give her last minute instructions.

Nana had been governess and nurse to the family for ten years. The proud, majestic woman was thoroughly trustworthy and competent. Furthermore, she was devoted to the children, extremely fond of Kate, and had long since won the admiration and respect of John. A tall woman, she moved with a regal air. She spoke with a slight accent, which seemed to be a combination of French and Austrian. She spoke little of her past and her life in Europe, and she tried her best to appear a proper New Englander.

"You can count on me, Mr. Collier," Nana stated. She always wore black, with a high collar and long sleeves. Her appearance rarely altered with the changing of seasons.

"Yes, I'm certain I can, Nana," John replied. "I must admit I have some reservations about leaving, with Mrs. Collier being plagued with that persistent cough. I will leave it to your discretion if you feel she requires a doctor. Don't hesitate to call Dr. Mumford—young Dr. Charles Mumford."

"Rest assured, Mr. Collier, I will look after Mrs. Collier and the children. With Nellie away, it should be an easy task."

"Why do you make such a statement? Have you come into conflict with Nellie?" John asked.

"No real conflict, sir," Nana replied. "Nellie is obviously a determined and sometimes stubborn child. When a person is so strong-willed, it makes it difficult to exercise authority over her."

John laughed. "Quite observant, Nana."

"And she does have an uncanny imagination," Nana added. "With the success of the Brontë sisters and that Alcott woman in Massachusetts, I should think it would be advisable to encourage Nellie to write down some of her more imaginative—well—tales."

"I should think that would be wise."

"I must admit there are times when she puts me ill

24

at ease," Nana continued, "with her singular ability of seeing into the future."

"Seeing into the future?" Again John laughed, but it was strained. "Nellie does have premonitions, I do have to say that for her."

"And those premonitions, Mr. Collier, are often quite accurate," Nana said. "Well, I understand that there have been others in the Phenwick family who have had such ability. Or is it a curse?"

"A curse?"

"Frankly, I am perfectly content not knowing what the future has in store," Nana declared. "If the good Lord above had wanted me to know such things, perhaps He would have given me that precognitive ability." She cleared her throat. "Rest assured, Mr. Collier, I shall take good care of your brood. And if there is any reason to call Dr. Mumford, you may depend on me doing so."

"Thank you, Nana."

John went to the upstairs sitting room, where Kate was lounging on the chaise, absently gazing out toward the sea. The trees were thick along the shore, making it impossible for her to catch more than an occasional glimpse of the water between the trees. Her husband kissed her lightly, tenderly caressed then sat beside her when she moved her skirts to make room for him.

"Nellie has already been in to kiss me good-bye," Kate said with a bright smile. "She is filled with such enthusiasm that my heart wants to dance with her."

"Are you certain, dearest Kate, that you feel quite well?" John questioned as he held her hands.

"Quite, my darling. You mustn't worry about me. You've business to which you must attend in Boston," Kate replied. "I trust you will give my love to Nancy and Stuart and all the other Phenwicks. Since Mother's death two years ago, we've not kept in continual contact with the Phenwicks. I've written notes for you to take to Nancy and the others." She laughed strangely. "I have

25

even scribbled one to Millijoy. I just had a feeling that I should. I was never close to Millijoy, but I did feel a kind of affinity for her."

"You're most considerate, dear Kate." John kissed her and held her for several minutes. After expressing his love and the depth of his affection, he rose and stood beside the chaise, still clinging to her hand. "Alas, we must depart shortly, or we'll not connect with the train in Portland."

"Then hurry along, my dearest. God speed you." Kate smiled up at him. Her eyes looked tired, and she turned her glance away.

"What is it, my darling?"

Kate looked back into his well-proportioned face. "It's nothing."

"But it is, Katie, I can tell by your expression." He sat again beside her.

"It's only that I will miss you."

"No more than I will miss you. If only you felt up to the journey—"

"But I don't, my dearest." Then she brightened. "Perhaps, if you have to travel to Boston in the fall, I'll have more strength."

"I'll postpone the trip until then."

"No, you mustn't." Kate pulled his hand to her lips and kissed it. After her lips pressed to each of his fingers, she brushed the back of his hand against her cheek. "I hadn't planned on telling you, but you might as well know. I've had several dreams lately in which Augusta has appeared."

"Augusta?"

"Augusta Phenwick."

"Her ghost is haunting you?"

"Not haunting. She speaks to me, and her words are most reassuring," Kate whispered. "Sometimes I wonder if I'm actually asleep when these dreams of Augusta occur."

26

Kate had good reason to believe that she was the reincarnation of Daniel Charles Phenwick the first. Whether she had actual faith in that theory was a questionable point; still, she felt there was sufficient evidence in that direction to make her think she *might* be the continuation of that soul, who had previously been born as Augusta's son, the only child of hers that grew into manhood. At the same time, there were strong indications that John Collier was the reincarnation of Danny's close friend in that other era, Michael O'Plaggerty. If, indeed, Kate had been previously incarnated as Danny, and the spirit of Augusta actually hovered over Phenwick House as it was reputed to do, it would seem logical that Kate would have a special awareness of the woman who had founded the Phenwick family and had determined to have a dynasty of Phenwick women.

"Did she come with the scent of violets?" John asked, after staring deeply into his wife's face.

"Oh, yes, very much so." Kate was smiling brightly. "Perhaps the odor was stronger these last few times than it has ever been in the past."

John kissed her again, taking her in his arms. "I shan't go."

"Don't be foolish, my darling. Of course you must go."

John's lips were at Kate's ear. "I love you so very much, my Katie. I always have, I always will."

"And I love you, my precious darling."

Tears had come to John's eyes as he walked from the room. He kept putting distressing thoughts from his mind, but they persistently returned.

With Nellie beside him in the carriage and his three younger children waving from the steps of the house, John gave orders to the driver, Alvin Paxton, to drive by the office of Dr. Charles Mumford before they took the road to Portland.

"You must remain in the carriage and visit with Mr. Paxton, Nellie," John stated. "I'll only be a few minutes."

Nellie watched as her father entered the doctor's building, then engaged the talkative Alvin Paxton in conversation. The delay bothered her, but she tried to hide her annoyance.

Charles Mumford was an attractive-looking man of twenty-six. Extremely intelligent, he had finished medical school in Boston the youngest in his class. Reddish blond hair and soft blue eyes gave him a look which inspired confidence. Charles had known John since he was a young boy. It was John Collier who had encouraged him to take up the study of medicine. It was also John who had arranged for him to have a substantial financial loan to see him through school. Naturally, Charles would let other patients wait while he consulted with his friend.

"I thought you were off to Boston," Charles commented as John entered his private office.

"I'm on my way. Fact is, Paxton has the carriage at your front door and Nellie is waiting in it."

"I trust you will remember me to John Phenwick," Charles said. "He was such a very good friend to me while I was at school. I suppose he is practicing law in Boston now. A brilliant man."

"Strangely, John Phenwick and I are not that well acquainted," John returned. "John was away at school so much of the time that I was in Boston. I know his brothers Thad, Paul, and Daniel Louis far better than I know John. Still, I will make a point of calling on him."

"Ah, dear Thad," Charles sighed. "I suppose it is traditional that we Mumfords envy the Phenwicks. As you know, Paul had already left home when I was in Boston. He's gone out west somewhere. Colorado—California— I don't recall where. But I suspect you didn't come to me to discuss the Phenwicks of Boston, did you, John?"

Previously, John had discussed the theories of reincarnation with Charles, and the possibility that both he and

28

Kate had lived former lives in Greenfield as the aforementioned Danny Phenwick and Michael O'Plaggerty. He had also related stories about the notorious Augusta Phenwick, and the legend of her spirit that was reputed to still remain earthbound after all these years.

"It's Katie, dear Charles," John sighed. "I worry about her health. She does seem perfectly well. Yet I notice that she appears feeble at times, listless and, I suspect, melancholy. I don't like leaving her alone."

"Rest your mind, John," the doctor said. "I promise I shall daily stop by Phenwick House and have a look in at Kate. We manage to get into some delightfully whimsical conversations. I don't have much of a sense of a humor, but that which I have is rarely appreciated by many people. Kate is one of the few who find me witty." He laughed.

"That will please me greatly, Charles." John shook his hand. "And, for your information, I've always thought you had quite a wit. Now I must leave. Nellie will be on tenterhooks."

"I would walk to the carriage with you, John," Charles remarked, "but I have an office filled with patients. For some peculiar reason there's been quite a rash of stomach cramps going around."

"Too many green apples, heh?" John joked.

"Yes, I suppose."

The two men embraced and patted each other as John departed.

"I wish," Charles said to himself before he called in the next patient, "that the explanation was as simple as 'too many green apples,' but I sadly fear it isn't." A religious man, he took a moment to pray before he beckoned the next person into his office.

Nellie delighted in the train ride from Portland to Boston. Since the entire trip was made during daylight hours, she kept her attention riveted on the passing scenery. Occasionally she engaged her father in light conversation, but John appeared to want to be left alone with his thoughts.

At one station along the way, a newspaper boy boarded the train long enough to sell a few papers. John purchased one and absently scanned it, unable to read easily with the vibrations of the moving train.

Periodically Nellie glanced over at the paper. "What's cholera?"

"How's that, my darling?" John asked. His eyes had only been running over the printed words, he had not been reading.

Nellie pointed at a caption on the page. "Cholera. It says fourteen died of cholera in Kittery."

"Oh, so they did," John said, focusing on the words. "And it appears six others died of it in Kennebunkport. I don't know what it is precisely, but I would guess it's some kind of disease that strikes in epidemic proportions." He flipped the page.

Nellie stared at the paper as an image came to her mind. It was a picture she recalled from a dream: a picture of a graveyard and four headstones. She violently shook her head and tried to put the image from her mind.

An hour before arriving in Boston, Nellie had become sleepy. Childlike, she cuddled up against her father and napped. John put his arm about her. A man sitting across the aisle asked if John had finished with the paper, and he gave it to him.

The monotonous rhythm of the train wheels over the tracks kept repeating one word in John's mind. He would ask Dr. Joseph Ornby what it meant when he arrived in Boston. Still, whatever it was, he knew it must be a dreaded disease.

Finally, as the conductor passed through the car, John

nudged Nellie. "It's time, my precious, for you to open those big eyes of yours. You don't want to look sleepy when you meet your cousins, do you?"

Nellie blinked, then smiled. "I'm awake, Daddy."

# Chapter Three

Nellie had obviously generated a tremendous amount of excitement by the time the train pulled into the station and had come to a stop. "Do you see them, Daddy? Do you?"

John had to stoop to observe through the window. "Not yet. But this is a long train, and they might be situated at another car." He lifted down the hand luggage. "Take my hand, Nellie. Boston is a big city and I shouldn't want us to become separated."

Three landau carriages had arrived at the station fifteen minutes prior to the expected arrival of the train from Portland. Nancy Phenwick, her hair graying and her face etched with age, was in the first landau with her youngest son, Daniel Louis. The second carriage carried the persons of still-handsome Stuart Phenwick, his lovely wife Ruth, and Stuart's two children by his first marriage, Danny and Ann Marie.

The passengers of the first two landaus were surprised to see the third arrive, and even more startled to recognize the grandly elegant figure of Millijoy Phenwick within it, in the company of her son Thomas. Although it was a warm day, Millijoy wore a wine-colored satin gown, a black-embroidered velvet cape, and an imposing hat with black ostrich plumes.

Nancy, who was clad in a dark green lightweight gown cut from a conservative pattern, gaped at Millijoy and tried to find a hospitable smile.

"What's she doing here?" questioned somewhat outspoken Daniel Louis. The seventeen-year-old had had more than one encounter with Millijoy, and he openly called her unkind names.

"Hush, Daniel Louis," Nancy shushed. "Millijoy is a Phenwick woman, too. Do try to be cordial and not make disagreeable sounds."

"I'll promise nothing, Mother," Daniel Louis said between his teeth. "Had I known she was going to be here, I wouldn't have come. And that brat is with her."

"Daniel Louis, I'll jab you with my parasol if you don't behave yourself," Nancy said under her breath. Then she turned to exchange a puzzled glance with Stuart Phenwick, before he reached to help his beautiful Ruth from the carriage.

"Wait, Tommy," Millijoy stated as she put her gloved hand on her son's black, curly hair. He looked up at her with big dark brown eyes. His skin was tan color and his features, while not displeasing, had Negroid characteristics. Millijoy had hoped that her son by Gordon Phenwick would be as light as she; but when it became apparent that Tommy was of mixed races, she reluctantly admitted that her father had been a black man, lest it be suspected that she herself had had an affair with a Negro and had tried to pass the child of that liaison off as Gordon's. Still, there was no mistaking that Tommy had the physical features and somewhat of the disposition of the late Gordon Phenwick.

"Am I not to join my cousins?" Tommy asked. "Danny and Ann Marie are my first cousins, you know."

"They will come to us," Millijoy replied. "It is best that way."

33

Tall, handsome, wordly-appearing Stuart Phenwick stepped to the carriage in which his sister-in-law was waiting. "Millijoy, my dear, what an unexpected surprise."

"Yes, isn't it, Stuart?" Millijoy extended a gloved hand.

"And Tommy, you certainly are growing." Stuart shook hands with the boy.

"Hello, Uncle Stuart," the boy responded.

"Your cousins are over there," Stuart stated. "Why don't you go over and speak with them?" He watched as Tommy went to where Danny and Ann Marie were standing. "I suspect you had very good reasons for coming to the station, Millijoy."

"The arrival of relatives should be reason enough, Stuart."

"Funny, it never occurred to me to think of you as being any part of a welcoming committee," Stuart stated.

"You forget that I did know John Collier in the past," Millijoy returned coyly.

Stuart tried to penetrate the meaning behind Millijoy's enigmatic expression. Her eyes had an odd sparkle that were filled with insinuation. "Will you come and join us?"

Millijoy glanced over at Ruth. Then her eyes met Nancy's. "Why, yes, why not?"

"Millijoy, so good to see you," Nancy exclaimed as she bent forward to embrace her. "My goodness, it's been ever so long since we've seen you."

Daniel Louis moved away and went to where the children had gathered. He shot a contemptuous glance back at Millijoy.

"Oh, Mrs. Phenwick, you always look so beautiful," Ruth gushed.

"And so do you, Mrs. Phenwick," Milljoy returned, a fine edge to her voice.

"We're having a little dinner next week at Edward house," Ruth went on. "You simply must come and be with us."

Millijoy cast Stuart a look. "Why, yes, that would be nice."

Daniel Louis was the first to spot John Collier and Nellie. Without calling them to the others' attention, he went to where they were standing on the train platform. "I suppose you remember me."

"Is it Daniel Louis?" John questioned. "It must be. I know Paul has gone west."

"It's me, all right," Daniel Louis answered. "And this, I take it, is Cousin Nellie."

"Since I sent word that only Nellie and I would be coming to Boston, that's a very good guess." John laughed and embraced the young man. "Did you come alone to meet us?"

"No, there's a whole horde of people," Daniel Louis commented, "including her questionable highness."

"I beg your pardon?"

"My late nephew's wife, Millijoy."

"Oh. Oh? Millijoy."

"I see her appearance here no more pleases you than it does me," Daniel Louis observed. "She never appears without a reason."

Nellie had been studying Daniel Louis. His boyish face and the crackling sound of his changing voice intrigued her. "Why do they call you Cousin Daniel Louis? Why not just plain Daniel?"

"Because my great-nephew is named Daniel Charles Phenwick," the youth explained. "It's the same name of my grandfather. He has inherited the nickname of Danny, while I must be Daniel Louis. I don't know whether that makes any sense to you—it doesn't make too much to me—but I live with it."

"I suppose I'll get it sorted out before too long," Nellie commented.

By then the others had arrived at the place where the visitors were standing. Introductions were made, along with hugs and kisses.

Even in the midst of all the confusion and excitement, John could not help but be aware of Millijoy's intense gaze in his direction. He had greeted her and introduced Nellie, but the woman was determined to keep her attention on him.

"There's room in our carriage," Nancy suggested. "We'll drive John and Nellie to Edward House. We can all meet there and have a cup of tea." She turned to Millijoy. "You will come, won't you, dear?"

"I think not," Millijoy replied. "Tommy has a piano lesson in a short while. It was only because we had time to kill that we decided to come to the station." Her attention again went to John. "I trust you will come and visit us at Triumph House, John."

John swallowed hard. "I'll make a point of it."

"Thank God she's not going to be at Edward House," exclaimed Daniel Louis as he rode on the backward-riding seat in the landau.

"She?" John questioned.

"Millijoy," Daniel Louis snorted.

"That's enough, Daniel Louis," Nancy said, putting her arm about Nellie, who was on the seat beside her. "You must forgive Daniel Louis, he is sometimes quite outspoken. You know, I never had a little girl of my own—and I always wanted one. I just had the four boys. Now Paul has gone to California. He was just nineteen when he up and went. We haven't heard from him in eleven months. And Thadius has gone to England and the continent—although he should be home before too long. My John lives in Cambridge, where he's doing graduate work. You know, I think you two should stay with us, not with Stuart and Ruth. Why, we've got that big house and only Daniel Louis is home."

"Perhaps we can spend some of the time with you, Miss Nancy," Nellie said. "I think I would like that."

Nancy pulled the girl tighter to her and smiled.

Masculine Phenwick beauty had carved the features of Thadius Phenwick. His hair had a golden sheen like the top of a wheat field, after weeks of being at sea and traveling about. His dark blue eyes glistened with the sun's reflection, sapphires in a sea of dreams. With a dislike for the bulky British fashions, Thad preferred to dress in lightweight, formfitting attire. He chose white and blues, usually, but occasionally he picked an outfit of brown and beige. Whatever he wore, he cut a handsome figure that could not help but draw attention to him.

Twenty-four. He had a kind of wanderlust that was not akin to melancholia, yet neither did it stem from desire for adventure. Often considered an inverse person, he was given to long hours of meditation and deep contemplation. Years before he had had a youthful crush on Ruth Eldridge, who later married his nephew Stuart. Thad had been wounded deeply by his thwarted love; as a result he joined the navy and served in the last part of the Civil War. During the years after he returned home, he had had a difficult time adjusting to what he considered limitations of family which required conformity to accepted ways of life. He was Nancy's eldest child, although he was his father's fifth offspring.

Like Peter, his father, and Danny, his grandfather, Thad had a mysterious love for the sea, for travel and romantic adventure. Although his nephew Stuart was a good fifteen years his senior, the young man had great respect for him. Even when he discovered that Ruth loved Stuart and not himself, he could not feel bitterness toward either of them.

During the years of growing up, Thad had been remarkably close to his brother John. The war years had separated them. He was proud of John and his scholarly accomplishments. He had not been as familiar with his younger brothers, Paul and Daniel Louis, but he felt an innate sense of family unity and was protective of them.

Now Paul had left home. Thad had considered going west with his next-to-youngest brother, but at the last minute he thought better of it.

A rugged older seaman, who called himself Kit Snyder, had taken a fancy to Thad on the voyage and had made a point of cultivating his friendship. Kit was thirty-six, bearded, and in possession of a salty vocabulary which he accentuated with a hearty, thundering laugh.

"You'll see land tomorrow, lad," Kit said as he came up to the railing alongside where Thad was standing.

"So soon?"

Kit put a thick arm about the youth's shoulders. "Aye, lad. I figure we'll see the skyline of Boston by about six bells tomorrow—eleven o'clock, landlubber time. It'll take an hour or two to get your land legs, then the city will be yours."

"I fear Boston nor any other city will ever truly be mine," Thad returned.

"Then why don't you make a life at sea, lad, as I've done?" Kit questioned, applying pressure with his arm. "It's not a bad life, and there's always something new and different. It's not like in the old days. And the ports are filled with lovely lasses just for the asking."

Thad laughed. "I'll tell you what. If I'm not married by the time I'm thirty, I'll give serious thought to becoming a sailor."

"Aye, but you're a Phenwick," Kit said. "You won't ever be a common seaman. Like as not you'll become a bloody captain. You know, that's something that's bothered me about you. Here you come from wealth, a prominent family, and I'm practically an orphan who grew up on the streets—still we've become friends. Such friendship could never happen on land—but at sea—well, that's a different matter, isn't it?"

Thad coughed, grabbing hold of the rail to support himself.

"Hey, lad, what ails you?" Kit asked.

"I've felt a little ill the last few days. I suppose it is the damp sea air."

"Then why are you standing out in it?"

"I cough below in my cabin as well," Thad explained. "Besides, I like to stand at the rail this time of the day, when the sun is setting. Then watch and wait as the sky grows dark and the stars begin to appear. It stimulates my thoughts."

"Are you a religious person?"

Thad turned to look at his friend. "I believe in a Supreme Power and that the Universe is run by a well-ordered plan. But, as for being religious in a church way, well, I don't think I am. My brothers and I were raised with definite Christian teachings. Somehow I've never been able to accept on faith everything I was told."

"That's me, Thaddy," Kit roared. "I believe there's something out there, but I doubt if it's the way all those church people say it is. That's why I like to look at the night sky, too. To me, there's a kind of reality in contemplating the vastness of all that's out there."

"Sometimes I stare at a particular star," Thad remarked a few moments later, "until it seems like its beam is shining right through me. And it makes me think that maybe a small ray of that Supreme Power is beaming through me. When that happens, I feel like I'm really part of the whole of the Universe."

"Aye, lad, I know the feeling," Kit commented. "You can see the same stars at night in Boston."

"I wonder if my awareness of them will be the same."

When Thad was alone later that evening, he went again to the ship's railing and stared up at the stars. His mind was clear, almost as if he were without thoughts, when a singular notion came to him—as if it were a voice speaking to him from somewhere out in the spheres. He could not describe the sensation that had come over

39

him, but he knew that he was returning to Boston for a definite reason, and that he would learn what his life's destiny was to be.

Thad coughed again and hurried down to his cabin.

# Chapter Four

It was obvious from the start that Ruth Phenwick was destined to become a close friend to Nellie. Stuart's wife was delicately pretty. She was lighthearted and always appeared to be happy. Her three small children were a joy to her, and she delighted in the fact that Nellie seemed to be so fond of little Peter, Polly, and Donald. Ruth spoke with music in her voice, her movements were as graceful as a dancer's. Infectious laughter caused Nellie to chuckle over the slightest incident.

"Are you always so good-natured?" Nellie asked, the second week after she and her father had pretty much settled into Edward House.

"I try to be," Ruth replied. "When I fell in love with Stuart, my entire world changed. And I knew, since I was his second wife and he had dearly loved Marcia Phenwick very much, that I would have to do my best to give him love and happiness. He's a very busy man. I try not to intrude. And I do feel he loves me as much as he did the previous Mrs. Phenwick."

"Cousin Stuart seems to be so much older than you," Nellie observed.

"What does the age of a person matter?" Ruth returned. "Sometimes I feel as if I'm ten years older than

41

he is, when in reality he is fifteen years older than I. And when I think of how much older Mr. Peter Phenwick was than Nancy, I consider myself extremely lucky to have a man as young as Stuart. Oh, don't mistake me. Nancy declares she was terribly in love with Peter Phenwick. Perhaps that is why she has never married again. But now that her sons are going out on their own, I do believe she should consider taking a second husband, don't you?"

"The notion never entered my mind," Nellie stated. "If Cousin Peter was so much older than Nancy, she must have known their life together would not be for a long duration."

"I'm certain she did," Ruth replied. "But one doesn't think of that when one falls in love."

A servant came to announce that Mrs. Phenwick had a visitor.

"A visitor?"

"A male visitor."

"Did he leave a card?"

"It's Mr. Thadius Phenwick, ma'am."

"Oh, dear, Thad," Ruth said, flipping her hands in the air. "He's been abroad on an extended journey. I didn't expect him back so soon."

"Cousin Thadius?" Nellie questioned, an interested smile drawing at her lips.

Ruth glanced at Nellie. What mystery was in the child's face? "I must say I'm delighted you are here. And you must promise to remain while Thad is present. I know he still clings to the old emotional feeling he had for me. I do like him very much, you mustn't mistake me. But I don't dislike many people. I always try to be friendly. I just don't want to encourage him, if you know what I mean. But how could you?—you're still such a young girl."

Nellie wanted to object. Instead she smiled and looked demure.

"Ah, dearest Ruth!" exclaimed Thad as he strode into the room.

"It is you, Thad," Ruth returned, "looking tanned, your hair bleached and, I must say, the very picture of a sea-going man." She permitted him to kiss the back of her hand. "I don't believe you know your cousin Kate's daughter, Nellie."

"Nellie Collier?" Thad turned his attention to the child. "What a pretty little cousin I have."

"That is kind of you to say, Cousin Thadius," Nellie returned. "It seems to me that I have a rather pretty cousin, too." She laughed.

"You mean dear Ruth, of course," Thad said.

"While I think Ruth is one of the prettiest ladies I've ever known," Nellie returned enthusiastically, "it was *you* to whom I was referring."

"You flatter me, Nellie."

"I find your brother, Daniel Louis, a nice-looking person," Nellie continued, "but I'm of the impression that you're far better-looking."

"I'm sufficiently sunburnt that you can't see that I'm blushing," Thad commented, "but I assure you that I am." He laughed, and the laughter evolved into coughing.

"Do take a sip of brandy, Thad," Ruth encouraged.

"So it will burn the cough away?" questioned Thad.

"I suppose that *is* the theory, isn't it?" Ruth poured brandy into a crystal glass. "I'm certain it will help."

A few moments later Thad's coughing had ceased.

"Are you ailing, Thad?" questioned Ruth.

"I've felt a bit listless during the return trip." He sneezed. "I was perfectly all right when I first entered this house. It's that damnable violet perfume that seems to be affecting me."

"Violet perfume?" Ruth looked from Thad to Nellie. "I'm not—Nellie, are you wearing perfume?"

"No." Nellie smiled as a vision came to her mind.

When Thad was about to sneeze again, she went to him and put her finger to his upper lip and pressed. "This will stop the sneeze."

"What, and blow out the back of my head?" Thad teased.

Ruth observed the two cousins. "I'll ring for tea, shall I?"

When John and Kate Collier first settled in Greenfield at Phenwick House, a large amount of restoration had had to be done. One of John's first projects had been to demolish and rebuild the old chapel that stood in the graveyard, beneath which reposed the bodies of Augusta the first, her husband, Charles Andre, and her son, Daniel. Believing sufficient time had elapsed since the demise of those beneath the chapel, John arranged to have their caskets buried in the adjoining cemetery. Because of his deep belief that Danny and Michael O'Plaggerty had been such close friends, he placed Danny's body next to Mike's, next to Danny's wife, Margaret. He had arranged to have new stones carved of marble and, for the most part, he had seen to beautifying the old cemetery as best he could.

On those spring afternoons, while John was in Boston, Kate often strolled about the grounds of Phenwick House. She would gather flowers and take them to the gravestones. If indeed her spirit had once occupied the body of Daniel Phenwick, why couldn't she remember any of the details of his life? She wasn't as convinced about that theory of reincarnation as her husband was. Still, she often found herself at Danny's grave as she almost hypnotically stared at the stone.

Kate had gathered lilacs, which were just coming into bloom. Of all the flowers, they were her favorites. Clad in a pale pink dress with long sleeves and a high neckline, she lifted her skirts with one hand as she brushed past the gravestones. A strange, vacant feeling came over her and the thought of her own death returned.

Pretty little Elizabeth had seen her mother in the walled cemetery, and ran to join her.

"Why do you come here so often, Mother?" Elizabeth asked.

"I find it very peaceful," Kate replied. "And then, after I've put flowers on the graves, I go into the chapel to meditate."

"You miss Grandmother Rebecca, don't you?" Elizabeth said.

"I was very close to my mother, dearest," Kate replied. "We had a close bond."

"Do we have a close bond, Mother?" Elizabeth asked.

"I believe we do, Elizabeth." Kate hugged her second child to her. "Now you run and play, little one."

"I've no one to play with," Elizabeth complained, "now that Nell is away."

"There's George and Rupert."

"They're boys," Elizabeth responded, with a tone of disgust in her voice. "They play far too rough for me." She clung to her mother's hand.

"I would prefer being alone, if you don't mind, Elizabeth."

Reluctantly the little girl went to find her brothers.

About fifteen minutes later, the children looked up to see a horse and rider approaching the house. Recognizing the rider as Dr. Charles Mumford, the children waved, but did not leave the game they were playing.

Charles rode up to the front of the house, dismounted and tied his horse. He was about to ring the bell when he glanced toward the cemetery plot and recognized Kate's familiar figure.

"Mrs. Collier," Charles said as he stepped through the gate. Two of the dogs had followed him, barking and licking his hand.

"Oh, Dr. Mumford."

"It's still Charles," he said as he crossed to where she was standing before the grave of Danny Phenwick. He took her hand and kissed her on the cheek.

"What brings you to Phenwick House, Charles?"

"I promised John I would have a regular look-in on you while he was away. I regret I've not been able to get away sooner," the young doctor said. "I suppose you've received letters from John and Nellie."

"Oh, yes. John writes every day, or so it would seem. The mail being the way it is, I get several letters at once," Kate informed him. "Then I have to sort them out by date to read them in the order they were written. Nellie is quite impressed with her Phenwick cousins."

"Who wouldn't be impressed with John Phenwick?"

"According to her letters, Nellie hasn't seen much of John Phenwick," Kate explained. "She seems to have enjoyed the company of both Daniel Louis and Thadius—especially the latter."

"Thad is twice Nellie's age," Charles commented.

"Oh, dear, you're surely not thinking— Goodness!"

"I didn't mean to imply— Forgive me. I was merely thinking that a girl of twelve couldn't have much in common with a man of—what is Thad now?—twenty-four." Charles kicked a dirt clod with his foot. "Perhaps we should discuss something else."

"Like what?"

"Your health, Mrs. Collier," Charles said, a cold seriousness coming to his voice. "How have you been feeling?"

"I confess I've not been my old self," Kate admitted.

"Can you be more explicit?"

"I have this lingering cough and periodic pains in my chest," Kate related. "It's nothing serious, I suppose. And I confess I've not had much of an appetite lately."

"You seem thinner than when last I saw you."

"I suppose I simply need a spring tonic. Sulfur and

molasses should pick me up," Kate said, and managed to project a smile.

Charles put his hand to her brow, then he reached down for her wrist to check her pulse. He made a concerted effort not to show an expression of concern. "I would like to suggest that you have Paxton drive you to my office in the next day or so—it's not urgent—and let me give you a thorough examination."

"Do you think it necessary?"

"We've had two cases of cholera in Greenfield. None of my patients. But, after conferring with the other doctors in town, I'm trying to see that none of my patients get the disease. The two who have contracted it were physically weak before it overtook them. A physical examination is merely a precautionary measure, Mrs. Collier, that's all."

"Cholera?" Kate questioned. She bent to readjust the lilacs at the headstone. "It was unfortunate that Edward hadn't been laid to rest here at Greenfield."

"Edward?"

Kate stood upright. "Edward Phenwick." She smiled dimly. "Edward and his sister Jane were adopted by Augusta Phenwick. Edward was Danny's stepbrother. They were quite fond of each other . . . and Jane was fond of them both." She had a far-off look.

"I've heard of Daniel Phenwick," Charles commented, "but I don't believe I ever knew of Edward."

"Edward was married to Patricia Phenwick, my grandmother. After Edward passed away, my grandmother married Elias Phenwick, Danny's eldest son."

"Elias *Mumford* Phenwick," Charles corrected. "His mother was never married to Danny. She was my greataunt Kate. There, you see, we must be distantly related."

Again Kate appeared distant. "Yes, I suppose we are, aren't we, Charles?"

Charles watched her a moment before he spoke. "Where is Edward Phenwick laid to rest?"

47

"In Boston. Grandmother insisted she be buried between both Edward and Elias." Kate blinked and forced a smile. "I suppose it doesn't make any difference about any of them now—I mean where they're resting. Still, it would have been nice if Edward could have been here near to Danny and Mike."

"Why do you concern yourself about such matters?"

"I don't concern myself, Charles. Still, I don't know why the thought keeps crossing my mind." She coughed. "Oh, dear!"

"What is it, Mrs. Collier?" He caught her with an arm about her shoulders.

"It's nothing, Charles, nothing." Kate sighed. "Perhaps I had better go back to the house now. I've exhausted myself."

Kate leaned on Charles's powerful strength as he helped her to the house. She suggested that she would be comfortable in the downstairs sitting room, since that was where she wanted to be anyway.

Charles realized she was simply too weak to navigate the stairs at that time. A rest was wanted. He saw she was comfortably positioned on the chaise longue beneath the portrait of Augusta. Then he remained with her and listened to her rambling conversation for nearly a half an hour.

When Charles returned home that evening, he wrote a letter to John Collier.

John Collier spent much time in the company of Stuart Phenwick. They had much business to discuss. And John had a curious interest in the Medallion Company. He and Stuart had long been friends.

"I've been giving much thought to what you've told me," Stuart said over lunch at a restaurant one afternoon. "And I've come to the conclusion that you need to take on a business partner."

"Are you suggesting yourself?" John asked, brightening.

Stuart chuckled. "No, not me. I'm far too busy to take on any more than I've already got. Oh, I could lend you money for an expansion program and become a silent partner, I suppose; but I should think you need a partner who can work alongside you in the furniture factory. The type of plans of which you speak will call for more than one man to handle the work. You may have the greatest trust in the world of your foreman, but it is dangerous to be away too long without overseeing all that is going on."

"I see your point, Stuart. But finding such a partner— I mean, the right one—could be difficult," John returned.

"I think you might do well to consider my uncle," Stuart said. "Thad hasn't found himself as yet, although I've a feeling he's been doing a tremendous amount of searching. Unfortunately, because of his feelings for Ruth, I've not been able to be as close to him as I would like to be. I feel there's still a silent resentment toward me. Yet I've noticed that he is extremely restless, and that he periodically has a need to travel. I suspect, although I cannot be certain, that it is difficult for him to be in Boston with Ruth so near."

"I can understand your reasoning, Stuart," John remarked, then sipped from a coffee cup. "I wonder if there isn't something more behind your words."

"Meaning that you think Thad's feelings for Ruth might be a threat to my happy home?" Stuart laughingly asked. "I have no doubt of my wife's affection and fidelity. And I know that, while Ruth is fond of Thad in a certain way, she has no deep personal interest in him. Why, if Adam Truff were another sort of man, I would consider him far more a threat than I do Thad. Adam is the only *other* man I believe my Ruthie has ever had a sincere affection for. But Adam is another matter altogether. Besides, he's rarely in Boston these days."

"Then you think I should consider taking Thad on as a partner?"

"I do. But I suggest you get to know him better and decide for yourself," Stuart said. He examined his watch. "We'd better consider drawing this luncheon to a close. The *Patricia* will be arriving in another hour or so, if she's on schedule, and I must be at the pier to greet her."

"The *Patricia?*"

"One of Medallion's finest ships," Stuart explained. "But it's one of her passengers I must welcome, not the ship herself."

"Ah! I didn't think it was your practice to meet every Medallion ship that came into port," John commented.

"Cousin Susannah is arriving."

"Kate's Aunt Susannah?"

"The same."

"Then, if you'll permit me, I'd like to join you," John said. "The old girl must be up in years by now."

"I suspect she's getting close to her eighties," Stuart replied. "She's a spunky old girl, and I doubt if she shows her age. When I learned she wanted to visit Boston again, I wrote to her son Gregory questioning the advisability of the trip. And Gregory wrote back saying that Susannah was set upon traveling and that that was that."

"I understand that Susannah and my late mother-in-law were not very much alike for being sisters," John inserted.

"*Half*-sisters," Stuart corrected. "I suspect she got much of her drive from her father, Uncle Edward, while Rebecca got a certain Phenwick quality from Uncle Elias. After all, Uncle Edward was really a Munsk by birth."

"Well, then, I must say I'm anxious to meet Aunt Susannah," John remarked as he motioned for the waiter to bring the check.

# Chapter Five

Obviously excited over the expected arrival of her Great-Aunt Susannah, Nellie stood at the upstairs window of Edward House on Beacon Hill watching for the appearance of the carriage and her illustrious aunt. Twice she had changed her dress in anticipation of making a good impression. Now she was considering making another change. And she might have, if the carriage had not pulled into the driveway. She ran to the upstairs sitting room, where Ruth was waiting. Then, after announcing the news, she was back at the front window to watch as Stuart helped the grand lady from the carriage.

As a young woman, Susannah had had a remarkable beauty, and she was possessed with an even more remarkable musical talent. For years she had reveled in fame and fortune as a concert pianist, the toast of the European continent. A widely celebrated person herself, she had associated with the world's finest musicians. Composers begged her to play their compositions. A first playing of a composer's work by Susannah Phenwick was considered almost assured success. Even after she had gone into retirement, Susannah had remained prominent in musical circles, her fame and reputation revered.

The elderly lady Nellie watched alight from the carriage still maintained a conscious grandeur, poise, and sophistication. The girl was certain that no queen could be as elegant nor as regal. Ruth had looked up in the family Bible and, according to her figures, Susannah had turned seventy-eight on the twenty-second of May. A faint unsteadiness could be detected in Susannah's walk and she appeared to lean on Stuart for support. Otherwise she showed no indications of being feeble.

"Mayn't I go down now?" Nellie asked as she returned to the sitting room.

"We'll wait until Mrs. Phenwick is situated in the first floor parlor," Ruth said. "I'm certain Mrs. Phenwick would think it fitting and proper that we made a well-timed entrance."

"You make her sound like a queen or something like that," Nellie observed.

"I imagine, from what I've heard, she's the closest thing to being a queen that I'll ever have the pleasure of meeting."

Nellie wiggled and fidgeted so in the next few minutes that Ruth nearly relented and let her dash down to meet her relative. Fortunately, John Collier appeared at the second floor sitting room and asked both Ruth and Nellie to join the others below.

"Is she nice, Daddy?" Nellie asked as she clung to his hand, as they climbed down the large front staircase.

"She is not at all like your grandmother," John assured her.

"I dearly loved Grandmother," Nellie said. "And she told me many things about her sister—her half-sister. And when I would say that I didn't believe such a person actually existed, Grandmother would say, 'You'll see, one day you'll meet her.' And now I am. Oh, Daddy, I'm so excited!"

"That, my dear Nellie, is obvious." He laughed.

Susannah was not thin; neither was she overweight. Still, she was heavy enough so that her skin did not sag and the wrinkles were not too deeply carved into her face. Loveliness exuded from her and she had a sense of composure that made her appear as if she were home in her own living room.

When Nellie arrived, Susannah stretched forth her hand. Diamonds glistened on her strong fingers above the fingerless gloves.

"My dear!" Susannah exclaimed. Her voice was firm and sounded to be that of a person half her age. "No doubt, John, this is your darling Nellie."

Nellie stepped to the chair in which Susannah was seated. She tilted her head to the side and stared. The woman was so familiar to her that she could not resist saying, "My dear Susannah, I would have known you anywhere."

"Nellie!" John went quickly to his daughter's side.

"I meant to say, 'my dear *Aunt* Susannah,'" Nellie corrected herself.

Susannah took the child in her arms and kissed her. "I must admit that Rebecca and I had little resemblance to each other when we were younger, but I suspect that in time we bore a certain similarity to one another. That being the case, of course you would know me anywhere. So you are precious Nellie, obviously a very sweet little girl. I have twin granddaughters who must be your approximate age. I'm very fond of them." She looked up at Stuart. "And, speaking of grandchildren, where are my precious Danny and Ann Marie?"

"They'll be here shortly, Mrs. Phenwick," Ruth explained. "You'll be pleased to know that Danny is taking a piano lesson, and Ann Marie is studying dance. They wanted to be here when you arrived, but I thought you would think it best for them not to miss their lessons."

"Quite right," Susannah exclaimed. She stared at Ruth, then she glanced at Stuart.

"You've not met my Ruth, have you?" Stuart said.

Susannah tried to smile politely as she offered her

cheek to be kissed. Her thought was that this was the young woman who had replaced her daughter Marcia's affection in Stuart Phenwick's heart. Although Marcia and her brother Gregory had been adopted by Susannah and Lex Phenwick, Susannah could not have loved either of them more if they had been born to her. She tried not to resent Ruth, nor to think morbidly of Marcia's early death while she was still in the prime of her life.

"Your Ruth is truly lovely, Stuart," Susannah found the words to say.

Nellie was staring at Susannah.

"What is it,, child?" Susannah asked. "What is it you wish to ask me?"

"When I look at you," Nellie candidly stated, "an expression comes to my mind."

"Well, what is it?"

"Sapphire."

"Sapphire?" John asked.

"And Raja Eye," Nellie added.

Susannah grew pale and placed a handkerchief to her mouth. "The Raja Eye?"

"Whatever happened to it?" Nellie asked cryptically.

Susannah flipped open a fan that was attached to her wrist. "Rebecca—that is, your grandmother—must have told you."

"I don't believe she did," Nellie replied.

"No, of course, Rebecca wouldn't have known about it unless Mother told her. And I shouldn't think she would have done that." Susannah stared at the child.

Nellie was obviously flustered. "I'm sorry. I don't know why I said that. It just came out."

Susannah held out her hand, beckoning Nellie nearer. A prickly sensation had come over the old woman. When Nellie stood very close to the old lady, Susannah said, "We've met before, haven't we?" It was hardly above a whisper, so no one else heard her words.

54

"I have the feeling we have, Aunt Susannah."

"We must talk in private later on when the others are not around," Susannah returned. Then, on impulse, she pulled the child to her and hugged her.

After supper that night, when the men had adjourned to the library for cigars and brandy and the ladies were in the sitting room taking tea and little cookies, Susannah asked that she and Nellie might be excused to have a look around the old house. Nancy offered to accompany them, but Susannah preferred only the company of the child.

"It was fortuitous that my granddaughter had other plans this evening, isn't it?" Susannah commented as she left the parlor in the company of Nellie. "Ann Marie is a sweet little thing, and she certainly has a mind of her own. I fear, however, that if she were present she would wish to occupy all of my time. And I do wish to get better acquainted with you."

Nellie held to the old woman's hand as they went down the hallway toward the front of the house.

"You know this isn't the same house in which I grew up, don't you?" Susannah continued. "The original Edward House was not on Beacon Hill, although it wasn't far from here. And, in fact, the original house was first called Barrywell House when it was built by my grandmother, Augusta."

"Barrywell House?"

"That was Grandmother's first husband's name," Susannah explained. "I, of course, never knew him. Nor did I know Joshua Phenwick, her second husband. Legend has it that Augusta liked old Joshua's name so much, she married him for it without more than a passing interest in the man who possessed it. Later, she met a French Canadian, prior to the Revolutionary War when the French were not welcome in Boston. She fell in love with and married Charles Signoret, who she forced to take the name of Joshua Phenwick in place of his French name. Besides, Grandmother was not about to give up the Phenwick name." She laughed merrily. "Grandmother was quite an old girl!"

"So I've heard," Nellie replied, catching the laughter. Susannah indicated the door to the ballroom and Nellie pushed it open. "Get a lamp from that table."

Nellie did as she was instructed. They entered the enormous ballroom.

"Ah, what memories this room brings back to me," Susannah said, "although this is merely a replica of the original ballroom. My mother, Patricia, had this house built. She called it Edward House for my father." She gazed at her reflection in the mirrors that lined the walls. "What wonderful parties and balls were held in here! My mother loved to entertain." She pointed to the large portrait at the end of the room. "Of course you've met Augusta, haven't you?"

"Yes, we have a painting similar to that one at Phenwick House," Nellie replied.

"Whew! I've eaten too much. Shall we sit on the settee while I catch my breath?" Susannah asked, still clinging to the girl's hand. "I'm afraid one more of those waltzes in here would do me in. But what glorious memories I have."

"I should like to hear about your girlhood sometime."

"Sometime—yes." Susannah sat, and motioned for Nellie to sit beside her. "I would like to ask you something, child."

"What is it?"

"When you first came to Edward House, did it appear familiar to you?"

"Why, yes, as a matter of fact it did," Nellie admitted. "I had the feeling that I had been here before. But of course that is impossible since this is my first visit to Boston."

"Yes, of course." Susannah arched her brow. She

glanced around her. The single lamp that had been placed on a small table, reflected in the many mirrors. "I don't know how to broach what is on my mind, Nellie. Perhaps I should preface it by telling you that I've been around the world several times. My life has been met with many and various experiences, and I've known many people, both ordinary and singularly different."

"My grandmother used to tell me about you."

"Ah, yes, dear Rebecca." Susannah sighed. "She was only my half-sister. Perhaps that is why we were so basically different. Still, in her way, I believe she understood me and my kind of life. Isn't it strange that we were both born of the same parent and yet were so dramatically different? Perhaps not."

"I find I'm quite different from the way Elizabeth is."

Pointing to the large portrait, Susannah said: "Augusta believed in the occult. She even hired a woman who appeared to be well versed in many phases of the mysterious to be with Aunt Jane when she was a young girl. I suppose all of us who have become Phenwick women have had some encounter with the supernatural —the unknown."

"The supernatural?"

"You've doubtless heard of the ill-fated Rachel Phenwick, who was allegedly possessed by the spirits of two disincarnate witches," Susannah said, as if she were speaking to herself. "Rebecca didn't like to think it possible, but I know she was convinced, as were others of us, that she was actually the reincarnation of Rachel."

Nellie stared without blinking.

"And it is said that your own mother, Kate, is the reincarnation of Uncle Danny," Susannah went on. "How that can be, I don't know. Or why there should be two —or more—incidents of alleged reincarnation in the same direct family line. I refer to Rebecca, then her daughter, and—well . . . " She sighed and softly belched. "I do love the taste of goose, but it always keeps coming back.

57

Where was I? Oh, yes. And if what I hear is correct, your own father, John Collier, is allegedly the reincarnation of Michael O'Plaggerty. Michael was a very good friend of both Uncle Danny and my father."

"Edward?"

"Yes." Susannah put a handkerchief to her face. "Now, if that is true—not that I'm saying it is—I mean about Uncle Danny and Michael—I suspect it's possible that as boys they willed themselves to return together into another lifetime. And if they did, might not my own father have done the same thing? Like a three-way pact."

"Your father? Edward?"

"Yes. Oh, dear, this really should be too deep for me to comprehend. Well, I don't—not at all. But if all this is possible, who might I have been in a past life? It boggles the mind, doesn't it, Nellie."

"You'll excuse me," Nellie said, "but I don't quite understand what this is all about. What are you getting at?"

Susannah turned to her. "Why did you ask me about the Raja Eye practically the moment we met?"

"I—I don't know. I didn't mean to offend you. It was just a thought that came to my mind. And even after I mentioned it, I didn't know why I had. It just came out. I believe I must have been as surprised about it as you were. I suppose I thought Grandmother had—"

"Nonsense! Nellie, you must remember I'm not like most of the women in the family," Susannah stated. "I've had too many experiences, have known too many persons who claimed to have known about the mysteries of the Universe. Too many stories from different sources have been presented to me—identical types of stories that indicate to me that there must be something to what I've been told."

"I don't understand."

"Nellie, the Raja Eye killed my father. It was a precious sapphire taken from a holy statue in India. A curse was put on it. Even I went into a kind of paralysis before the curse was removed. No person who is alive today knew my father had the Raja Eye in his possession at the time of his death. Mother may have known about it, but I'm certain she would never have told Rebecca about such a thing, particularly since Mother never mentioned knowledge of the sapphire to me after my father's death."

"Aunt Susannah, I don't know what you're talking about," Nellie stated. She was obviously frightened.

"In short, what I'm getting at," Susannah added, lightly stroking the girl's hair, "is that *only my father* would have mentioned the Raja Eye to me—or would have been the only person who knew it was a sapphire."

Nellie rose to her feet, jerking away from Susannah's touch. "I don't want to hear any more! You frighten me, Aunt Susannah! Please, let us go back with the others."

"Forgive me, little Nellie," Susannah called. "I didn't mean to upset you. But don't you see—"

"I see that you need help," Nellie returned as she scampered toward the door.

"Don't you see that if Danny and Michael fulfilled their agreement to return to be together in another life—and in that as husband and wife, Katie and John—then—then—"

Nellie was at the door. She wanted to close her ears.

"Then wouldn't it be logical that Edward would come back as their—as their child?" Susannah asked.

"No!" Nellie screamed as she ran from the room and down the hallway toward the parlor.

"Nellie, you—try to understand," Susannah said loudly.

The men had heard Nellie's close-to-hysterical screaming as they sat over brandy in the library. Stuart was quickly to his feet to investigate, with John Collier directly behind him and Thad in the rear. Stuart caught a glimpse of Nellie as she flew up the hallway. He motioned for John to go to her.

Susannah was staring in a daze when Stuart and Thad reached where she was seated.

"Cousin Susannah?" Stuart questioned.

"It's all very clear to me, don't you see?" Susannah stated. "Now I can see the logic behind it. I didn't when it was Katie and John, but now I do." She belched again, loudly this time. "The food was greasy, Stuart—delicious, but greasy."

"Thad will help you to your room," Stuart instructed. "You'll want to rest."

"Yes, I believe I should," Susannah replied. "I'm afraid you'll both have to help me up."

As Thad helped Susannah up the stairs, Stuart went to the kitchen and the servants' quarters beyond. There he gave instructions that a carriage and driver be made ready. He would personally go to the home of Joseph Ornby and get the doctor to come examine Susannah.

"No, Thadius, I'll not undress," Susannah said. "Just unloosen a few places that are tight so I can breathe easier. I fear the goose didn't agree with me at all."

Thad did all he could do to make her as comfortable as possible. He even got a wet cloth and put it to her head. Susannah appeared to be a bit more comfortable than she had been.

"Do you wish to sleep?" Thad asked after Susannah had been silent for several minutes.

"No, Thadius, I've merely been catching my breath," Susannah returned, removing the wet cloth from her eyes and pushing it onto her forehead. "There is something I must tell you. I don't know how you can prove it one way or the other. But I feel I must confide in you, and somehow hope that you will understand. When I was a young girl, I met a man who gave me a sapphire. The sapphire was called the Raja Eye."

Thad pulled a chair up to the bed and sat to listen as the old woman told her story.

"Can't you tell me what is wrong, Nellie?" John asked as he held her close to himself. They were in the dining room, just off the parlor, where John had caught her before she had burst in on the ladies.

"She frightened me. Aunt Susannah frightened me!" Nellie blubbered, sobbing between words.

"How did she frighten you?"

"I can't tell you," Nellie cried. "I don't want to stay here. I want to go home."

A light tap came at the door. It was pushed open and Nancy appeared.

"What is it, John? What is troubling the child?" Nancy inquired.

"She appears to be frightened. That's about all I can get out of her."

Nancy went directly to where they were standing. She put her hand to Nellie's face. "Can you tell *me* about it, Nellie?"

"I would rather not," Nellie sobbed, "not now."

"She is obviously deeply distraught," Nancy remarked. "I thought she was with Susannah."

"It was Susannah who—"

"I don't want to stay in this house!" Nellie exclaimed. "Please don't make me stay here another night!"

"Nellie, you're not being reasonable," John said.

"Please, Miss Nancy, can't you help me?" Nellie pleaded.

"Of course, I can, child, of course, I can," Nancy soothed. "Come to Cousin Nancy. Let me hold you."

Nellie relinquished her hold on her father and practically leapt into Nancy's waiting arms.

"You'll come to our house. We've plenty of room. It will be better, with Susannah here. John, you may come, too."

"Yes, under the circumstances, I suppose that would be best," agreed John. "I'll have to speak with Stuart."

Nancy comforted Nellie until the girl had calmed; then she made arrangements for Nellie and John to stay with her.

Dr. Joseph Ornby examined Susannah. Believing her to be tense because of the sea travel and the excitement of the evening, he gave her a sleeping draught and suggested that Thad remain with her until she lost consciousness.

"What do you make of it all, Joe?" Stuart asked his cousin as they left the old lady's room.

"She is up in years," Joseph replied. "And she may well be verging on senility. I'll have a come-look-in on her tomorrow. Also, because of the child's distressed state, I would like to confer with her, too, in my office. I'll not stay longer, Stuart. Good night."

Stuart closed the door behind the doctor. He was about to go toward the parlor when Thad appeared coming down the stairs. "Is she asleep?"

Thad nodded his head. He wore a strange expression. "What is it, Thad?"

"Only the ramblings of an old lady, I suspect." Thad shook his head and went to put his hand on Stuart's shoulder. "We Phenwicks are a strange lot, aren't we?"

The following morning when the maid went to awaken Susannah, there was no response to her knock on the door. Instead of entering, she went immediately to get Stuart.

Ruth was waiting outside in the hallway when Stuart came from Susannah's room. He stared vacantly at his wife.

"Cousin Susannah has passed away. I'll send for Joseph."

# Chapter Six

A simple memorial service was performed in Boston, obviously for the benefit of the family. The body was embalmed and sent on the next ship back to England where Gregory would make concluding arrangements for his mother. Susannah had many, many friends. It would be a large gathering.

A letter from Charles Mumford had arrived in Boston the day of the memorial service for Susannah. Because of the confusion and emotional state in which the family found themselves, the letter remained on the hall table at Edward House for two days before it was given to John Collier.

Dear John:

I do not wish to alarm you, but I feel you should be advised of the situation here in Greenfield.

First, your beloved Kate has not been a bit well these last two weeks. She appears to have excessive congestion in her lungs. It started with one, then moved over to the other. I have ordered her to bed. She is a devoted mother and cannot resist responding to the needs of her children. Hence she is up and down.

Strangely, young Rupert seems to have developed

a similar condition. Believe it or not, he is easier to keep in bed than Kate is. I call on them both at least twice a day, and Mrs. Carlyle is in constant attendance.

The other development, which is most discouraging, is an outbreak of seven more cases of cholera in Greenfield. That brings the total to fifteen. Fortunately there have only been two deaths as a direct result of the dread disease. My colleagues and I have agreed that it has reached epidemic proportions here, which means we are all kept busy tending to those who have it and those who show the least indication that they might have it.

Although I don't believe it is necessary for you to rush back to Greenfield immediately, I would suggest that when you do return that you leave Nellie in Boston for a while until this thing is contained.

We were all sorry to hear of the passing of Mrs. Phenwick and send our condolences to you and the rest of the family.

> Yours faithfully,
> Dr. Charles Mumford
> [It was signed *Charles*.]

John reread the letter three times. While the words did not have a sense of urgency to them, he felt as if he were reading between the lines, where he discovered implications of fear that verged on panic. Charles was a sensible man who did not seem to be ruled by emotions. Perhaps that is why he had not insisted that John return immediately.

"Something wrong?" Thad asked as he came upon John reading the letter in the front hallway.

"Wrong?"

"You look pale."

John listlessly handed the letter to Thad. "I just received this."

Thad scanned it, then handed it back. "What are you going to do?"

"The first thing is pray," John replied. "Then I think I'd better have a talk with Stuart."

"He won't be back from Portsmouth until late tonight or early tomorrow," Thad explained. "He was called up there yesterday afternoon."

"I see." John scratched his head. "What are your plans for the day?"

"I've nothing definite ahead of me," Thad replied. "I thought I would go down to the Medallion office for a while. But it isn't important. I can do it later. Do you have something on your mind?"

John fluttered the letter in Thad's direction.

"I mean, besides that."

"How about a long walk on the Common? Just you and me," John suggested.

"If that is what you would like," Thad returned. "Mother said she was taking Nellie to see Dr. Joseph today, and Daniel Louis is off doing something or other. We could just stay here and talk."

"I'd rather walk, if you don't mind."

"Sure. I'll change my boots. These aren't for long-distance walking," Thad said with a laugh. "I'll just be a few minutes."


"Let Nellie remain here with me," Joseph told Nancy, "while you run errands for two or three hours."

Nancy was reluctant to leave the girl alone, yet she realized that keeping herself occupied during the time Nellie was with the doctor was far better than sitting about fretting. She also needed to keep busy to get her mind off of Susannah. Although she had not known the old lady very well, Susannah's passing had affected Nancy.

Nellie sat in the big overstuffed chair and stared about the office at the books, the pictures, the various items of interest that caught her attention. Then she gazed concertedly at Dr. Joseph Ornby as he stroked his beard while he sat behind his desk. After cleaning his glasses and readjusting them on his face, he smiled broadly at the little girl.

"Cousin Nancy tells me that you have been having some bad dreams since you've been staying at her house," Joseph began.

"I've always had many dreams," Nellie replied. "I dream practically every time I go to sleep. And they're not *all* very nice."

"You have what they call nightmares?"

"Yes. Often. But there is a certain kind of dream that really disturbs me."

"What kind is that?"

"Well, I know it, whether it's good or bad, by the fact that I remember it all day after I've dreamed it the night before. Sometimes it stays with me for a long time. The usual dreams just go away—or are forgotten shortly after I awaken."

"Why do you suppose those other dreams remain?"

"Because I believe they foretell something that is going to happen."

"Prophetic dreams?" Dr. Joseph asked.

"I guess that's the word," Nellie replied.

"Are these prophetic dreams always bad?"

"Oh, no. Sometimes they're very good, and I feel happy thinking about them. Most aren't gloomy at all. And ever so many of them turn out like I imagine they're going to—I mean in reality."

Joseph Ornby leaned back in the chair and tried to appear very fatherly. "As you know, dear Nellie, my brother Augustus and I have for many years been interested in the workings of the mind. Aug has spent much time abroad—and, in fact, is now in India doing further

66

research. We both have long had theories about dreams, as have other doctors who have analyzed the psychological aspects of man. We feel that dreams are produced by mental activity that happens in a sleep state. That is to say, when your conscious mind is asleep, your subconscious mind is free to roam wherever it likes in time and space. It can go forward or backward, and it seems to gather little bits and pieces along the way. Sometimes when we doctors put patients into a sleep state—it's called hypnosis—we're able to get the subconscious mind to project forward or backward in time-space to bring us some very interesting pictures."

"It sounds very complicated," Nellie commented.

"Well, where else do you suppose these premonitions you have come from?" he asked, leaning forward.

"I don't know."

"But you *do* know that you have dreams, or notions while you're awake, that do happen."

"Yes." Nellie squirmed in the chair. Her feet could not touch the floor. "I know I came to Boston for a very definite reason."

"What was that reason?"

"*That* I don't know exactly," she replied. "But I do believe it was for the purpose of meeting someone."

"For meeting someone? Who do you suppose?"

"That hasn't been made known to me yet."

Dr. Joseph Ornby pushed back in his chair. "But you believe you will know who or what it is before you leave Boston, is that the case?"

"I believe so, yes."

Joseph rose. A hulking man with graying hair and a large round face, he paced to the window and seemed to circle around the room before he spoke again. "Nellie, I have been told that you said something to Susannah Phenwick upon first meeting her that was enigmatic, perplexing."

"I had an urge to say *Raja Eye*," Nellie replied, "and almost instantly I knew it was really a sapphire."

"Have you ever seen a sapphire?"

"No."

"Do you know what a raja is?"

"No."

"Had you, then, never heard of either a Raja Eye or a sapphire prior to meeting Cousin Susannah?"

"That is correct."

Joseph sat on the edge of the desk, only inches from Nellie. "When Nancy first told me of that incident, for she had overheard what you said to Cousin Susannah, I merely casually passed it off. Then I began to focus my attention on it—for it wouldn't leave me alone. And the conclusion I reached is that Cousin Susannah must have attached some great significance to the sapphire Raja Eye."

"I know she did."

"Cousin Susannah's mother, whom we all called Aunt Patricia, was herself a writer of sorts," Joseph continued. "During her last years, when she was bedridden and infirm, she dictated a kind of family history to Marcia Phenwick and later told other stories to Gregory Phenwick's wife, Ilene, when she was attending the old lady. Marcia, who, as you know, was Stuart's first wife, had carefully chronicled the stories Aunt Patricia told her. Later, after the old lady's passing, Marcia had the family history published in a limited edition. My Aunt Jane Augusta left me a copy of the history. When I began to delve through it, I discovered the story of Cousin Susannah and the events that happened in her youth, when she was presented a mysterious sapphire, which was known as the Raja Eye."

Nellie blinked. "She gave it to her father to keep for her."

"Yes. How did you know?"

"It was just a thought that occurred to me."

"Uncle Elias?—" Joseph baited.

"No, Edward. Elias was Patricia's second husband," Nellie corrected.

"Yes, I was mistaken." Joseph stared deeply into her eyes. "What did Cousin Susannah say to you that so terribly upset you, Nellie?"

"I don't wish to tell you," Nellie replied. "That was between Cousin Susannah and me."

"I see." Joseph stretched his legs and went back around the desk. "I shan't press you for an answer. That would be prying, wouldn't it? Cousin Susannah had lived to a ripe old age. Her life was full and complete. I suspect senility had begun to creep into her thinking. I once had a teacher who told me that both the flesh and the mind begin showing desire for change prior to the time a person passes. What a relief it must be for a person who has suffered either physically or mentally to be free of such painful conditions! Dear old Aunt Jane Augusta was in sheer misery before she went. And my father confided that Aunt Patricia prayed for death in her last years—living was that uncomfortable for her."

Nellie was looking down. She acted as if she had not heard Joseph's words. Lifting her head, she smiled at the man. "I dreamed that I was to come to Boston with my father."

"Did you dream that more than once?"

"I don't recall."

"Have you had any recurring dreams?" Joseph questioned. He realized that Nellie had purposefully turned away from their previous subject of conversation.

The child paled. "There is one."

"Would you care to share it with me?"

Nellie related about the dream in which she stood in the cemetery in Greenfield and gazed down at the tombstones of her mother and her siblings. "The night before last, I was in the cemetery again. There I found my father grieving. I forced myself to awaken and went into his room to comfort him."

Joseph sat with his hands folded beneath his chin, index fingers pointing up to his lips. He, too, had feelings mixed with impressions that came to his mind. He was aware that the little girl's words were true and could well carry an explosive impact. Then he smiled reassuringly at Nellie. But his exterior facade could not erase the sense of awareness he experienced at that moment.

The Common was early-summer green. The trees stood tall, with richly colored foliage, and cast shadows to make shade from the warmth of the sun. A soft wind had been whispering over the uneven terrain. Birds sang and chattered. Squirrels scampered and frolicked. It couldn't have been a nicer day.

John had confided the feelings of urgency that had come over him, and the nagging desire he had to return to Greenfield. Thad had been a good listener. They had walked for nearly two hours. Finally, as they both felt the need of rest, they found cool shade beneath a large oak tree. They removed their coats and untied their cravats.

"You won't take Nellie with you, will you, John?" Thad questioned.

"What? No. I feel very close to little Nell," John related. "And if I could, I would bring my other children and Kate to Boston until that dreadful thing is over up there."

"I'm certain Mother would be pleased to look after Nellie," Thad said. "And I would see that she was protected."

"That is kind of you, Thad." John patted the other's hand.

"I will consider it an honor."

John stared deeply into Thad's face. "We've spoken enough about me. I'm weary of it. Tell me about yourself."

"I beg your pardon?"

70

"I know you recently returned from being abroad," John remarked. "Stuart tells me you're restless and haven't quite found yourself yet."

Thad ducked his head. "You might say I've long been having an internal battle of emotions. I still have deep feelings for Ruth—I suppose I always shall. She is often on my mind."

"But she is Stuart's wife. And Ruth deeply loves him. That is apparent."

"Yes, I know." Thad gazed into the distance. "I spoke with my half-brother, Joshua, in London. He invited me to come live there and become a partner in Medallion Enterprises of London. It was an interesting idea—and I must admit I found myself becoming strangely attracted to Gregory's twin daughters, Isabelle and Elena. They're identical. Yet they're still very young—near the same age as Nellie, I suspect. And Joshua's daughter Carrie seemed to find me appealing. But I could only foresee an emotional entanglement there. Besides, I wanted to return to Boston to see that Mother was doing well. Brother John is still close at hand, but I worry about her."

"Then you plan to remain in Boston?"

"No, John, I don't," Thad said emphatically. "For as long as I am here, I will be too near to Ruth for comfort—mine and hers."

"Running away from your emotions, Thad? That's an impossibility."

"I know that, too." Thad sighed. "I've visited Portland on several occasions. Now that Leo has taken over the operation of Medallion there and Crandall Ornby has gone into retirement, I've considered working with my nephew. Leo and I are close to the same age."

"Leo?"

"You probably know him as Mike. He's happily married to Ann Ornby," Thad related. "But I've never really been well acquainted with Leo."

"What would you like to do with Medallion?"

71

"I don't know. Perhaps I could work in somewhere."

"When was the last time you were at Greenfield?"

Thad thought a moment. "I can't remember. It's strange, I've often thought of Greenfield and wondered what it would be like to live there."

"It's my favorite place in the whole world," John confessed. "My business is doing well. In fact, it is increasing so rapidly that I can hardly keep up with it. I shouldn't be away so long now. I trust the men who work for me, but I like to be close at hand to oversee. Still, trips like this to Boston are necessary, too."

"You need an assistant."

"Well I know." John again observed Thad's still somewhat boyish face. "My sons, George and Rupert, are only small boys, a good many years away from becoming actively involved with the business. Nellie helps as best she can. And I have to admit she has a good business sense about her."

"I've already become quite fond of Nellie," Thad expressed.

"Of course she is still a child."

"Of course."

John smiled. "Perhaps you would be interested in coming to Greenfield again. If you do, I'm liable to put you to work making furniture." He laughed.

"Don't laugh, John, I might like that," Thad said. "Yes, I might." He cleared his throat as if he wanted to change the subject of conversation. Then he glanced to the west and saw the figure of a boy coming toward them on a bicycle.

John followed the direction of Thad's attention. The boy was waving his hand. A stab of anxiety went through John, a creepy feeling that told him the boy was searching for him with an unhappy urgency.

"It's Danny Phenwick," Thad exclaimed, rising to his feet. A moment later he was dashing to meet the boy.

"I've brought a wire for John Collier," Danny explained. "It was delivered to the Medallion office. My father sent me with it."

The handsome, physically attractive youth of thirteen breathlessly propped his bicycle against the tree and fumbled through his pockets for the telegram.

With a sense of dread, John unfolded the paper. "Oh, no!"

Thad took the paper from him.

DEAR JOHN

ELIZABETH HAS CHOLERA STOP SUSPECT GEORGE IS COMING DOWN WITH IT STOP BOTH RUPERT AND KATE HAVE GROWN WEAKER STOP LEAVE NELLIE IN BOSTON STOP URGENT YOU RETURN HOME IMMEDIATELY STOP

CHARLES

"Oh, my God!" exclaimed Thad. He put his hand to John's shoulder and held tightly.

Tears streaked down John's face. "My dearest Katie— my children."

Thad moved around to face the man and stoutly embraced him as John broke under the emotional impact and began to cry. The telegram fell to the ground. Danny picked it up and folded it.

"Shall I go with you, John?" Thad asked several minutes later.

"No. I must go alone. You mustn't jeopardize your own health," John sobbed. "Look after Nellie for me."

"I will. You know I will," Thad returned.

"I mean—if—"

"Don't think such a thing, John."

"But if it should happen, I want you to promise that you will see to Nellie's well-being for as long as you live," John stated. "Is that a promise?"

"It's a promise. Danny is my witness." Thad tightened his embrace.

"Now I must go," John said, wiping the tears from his eyes. "May I use your bicycle, Danny?"

"By all means, Cousin John," Danny replied. "It's easy to ride."

John took the telegram, tucked it into his pocket, then got on the bicycle and drove as directly as possible across the Common.

"I knew it must have been important," Danny said. "That's why I came so fast."

Thad stared at the young boy. Then he put his arms about him. Tears came to Thad's eyes and Danny could feel the sobs welling in him as Thad leaned heavily against him.

"I may have been better off to remain in London," Thad remarked a short while later. "Still, I wonder what this thing called *destiny* is. There must have been a reason for me not staying abroad. Events and times change. I feel as if I've been drifting about for years now, and suddenly fate or whatever has cast me into a new role. It is a time of death, Danny, still life must go on. Tragedy strikes, and out of its turmoil new horizons appear."

"I was so young when my own mother died," Danny commented, also reacting with sorrow to the situation.

"Come, Danny, we must get back and help John if we can," Thad stated, his arm still about the boy's shoulders. "And most of all, we must help Nellie. She obviously is the one who will need most comforting."

The two walked together over the green grassy knolls. The sun was brightly shining, but tears made rainbow prisms in their vision.

# Chapter Seven

Obviously Nellie could not be consoled, although both Nancy and Thad tried their best to comfort the girl. After a tearful parting with her father, the child went to her room and asked not to be disturbed. She knew within her heart of hearts that her prophetic dreams were manifesting.

The train ride from Boston to Portland seemed to take an eternity. John went immediately to Falmouth House and arranged with Leo to borrow a carriage and horses. Both Ann and Leo wanted to accompany him. But John would not permit it.

Rain fell as John traveled the road from Portland to Greenfield. He would not spare the horses. Rain was still drizzling when he reached Phenwick House. Paxton took care of the horses and shortly thereafter went to fetch Dr. Mumford.

Nana Carlyle met John at the front door. She wore a piece of cotton tied about her face and mouth. She had another piece of material for John to tie about his face.

"It's a precaution, Mr. Collier," Nana explained. "It allegedly keeps one from coming in direct contact with the germs."

"Have the children worn these?" John asked, as he tied the cloth about his head.

"We tried to get them to, Mr. Collier," Nana said. "But you know how stubborn George can be. And Elizabeth complained that it suffocated her. Now they are both in bed, deathly ill."

With Nana at his side, John went to the rooms in which his three younger children were isolated. Rupert was asleep. George, while conscious, seemed delirious and did not recognize his father. Of the three, only Elizabeth perceived that her father had arrived.

"Don't come closer, Papa," Elizabeth whined. "I don't want you to become infected."

"Oh, my precious Elizabeth," John moaned. "How weak and pale you look."

"Please, Papa, don't come nearer, please," the child begged.

John could not believe his eyes when he went to the door of Kate's room. Her face was gray, eyes sunken in and circled with deep brown marks.

"Oh, my darling, my darling!" Kate feebly exclaimed. "You've come home at last."

Refusing to heed Nana's warning, John went directly to the bed and took Kate in his arms. "Katie—Katie—"

"I'm infected, my dearest. You mustn't catch what I have," Kate complained. "You mustn't die too."

"Don't speak of death, dearest Katie," John whispered, the cloth mask between his lips and her ear. "We're soul mates."

"That doesn't mean we must die together, my darling," Katie sighed.

"How can I live without you?"

"You've done it before, John—you can do it again."

"No, no, Katie."

"Nellie—?"

"Nellie remained in Boston," John explained.

"Good." Kate tried to smile. "They haven't told me the

truth, but I know my other children are also grievously ill. It tears at my heart to think they are suffering." She coughed.

"You mustn't talk too much," John coaxed.

"I love you, John. I always have, I always will," Kate stated. "I'm so very tired. If this is my debt for behavior in former lives, then I trust it is sufficiently awful to wipe the slate clean. I have suffered, long before you ever knew I was in great pain. The one thing that has made this life worth while has been your love, dearest John. Oh, my darling, although I hate to leave you alone in the physical world, I am anxious to depart from the torment of the flesh."

"Please don't speak of such things now," John begged. "You will get well. You'll be strong again, you'll see."

"I think not, my darling," Kate sighed. "But I do promise you this, that I shall not leave this earth plane as long as you are alive. I will somehow manage to hover about you and love you from the other side."

"Oh, Katie—" John was crying.

"But because I love you so very much, my darling," Kate continued, "I want you to promise me that, when the time is right, you will consider taking another wife. The thing I can't bear is the thought of you being without someone with whom you can express the deep love that is in you. I've been wonderfully blessed with the beauty of your physical gratification, and in pleasing you, I've pleased myself. You must continue, in time, to have that physical release, that experience of loving. I promise not to watch you during intimate moments." She chuckled, but that quickly evolved into a fit of coughing.

Nana rushed into the room and practically pried Kate from John's embrace. "You must go now, Mr. Collier. I'll tend to Mrs. Collier. I know what to do."

John slowly drew his hand from Kate's until only their fingertips touched. He wanted to fall onto the bed, but Nana gave him a look of warning that discouraged him.

A lost man, John climbed down the stairs. He was crying, and periodically he fell against the wall to brace himself.

Dr. Charles Mumford was ushered into the library by Paxton. John was seated in the large, leather-upholstered Queen Anne chair, his face buried in his hands. If he was aware of the doctor's presence, he made no acknowledgment of it.

Charles stepped to the seat and put his hand to John's shoulder. "You've arrived home safely."

John glanced up. He was still wearing the mask, as was Charles. "My heart is breaking."

"I know, John, I know," Charles said. "There have now been twenty-seven deaths from cholera in Greenfield. Your foreman, Horace Boggs, isn't expected to live through the day. This is the most terrible disaster that has hit Greenfield."

"How can it be stopped?"

"I wish I knew." Charles drew a chair up in front of John. "I've been working day and night for the last several weeks. I do my best to keep my strength up, but I am weakening."

"Katie—the children—?"

"Both Kate and Rupert have something other than cholera," Charles stated. "Although I suspect they each have touches of cholera, too. George and Elizabeth both have the disease. I hold a slight hope for them."

"Hope only for George and Elizabeth?"

"Only a *slight* hope, John." He took John's hand and held it.

On the morning of July third, Nana sent Paxton for Dr. Mumford. Rupert had died during the night.

"He must be buried quickly, John," Charles advised. "Hopefully we will bury the germs with him. Reverend Ketchum will perform a simple service. Later, after this is all over—"

"After? Will it ever end?" John questioned.

Charles patted the man. "It would be best not to tell Kate of Rupert's passing. The emotional strain would severely weaken her."

"Charles, will you be so kind to make arrangements with Reverend Ketchum. You know what to do, I don't," John said.

"Yes, of course."

When John arrived at Kate's room a short while later, he found her bed empty. Charles was in examining Elizabeth, when he heard John's frantic screams.

Kate was standing at the door to Rupert's room. The sheet covering her youngest child's face told her all she needed to know. When John reached her, she collapsed in his arms. He carried her back to her bed, with the assistance of Dr. Mumford.

Toward late afternoon that hot July day, John had fallen asleep in the rocker in Kate's room.

"Mickey, it's time to go now."

John shook himself into consciousness. Kate's eyes were open and she was staring into the distance. He went to the bed. "Katie?"

"It was Katie this time, wasn't it?" She smiled. "Before, it was Danny. And who knows what it will be next time. My Mickey, my John." She reached for his hand, but before their fingers touched, Kate's hand fell limply to the bed.

"Katie? Katie?" John panicked. "Nana, come quick!"

At noon on July fifth, George Collier stopped breathing. Effort was made by Nana to revive him, but it was useless. Both Dr. Mumford and Reverend Ketchum were sent for.

John, Nana Carlyle, and Paxton witnessed the third funeral in three days. Charles was also present.

"I'll not wear this damn thing any longer!" John declared, violently ripping the cloth mask from his face. "Let me catch the vile disease and go to join my family!"

"You still have two daughters, John," Charles said softly, comfortingly. "And even if Elizabeth—"

"*If?* Is there any doubt in your mind, Charles?" John ranted. "I came from her room less than an hour ago. She has the same look in her face that the others had."

"John, there are no words that can comfort at a time like this," Charles stated.

"The only comfort I can ever possibly know is death!"

"Perhaps—and perhaps not." Charles shook his head. "You believe that you and Katie were soul mates. If such things do exist and people come back to earth time and time again, doesn't it occur to you that you also have soul attachments to the others who are with you? Perhaps you even have some kind of bond to me. And goodness knows, there has always been a remarkable closeness between you and Nellie. Think of little Nell. She needs you now more than ever, John. You can't give up, can't escape through death—you would be running out on her. Isn't it obvious to you that Nellie needs you; obvious that you must make every effort to go on living?"

"Obvious? Obvious? The only thing that is obvious to me now is pain, torment, inner emptiness!" John exclaimed. "I intend to sit with a naked face in Elizabeth's room the rest of the day and through the night. I will hold her, kiss her, breathe her breath—until I am contaminated with her germs. I don't want to live, Charles, I don't! Nellie will manage!"

When Charles arrived the next day, he found John sitting in Elizabeth's room. He was in a daze. The mask he had worn was shredded in tiny bits.

"John?"

John did not react.

Charles felt his brow and took his pulse. Then he went to his medical bag and withdrew a hypodermic syringe. John barely reacted to the injection. Yet by the time

Charles had examined Elizabeth, John was unconscious. Paxton helped Charles carry the man from Elizabeth's room.

On the morning of the seventh, Charles arrived early at Phenwick House. He first examined John. He showed no signs of having symptoms of the disease.

Charles returned at two in the afternoon. John was resting comfortably under sedation. Still no indications of cholera.

Then Charles went to examine Elizabeth. He deduced that she had died within an hour of his arrival.

The doctor made arrangements for the burial, then ordered that John be taken to his house, where a special room was prepared for him. There he was kept under heavy sedation for the next week.

The telegram arrived in Boston on the afternoon of the twelfth of July. It was addressed to Stuart Phenwick in care of Medallion Enterprises.

MY DEAR STUART

. IT IS WITH DEEP REGRET THAT I MUST INFORM YOU THAT THE WIFE AND THREE YOUNGER CHILDREN OF JOHN COLLIER HAVE SUCCUMBED TO THE FATAL DISEASE OF CHOLERA STOP EMERGENCY BURIAL WAS EXECUTED AND FORMAL SERVICES MAY BE PERFORMED LATER STOP JOHN COLLIER HAS BEEN KEPT UNDER SEDATION SINCE PRIOR TO THE LAST DEATH STOP HE SHOWS NO SIGNS OF HAVING TAKEN THE CHOLERA STOP FROM ALL INDICATIONS THE EPIDEMIC HAS GREATLY SUBSIDED AND THERE HAVE BEEN NO DEATHS IN THE PAST THREE DAYS STOP AT ALL COSTS IT IS MY MOST CONCERTED ADVICE THAT NELLIE REMAIN IN BOSTON FOR AN EXTENDED PERIOD OF TIME UNTIL THIS TERRIBLE THING IS COMPLETELY CLEARED AWAY STOP YOURS FAITHFULLY            CHARLES MUMFORD

Stuart read the wire several times before he made

arrangements to leave the office and go directly to see Joseph Ornby. The doctor accompanied Stuart to the home of Nancy Phenwick.

Nellie had spent the morning playing with Ann Marie Phenwick at Edward House. She had returned and was in the midst of bathing when Stuart and his cousin arrived. The telegram was shown to Nancy.

"Oh, dear God! What will we do?" Nancy asked.

"Do our best to control ourselves," Stuart replied. "We must help the child as best we can."

Thadius returned shortly before Nellie appeared, fresh from her bath. After reading the wire, he quickly took a drink of brandy.

The four were waiting at the foot of the stairs as Nellie descended. She was wearing white with a bright blue ribbon in her hair. Her perceptive eyes moved over the faces before her as she stopped four steps from the bottom.

"What is it?" Nellie asked. "Why is everyone here?"

Stuart said, "Nellie, there is something we must tell you."

Nellie stepped down one more step. Her eyes went to each of the four pairs watching her. A smile. Then a frown. Tears welled at her eyes. "They're dead, aren't they?"

"How did you—?"

"They've been dead for seven days, haven't they?" Stuart nodded.

"Not your father—" Nancy inserted.

"Yes, I know," Nellie said weakly. "I was there. I saw each of them being buried."

"You were there?" exclaimed Joseph.

"I don't know how I got there or when I arrived back," Nellie stated, "but I saw it. Mother called my daddy *Mickey* at the end. If that is so, then you will know I was there. Now, if you will please excuse me, I'll go to my room."

They watched as the brave little girl climbed the stairs. Not until the door was heard closing did Thad go in the same direction.

"She is obviously in a state of shock," Joseph said.

# Chapter Eight

He was obviously as handsome as ever; slightly more mature-looking. Tall. Black hair that glistened, with a twist of curl in it. He was as beautiful to behold as he was magnetic in the way his charm seemed to reach out and engulf people. Despite his years of adventure and his clandestine experiences during the Civil War, a kind of joy emanated from within his personality. A mishap during the war had left him with a slight limp, which was hardly noticeable unless attention was drawn to it. Only occasionally did he experience pain when he walked, and then only when he was tired.

After he had paid the cabman, he stood a moment to gaze up at the glorious white mansion that was perched on top of a bluff overlooking the sea, just north of Boston. There was a time when he had considered that the building was ostentatious and looked far too much like a European castle to be located so near to sedate Boston. The afternoon sun shone on his beige and white attire. The sole casual affect to his entire costume was the straw hat he wore, which had a broad brim and a short crown and was trimmed with brown partridge feathers.

The doorbell was noisy. He could not help but laugh as he heard its familiar ring.

The stiff, balding butler opened the door. He was perhaps the most proper-looking butler in Boston. "Yes?"

"I wish to see Mrs. Phenwick, if you please."

"Is Mrs. Phenwick expecting you, sir?"

"You're new here, aren't you?"

"Yes, sir. Carrier is the name: Amos Carrier." The butler appeared unruffled. "Who may I say is calling?"

"Then she is in. I wish to surprise her. Merely tell her an old friend is here." He handed the butler a red rosebud. "With my compliments to Mrs. Phenwick."

Carrier closed the door and crisply walked over the marble floor of the foyer and the entrance hallway. His footsteps echoed as he moved up the curved stairway with the cupola above it. On the second floor he moved catlike to the large doors that opened onto the sitting room. It was here that the lady of the house spent much of her time during the day hours. An expansive view of the ocean glistened beyond a wall of windows.

"Mrs. Phenwick, there is a caller," Carrier said after his mistress had bade him enter.

"A caller? I'm expecting no one." The lady stretched her long legs beneath the rose pink satin house gown, revealing a glimpse of ankles as she did.

"The gentleman refused to give his name," Carrier explained, "but he did ask me to give you this red rosebud."

Millijoy took the flower from Carrier, stared at it for a moment, then burst into an hilarious gale of laughter. Before Carrier could interpret her reaction, she was quickly to her feet and hurrying toward the door. "It's all right, Carrier. Thank you."

With the graceful swiftness of a ballerina, Milljoy took the steps with great speed, dangling her hand along the marble banister to assure her balance. A moment later she was gliding across the floor of the foyer, one hand holding her skirt to give her freedom of movement. The door was flung wide.

"Adam Truff! I knew it had to be you!" she exclaimed. "Who else would make such a mysterious, well-timed entrance."

"I'm not in yet."

"Don't stand out there. You'll let in the heat of the afternoon," Millijoy stated, reaching to pull him inside the house. Then, with the familiarity of old friends, they embraced. She kissed him on the cheek. "Oh, Adam! I sometimes wondered if I would ever see you again."

"Unless you've gone blind," Adam commented lightly, "it would appear that you're getting a frightfully good look at me now."

"Come upstairs. You do have time for a visit, haven't you?"

"I have made no plans for the rest of the day."

"And for the evening? The night?"

"Nothing," Adam said as he followed her to the stairs. "I've left my baggage at the railway station and I've contacted no one in Boston. You're the first to know I'm here."

Carrier was instructed to bring cool drinks and serve them in the sitting room. The stoic butler eyed Adam curiously and kept thoughts to himself.

"Let me look at you, Adam!" Millijoy remarked, as she held his hands and stood back at arm's length from him. "Have you aged? I wonder."

"You certainly appear the same as when last I saw you."

"I'm getting up in years, Adam. I'm in my thirties now—just barely. But don't breathe that to a soul," Millijoy warned.

"I'm a year away from thirty," Adam said.

"Really? You always seemed so much younger than me in the past."

"Enough about age. It's relative anyway." Adam smiled. "May I sit?"

"You may do anything you please, Adam Truff."

Adam sat on a lounge near the window. In a moment he became casual and appeared to recline on the ornate piece of furniture.

"Now tell me what you're doing back in Boston," Millijoy said.

"What am I doing in Boston? Or why did I come first to Triumph House?" Adam asked.

"You know I'll expect an answer to both questions, so choose which will be first."

Adam laughed.

Carrier served the cool drinks and properly left the room.

"He's new," Adam observed.

"Carrier is a gem. You know I can't keep butlers long. Never mind that. Get to the subject."

"Well, my dear Millijoy," Adam said after sampling the drink, "as you know, I've been traveling much since the end of the war. And quite frankly, I've gone through a large sum of money."

"You're broke?"

"Not quite. But my bank account has reached a touchy state," Adam explained. "I don't care to work for Medallion—or at any job where I must put in regular long hours. So I must find something to supplement my finances."

"And why have you come first to me?"

"To discover the latest about the Phenwicks," Adam replied. "Who better knows of the affairs of the Phenwicks than you?—even if you do sit on the outside looking in. Or have the Phenwicks finally given in and accepted you as one of them?"

"Our relationship has always been strained. My brother-in-law makes a point of being cordial and sometimes solicitous," Millijoy related.

"Stuart was always cordial. A dear person."

Millijoy raised an eyebrow. She sipped from her drink. "And Miss Nancy has continually tried to be sweet. Can she be any other way?"

"I love Nancy dearly," Adam declared. "I take it the two mentioned overlook your reputation."

"My reputation?" Millijoy rolled her head back and laughed. "We *do* understand one another, don't we, Adam?"

"I understand you," he said. "Sometimes I wonder if you truly understand me."

Millijoy eyed him again. Then she proceeded to bring him up to date on the affairs of the Phenwicks.

"John Collier?" Adam questioned. "Yes, I remember him."

"I understand he is doing well in the furniture business in Greenfield," Millijoy continued. "It seems, from what I can gather, that he is in Boston, both trying to do some business and in search of a business partner. I used to get quite a bit of information about the family from Paul. But he's gone out to California. Then I attempted to establish a rapport with Daniel Louis—but he took offense at some of my actions and got uppity."

"You're rambling, dear heart."

"There's little more I can tell you, unless you're interested in becoming John Collier's business partner," Millijoy stated. "The last I heard, he had returned to Greenfield. There's been an epidemic of some kind, which apparently has struck his family. He left his eldest daughter, Nellie, with Miss Nancy."

"Nellie?"

"She's all of twelve," Millijoy replied coldly.

"Speaking of children, where is young Tommy?" Adam asked.

"I will spend an hour with him later this evening," Millijoy explained. "I suspect he's practicing now." She glanced at the large clock standing near the door.

"Practicing?"

"The piano. He's also studying organ. However, I've not got so extravagant that I've purchased that musical instrument for him," Millijoy said.

"It sounds as if he's becoming quite a musician, this son of yours."

Millijoy frowned.

"What is it?"

She shook her head and smiled. "Sometimes I can see very much of Gordon in Tommy."

"Gordon? Why not? Gordon Phenwick was his father."

Millijoy's expression became vacant. "Poor Gordon, he did *so* want to be important. But he was so confused. Tommy practices on the organ in one of the larger churches of Boston. They require an outrageous sum for the use of it. But Tommy is determined."

"He gets his determination from you, Millijoy." Adam altered his position. "Why does it concern you that he must use a church organ?".

"Why? Because that particular church has a rather hysterical doctrine—I mean fanatical—like Gordon was." Millijoy rose and paced to the window. "It worries me that Tommy might be more like his father than I would want him to be." She stared out at the water. "You will stay for supper, won't you?"

"I'll even stay the night, if you have a spare room," Adam said playfully.

Millijoy excused herself on pretense of giving the servants instructions for the evening meal. Adam quietly watched as she left the room. She was disturbed, and he suspected it was brought on by thoughts of her son. A short while later, Adam rose and went to the window. He liked Triumph House. It was the sort of place that appealed to one aspect of his character. He enjoyed the feeling of luxury, the artistically decorated rooms and carved woodwork. Most of all, he felt comfortable in the spaciousness of it. And the view of the sea was the crowning touch. Were he another sort of man, he might create an intimate liaison with Millijoy. Were he underhanded, he could well charm her out of her fortune. But he believed in his way of life, his persuasions, his unorthodox ideas. No, his friendship with Millijoy Phenwick would always remain platonic. It could be no other way.

Millijoy had a second unexpected visitor that evening. While she and Adam were dining on the terrace, enjoying the cool, refreshing sea breezes, Carrier announced that Stuart Phenwick was waiting in the foyer.

"Stuart here?" Millijoy arched an eyebrow and cast a worried glance at Adam. "Tell Mr. Phenwick that I'll see him in the parlor in five minutes, Carrier."

"Yes, Mrs. Phenwick." The butler went to deliver the message.

"Why not invite Stuart out here to have a cup of coffee with us, or a glass of brandy?" Adam questioned as he toyed with a stemmed wine glass.

"I wasn't certain you wanted to see him right away."

"But that's silly, Millijoy. You know I'm always anxious to see Stuart," Adam stated. "After all, I worked directly under him during the war when I was employed as a spy for the North."

"I thought, because you came first to see me, that you were perhaps not on as good terms with Stuart as you had been," Millijoy commented, a tone of skepticism in her voice.

"If you must know the truth, my dear," Adam explained, "I simply didn't wish to go to Edward House for fear I might encounter Ruth by herself."

"Ruth?"

"Although she professes to be deeply in love with Stuart," Adam added, "I don't believe she has ever fully gotten over that remarkable emotional reaction she had to me."

"Does anyone ever get over such a reaction to you, Adam?"

Adam laughed. "I'm serious. I'm too fond of Stuart to put myself in the position of creating a problem in his house."

Millijoy raised her wine glass. "In that case, Adam, why don't *you* go to the parlor and invite Stuart to come join us?"

"A lovely thought." Adam stood, smiled down at the lady, and quickly left the terrace.

Stuart Phenwick had a remarkable way of not displaying reaction to emotional problems, especially when such involved death. Still, he appeared restless as he waited in the parlor. Conscientiously he put thoughts of the tragedy in Greenfield from his mind. When such images would occur, he would instantly think about something else—anything else. Still, he could not help worry about how John Collier was taking the unhappy situation.

Stuart responded to the sound of the door being opened. He did not turn immediately around. "Millijoy, I apologize for appearing unexpectedly this way."

"You needn't apologize to me, Stuart."

"Adam!" Stuart was quickly across the room to embrace his old friend. "Adam Truff! What in the devil are you doing here at Triumph House? When did you arrive back in Boston?"

"I'm having supper with Millijoy is the answer to the first question," Adam said brightly. "And this afternoon should suffice for the second."

"Why didn't you come instantly to see me?"

"I did go to Medallion, but you weren't there. Rather than to go to Edward House and not find you there, I came here."

Stuart knew only too well why he had not gone to Edward House.

"We received word of tragedy this afternoon." He explained the situation.

"I'm terribly sorry to hear of that," Adam said. "I grieve for John Collier. You have my condolences as well, Stuart. After all, Kate was your cousin."

"Distant cousin," Stuart corrected. "I've come to give the news to Millijoy."

"She's awaiting us on the terrace," Adam explained, and motioned for him to go ahead.

The news related, Stuart relaxed and accepted the offered brandy. Sensing his friend's uneasiness, Adam changed the subject of conversation.

"I've recently come from Savannah," Adam informed them. "Savannah in the spring is beautiful; but Savannah in the summer is far too hot and muggy for comfort. Jim Phenwick asked me to relate that he is beginning to get Medallion, Savannah, into working order."

"I'm pleased to hear that," Stuart commented.

"As am I," Millijoy interjected.

"You are?" Adam questioned.

"Millijoy is one of the principal stockholders in Jim's company," Stuart stated. "She has uncanny luck with investing. No wonder she lives in such a luxury palace."

"You might be interested to know," Adam continued, "that I have located the whereabouts of Alexander Augustus."

"You have?" Stuart sat forward.

"Who is Alexander Augustus?" Millijoy asked at the same time.

"He's the late Barbara Phenwick's son," Adam said.

"By Prentise?" questioned Millijoy.

"No, my dear," Stuart returned. "Alexander Augustus is my son. He was conceived while Barbara was married to Uncle Prentise, and her father—and I suspect the rest of the family—believed the child was his. Does Jim know where the boy is?"

"I believe not," Adam replied. "Before his death, Milton Callahan made arrangements for the boy to leave Savannah."

"I want that boy. He *is* my son. I wish to raise him with my other children," Stuart declared.

"It will take money," Adam suggested.

"Whatever it costs."

Millijoy poured brandy. "And naturally Adam must be paid well for his effort."

"I wouldn't have it any other way," Stuart said. "Can you come by the office in the morning, Adam? We'll discuss the matter then. In the meantime, I may have another job for you."

"That's nice, Stuart," Millijoy commented. "Since Adam isn't as aggressive as I am, I'll tell you he desperately needs to have his bank account refortified."

"Millijoy!" Adam exclaimed. "*Desperately* is putting it a bit strong. I'm not desperate—yet."

"Then, by all means, we must discuss business tomorrow morning," Stuart returned. "I would love to sit and visit the rest of the evening, but I think I had best get back. I want to stop by Nancy's house and have a look-in on Nellie. She seemed to be in a state of shock when I left her. Joseph Ornby gave her a sedative. Poor child, losing practically her entire immediate family in such a short span of time."

"I'll stop in to see Miss Nancy tomorrow, Stuart," said Adam in a casual way. "I would appreciate it if you would let me surprise her by not letting her know I'm back in Boston."

Stuart laughed as he agreed.

"Now then, Adam," Millijoy said, after he had seen Stuart to the front door, "what plans do you have for the rest of the evening?"

Adam smiled coyly at her. "Sleep. A warm bath would be nice."

"And nothing more?"

"You know me, Millijoy. I've not changed. *And nothing more.*"

Millijoy shrugged. "I have to admire you, Adam. Admittedly I don't understand you—but I have to admire you." She kissed him on the forehead. "When you're ready, I'll give Carrier instructions to help you."

Adam returned the kiss and thanked her.


Distressed and in an emotional state, Nancy left the house early the next day. Nellie was soundly sleeping when she looked in on the child. Nancy would run a few errands and hurry back, hopefully to arrive before Nellie awakened.

Thad had promised Stuart that he would stop by the Medallion office that morning, after first going to Joseph Ornby's office. Daniel Louis, also, had a reason to be away from the big house on Maple Street. The servants tiptoed about, not wishing to disturb the grieving child.

Nellie awakened to the sound of a mockingbird singing outside her window. She had had a happy dream. Tears had come the night before. Only an empty feeling came over her that day.

The child had dressed and was on her way to the kitchen to find a bite of breakfast when she heard a knocking at the front door. Since the bell had not rung, she assumed that it was one of the family. Opening the door, she gazed up into the handsome face of Adam Truff.

"Miss Nancy, please," he said.

"Miss Nancy?" Nellie seemed confused. "I don't know where she is. I'll get one of the servants."

"One moment, little one. With whom do I have the pleasure of speaking?"

"I'm Nellie Collier. With whom do *I* have the pleasure of speaking?" she mimicked his tone.

"I'm Adam Truff, an old friend of the Phenwick family." He smiled brightly, exuding a charm the child could not avoid. "May I come in while you have a look for Miss Nancy?"

"You may come and help me look, if you like, Mr. Truff."

"I know it's proper for a child to address a gentleman as *mister*," Adam commented. "But, my dear Nellie, I would be pleased if you would simply call me Adam."

"Adam?" Nellie smiled. "Oh, so *you're* Adam."

"I beg your pardon?"

"For at least the last two weeks, maybe longer," Nellie related, "the name of Adam has kept coming to me."

"The name has—?"

"As if it were being spoken from out of nowhere," Nellie answered. "That may sound peculiar to you, but I often hear things—well, not exactly hear them—I just suddenly become aware of them. I suppose that doesn't make much sense to you, and you probably think me a strange little girl."

"I don't think you strange in the least, Nellie Collier."

"Just plain Nellie, if you don't mind."

They both laughed.

"Who do you suppose mentioned my name to you?"

Nellie shrugged. "It just came." She reached to take his hand. "Come along, let's look for Miss Nancy."

Adam's hand seemed so big next to the child's.

When the servants informed them that Nancy, Thad, and Daniel Louis had all three left the house, Nellie invited Adam to have breakfast with her. He accepted the offer of a piece of breakfast cake and a cup of coffee. The servants, having been informed of the tragedy in Greenfield, were surprised to see the little girl in such a bright mood.

"You're a very brave man, aren't you, Adam?"

"How do you mean?"

"In the war and doing all that you did."

"Did Stuart tell you about me?"

"No."

95

"It must have been Thadius or Nancy, then."

"No. I just know."

"How do you know?" Adam asked.

"I don't know. I sometimes get impressions of people I'm with," Nellie admitted. "Like now. An unusual name suddenly comes to my mind." She seemed to be listening to an unheard voice. "Schuyler."

Adam paled. *"Schuyler?"*

"He was your friend, wasn't he? He died in your arms. He wanted you to shoot him because he was suffering so, but before you could work up nerve to carry out his wishes, he died." Nellie smiled. "Obviously I'm a strange little girl, aren't I?"

Adam simply stared in disbelief.

"May I tell you something else, Adam? We're going to become very good friends, you and I. It is meant to be." She smiled and reached to touch his hand.

# Chapter Nine

"I am led to believe that something obviously traumatic happened to Nellie the day she met Cousin Susannah," Dr. Joseph Ornby remarked three days later, as he took time to have a short social session with Stuart Phenwick. "Yes, something traumatic."

"Traumatic?" questioned Stuart. He had informed his cousin of the noticeable change he had observed in Nellie.

"And her trauma was indeed compounded by word of the deaths in her immediate family," Joseph continued. "The jolt of the shock to her emotions, and perhaps to her mind, seems to have jarred her precognitive perceptivity and somehow magnified her ability with it."

"I'm afraid I don't understand, Joe," Stuart remarked, a puzzled expression altering his handsome face.

"I confess I'm not as knowledgeable about such things as I would like to be," Joseph returned. "What I've discerned is that Nellie apparently was born with a certain psychic awareness. The fact that she has had prophetic dreams for as long as she can remember is indication of that. I do wish Aug were here. He knows far more about such things than I. The psychic world is his department. I've concentrated on the psychological aspects of the human creature. My brother, the august Augustus, has had other inclinations in his pursuit of study; and he would have me believe that there is a concrete connection between the psychological and the psychic experience."

"I'm completely in the dark about such matters," Stuart related. "I suppose, because of my brother Gordon's fanatical outlook toward religion and aspects of the occult—negative aspects, I must add—I've shut my mind to such things. Yet if I can accept the omnihovering presence of the spirit of our mutual Great-grandmother Augusta, I suppose I should at least be able to open my mind to alleged occult theories."

"You're a very practical man, Stuart," Joseph commented, reaching for the teacup. "You're basically what we call 'of the earth earthy'; meaning you rely on the perception of your outer senses. Not that you don't have feeling and sensitivity—ah, that I readily admit. But, as you say in reference to Gordon, you have closed your mind."

Stuart chuckled awkwardly. "Very well, I'll open it. Explain your theories about Nellie's condition."

Joseph took a sip of cool tea and motioned for Stuart to refill his cup from the china teapot. "If we can agree that Nellie was born with a certain precognitive sense, it is my belief that whatever occurred between her and Cousin Susannah simply triggered something within her. Perhaps I should say 'awakened.' Aug was telling me, the last time we had an in-depth visit, that there are those who can project their minds, or at least a part of themselves, out of their bodies into a distant place."

"How is that possible?"

"I don't know. Aug said it was called *astral travel*," Joseph explained. "As best as I can comprehend, it has to do with the fact that the subconscious mind is released when the conscious mind goes into abeyance—or is asleep. Some persons have trained their subconscious—

or, as Aug called it, their *astral self*—to extend out and beyond time-space barriers."

"I'm completely lost."

"How may I simplify this?" Joseph drank again. "I suppose it's rather like the wireless. It must travel over invisible lines in a vibrational frequency that is less dense than that what we know as the physical."

Stuart's laughter sounded embarrassed. "I don't even know about the wireless."

"In that case, I can only ask you to attempt to accept the theory that such things *might* be possible," Joseph replied.

"I'll try."

"If Aug's astral theory is correct, or even in part possible," Joseph suggested, "then it would be the only reasonable explanation for Nellie's insistence that she had been present in Greenfield when each of her immediate family members were buried. You see, what I'm getting at is that her psychic ability was somehow increased by whatever that traumatic experience was when she met Cousin Susannah. That is the only explanation I can reach."

Stuart stared off into space for a few moments. Naturally he would do all he could to help Nellie and her father, but her psychic perception was beyond his ken. Joseph reached over and patted his hand. "Nellie has strength, Stuart. I have confidence in her."

Ann Marie had inherited many of Stuart's physical characteristics. She also showed much of the personal quality that her mother had had. Unlike Marcia, she had been given every opportunity of material comfort from the time of her birth. Ruth was her stepmother, and the young girl refused to consider her in any other way. A personality conflict had arisen between the two that at times seemed insurmountable. Ruth made every effort to be a good mother to both of Stuart's older children, but

99

her time was largely devoted to the three she had had by him. Ann Marie's resentment had increased as she had grown older.

It would be incorrect to say that Nellie had become good friends with Ann Marie. They played together and shared certain ideas, but Ann Marie thought of Nellie as yet another intruder who managed to capture some of her father's attention. Furthermore, she disliked the friendship that Adam Truff had obviously established with her distant cousin.

That hot August afternoon, the two little girls had taken lunch beneath the wisteria arbor behind Edward House. Throughout their play period they had had several minor disputes. Ann Marie found it difficult to agree with anything Nellie suggested.

"I quite frankly don't think you much like me, do you, Ann Marie?" Nellie said.

"I was wondering if you had noticed that," Ann Marie returned, a look of hatred in her eyes. "I don't much enjoy playing with you—but you're better than having no one at all to play with."

"Well, you won't have to put up with me much longer," Nellie stated. "I'm planning on going back to Greenfield."

"My daddy says you can't go back because there are still germs at Phenwick House," Ann Marie said. "You're held a captive prisoner in Boston."

"I am not. And I can go home any time I please," Nellie assured her. "If no one will take me home, I'll run away and go by myself."

"Then why don't you do that?" Ann Marie asked saucily. "It'll be good riddance as far as I'm concerned."

"Someday your hateful attitude will bounce back on you, Ann Marie. I pity you."

"Don't pity me, Nellie. You envy me, that's what you do!"

Nellie glared a moment, then lifted her skirts and ran toward the house.

Later that day, Adam Truff had occasion to stop by Edward House. He was met by Danny, who explained that his sister was upset and sulking beneath the wisteria arbor.

Adam went to find Ann Marie, who, upon seeing him, sprang into his arms. He soothed her.

"What is it, Ann Marie?"

"Nellie. I don't like her."

"Do you have a reason?"

"I *just* don't like her. I'll be glad when she's gone back to Greenfield."

"Why is that? I thought you were playmates," Adam said.

"I play with her because I have to," Ann Marie stated. "I believe it is impossible to force friendship on anyone, don't you?"

Adam sat in a comfortable wicker chair and studied the little girl for a few minutes. She was pouting. "Dear Ann Marie—I don't like to see you unhappy this way."

Ann Marie stared down and drew a line with the toe of her shoe.

"Your Uncle Thad was wanting to take Nellie back to Greenfield," Adam related a short while later. "But he has had irritation in his chest, and your grandmother doesn't feel it would be advisable for him to make the trip."

"Miss Nancy is my step-grandmother," Ann Marie fired, "just like Ruth is my stepmother!"

"Whether or not you're related to either Miss Nancy or Miss Ruth by blood, they are still very fond of you and look upon you as though you were their flesh and blood."

"I question that," Ann Marie snapped.

"Be that as it may," Adam continued, "what I was about to explain is that I've just come from a conversation with your father, and it has been decided that I shall accompany Nellie home."

*"You? Why you?"*

"Because, my dear Ann Marie," Adam said, "I do work for your father occasionally. With Thad incapacitated, there is no one else to go with her. And, I will admit, I do need the position. Besides, I would like to see Greenfield again."

"You like Nellie better than you like me!"

"That isn't true, Ann Marie," Adam replied. "I have known you longer, therefore, I feel a deeper attachment to you." He took her in his arms and hugged her. "I try to have love for all people. Even during the war, I tried not to hate anyone. Yet I knew I had a job to do and I did it. People were hurt, and it distressed me. Sometimes people mistake the motives behind my attitude of love—and that has put me in some very embarrassing and often compromising positions. I love your father and your stepmother; in fact I love all people. I don't have to like what they do, but I believe I must love them in spite of their human weaknesses."

"I don't understand you, Adam," Ann Marie said quietly, tracing her small finger over his big hand. "I only love my daddy—and sometimes Danny."

"Then you must learn to love other people," Adam stated. "Love, and love will come back to you. The same thing is true of hatred. Remember that."

"Even love Nellie?"

"Especially love Nellie."

Ann Marie held to him. "I love you, too, Adam. I really do."

Adam hugged her again, rose and, taking her hand, walked to the house.

"We will miss you, Nellie," Nancy said on the day of the little girl's departure. "You know you will always be welcome in our house. I was hoping you would stay longer. I was just getting used to having a little girl around."

"I've been away from my father too long," Nellie returned. She, too, was fond of Nancy. "I like it here, but he needs me."

"I understand," Nancy commented, then kissed her.

As Nellie kissed Nancy, a thought came to her—a picture, which she quickly pushed from her mind. "I had better say good-bye to Daniel Louis and Thad."

Nancy smiled understandingly.

Thad coughed as Nellie entered his room. "Ah, Nell! How pretty you look!"

"I've come to say good-bye, Thad."

Thad reached for her hand. "I'll miss you, Nellie."

"And I'm certain I'll miss you, too, Thad. But it won't be for long," she remarked.

"Why do you say that? Will you return to Boston soon?"

"I think not." Nellie smiled sweetly. She had received another impression. "Perhaps you will someday come to Greenfield."

"I'm certain I shall," Thad replied.

"Adam will be coming soon," Nellie added. "I don't want to miss the train." She stepped to him and kissed him on the cheek. His arms were immediately around her and she hugged him with all her might. "I like Adam very much, but I like you more."

"And I have a wonderfully good feeling toward you, too, Nellie."

"My father needs me now, and I must go to him," she murmured. "Still, I believe we will see one another very soon." She kissed his cheek and clung to him. "I *know* we will."

Thad accompanied Nellie downstairs and waited while she briefly spoke to his brother. Daniel Louis was not indifferent to her departure, but he apparently did not have the close tie to her that Thad had. They shook hands.

"We'll all go to the station," Thad suggested.

"I would rather you didn't," Nellie returned. "I wish to remember you all here at the house."

The carriage had pulled up to the door. Daniel Louis carried the girl's suitcase out, while Nancy gave her a final embrace.

"I'll walk out with you," Thad stated.

"We don't want to keep Adam waiting," Nellie commented.

"You've plenty of time."

Thad plucked a pink rose from a vine that covered part of the front porch. In so doing, he pricked his finger. A drop of blood appeared.

"You've hurt yourself," Nellie exclaimed.

"It's nothing. Here, this is for you, Nell." Thad placed the rose in her hand. "Whenever you see pink roses, remember me."

Nellie put the flower to her nose. "I will. Isn't that funny, it doesn't smell like a rose at all."

Thad smelled the flower. "Impossible! How could a rose have the fragrance of violets?"

"Did you say *violets*, Thadius?" Nancy called from the porch, where she was waiting.

Nellie giggled. "It was only our imagination—wasn't it? Now it smells very much like a rose."

"Yes, it does—but for a moment—" Thad looked perplexed.

Nellie ran to Adam, who helped her into the carriage. She waved back from the window.

Thad watched until the vehicle was out of sight, then he slowly moved back toward the house.

"What is it, Thadius?" Nancy asked.

"It's nothing, Mother."

"I thought I overheard you say something about violets."

"It was our imaginations, I guess," Thad replied. "The rose really did have the fragrance of a rose, after all."

"But you thought it had the scent of violets?"

"Both Nellie and I did—at first."

Nancy smiled to herself and remembered when she had first encountered the mysterious scent of violets. She held to Thad's arm as they returned to the house. Then, when her son had excused himself, she went to the large portrait of Augusta that now hung in the parlor.

Softly Nancy said, *"Violets."*

# Chapter Ten

An obvious sullen attitude had fallen over Nellie during the return trip to Greenfield. It was only a matter of about three and a half hours to Portland, where she and Adam arrived shortly after noon. The twenty-odd miles to Greenfield would take nearly as long by carriage. Arrangements were made for transportation with Leo Phenwick at the Medallion Company. Leo, however, was busy and only had time for a brief chat with Nellie and Adam.

"It would be best if we took lunch here in Portland," Adam advised, "before we journey on."

"I've not much of an appetite, Adam," Nellie replied, a wistful expression crossing her pretty face.

"You may have a little something while I eat," Adam said.

Nellie agreed and accompanied him to a small restaurant.

"You've been remarkably quiet today, Nellie," Adam observed as they sat at the small table near the window.

"I've been thinking much about my father," Nellie returned. "I am so very worried about him. He doesn't understand as I do."

"Doesn't understand *what?*" Adam questioned as his lunch arrived.

"That Mother, Elizabeth, George, and Rupert have merely changed," Nellie explained. "They aren't gone forever, they've only been transformed in dimensions. They've finished with the bodies that they had, which were temporary structures to begin with—just as ours are. They're still close by."

"How do you know all this?" Adam questioned.

"I wonder if you would believe me if I told you," Nellie commented. She gazed deeply into his eyes. "Perhaps you would. I was reading *The Mysteries of Rosea Hackleby*, a copy of which Cousin Nancy has in the library. In one section it told about people who were clairvoyant and could see into other dimensions."

"Other—?"

"Well, could see the spirits of those who have gone beyond," Nellie continued. "I believe that I have become clairvoyant."

"*Become clairvoyant?*"

"There's a good chance that I always have been," she replied. "It is highly probable."

"And how did you arrive at this conclusion?"

"What else could it possibly be? The dreams were one thing. I suppose that is the way clairvoyancy developed," she said. "But lately I've become aware of people—well, you might call them spirits—who appear to me. It first happened one day when I was playing with Ann Marie. Suddenly I looked up and saw this beautiful woman standing nearby. She was watching Ann Marie. But I could tell that Ann Marie was unaware of her presence. I went closer to where she was to get a better look. Then I recognized her face as that of the picture of Marcia Phenwick that hangs in the library. I don't think she realized I saw her. A few moments later she just disappeared."

"It could have been your imagination."

"That's what I thought at first," Nellie continued. "But the following night, while I was in my room at Cousin Nancy's house, the vision appeared again. I spoke with her and she explained that she indeed was Marcia Phenwick. She told me she went to Edward House often to look after her children—she meant Ann Marie and Danny. She also told me that she was present when Cousin Susannah died and that was the real reason she had been drawn to the house. She had come to help Cousin Susannah make the transition. Then she told me she had seen my mother, my sister and my brothers, and reassured me that they were happy and doing well. But she warned that my father was not in the best frame of mind and that I should return to him, that he needed me. That is why it was urgent for me to return to Greenfield. I, of course, couldn't tell this to Cousin Nancy or even to Cousin Thad. And I wouldn't have told you except—"

"Except?" Adam held a fork suspended in midair as he stared curiously at the little girl.

Nellie reached across the table and touched his other hand. "During the trip here from Boston, I saw someone on the backward riding seat opposite us, next to where you occasionally rested your bad leg."

"There was no one opposite us the entire trip," Adam stated.

"Not in solid flesh," Nellie said. "He was a tall, thin young man with a long, not particularly handsome face. He appeared in a Confederate uniform and he seemed to gaze at you with tremendous compassion. Although no words were exchanged, I received the impression that his name was—" She hesitated and curled her fingers about his hand. "His name was Schuyler."

"Schuyler?" Adam paled.

"Schuyler Callahan," Nellie added.

Little bumps rose at the back of Adam's neck, and the

tiny hairs seemed to stand on end. His jaw was dangling and he appeared confused.

"You know who Schuyler is, of course."

"I knew—knew who he *was*."

"He still very much *is*." Nellie smiled understandingly. "I was aware that he was there only for a short time."

"You couldn't have possibly known about Schuyler," Adam blurted, pushing his plate from him, his appetite gone. "He's been dead at least five years, and I don't believe anyone in Boston—with the possible exception of Stuart—even knew of his existence. Or, if they did, they had completely forgotten about him. Schuyler was not the sort of person who made much of an impression on people one way or the other."

"Still, he was your friend," Nellie said quietly. "You grew up together. Then when his father felt you were having an adverse influence over him, you were sent away. But Schuyler was always a faithful friend and he loved you."

"Loved?"

"As one faithful friend loves another," Nellie replied. "Oh, Adam, I hope I didn't upset you by telling you this."

"I'm a bit shaken by the shock of it," Adam commented, "but I'm far from being upset. I suspect, if Schuyler really did appear to you, that he did so for the purpose of letting me know the truth about your powers."

"My powers?"

"Your clairvoyance. Little Nellie, I don't pretend to understand," he remarked before taking a sip of water, "but I do believe there was a strong reason why you and I became friends. I don't even believe it was an accident that Thad took sick and I had to replace him to accompany you home. There must be some Divine, Infinite plan that works these things. And, for as long as I live, I will respect whatever powers you have and do my utmost to defend them when others chide you. You see, I've always kept an open mind, and I believe that such things are possible. I just didn't think I would see them manifest in such a little girl."

"I knew I was different from other children when I was very young," Nellie explained. "Now I would say that it is obvious that I am clairvoyant. It's something I just know."

"I have an Indian friend by the name of Jamatu," Adam related. "He has risked his life over many years for me. I'm indebted to him."

"A red Indian, isn't he?"

"Yes. How—?" Adam laughed uneasily and shrugged. "All right, I won't ask. Jamatu told me that some people have the power you apparently possess. And it is a power, Nellie, don't ever forget that. I suspect that Jamatu had a little of it himself, although if he did he never confided that information to me. And, come to think of it, he once told me that I would meet a young lady who would impress me with her psychic abilities— and that we would become good friends. I, of course, thought he was alluding to a romantic situation and a far older lady. When I asked him if that was the case, he merely smiled enigmatically and changed the subject. Since Jamatu was rarely known to smile, I took that to have special significance."

Again Nellie put her hand to his. "I know why you were alarmed at his statement—you simply didn't understand. You were frightened of the fact that he might be insinuating that you might have romantic complications with that young lady. I know that will never happen, Adam. I don't understand, but I know."

Adam squeezed her hand. "I think it's time we were going, little Nellie."

"Yes, it is urgent we get to Greenfield soon."

John Collier was seated beneath the grape arbor, vacantly staring at the earth. A beard had sprouted on his face, which he had not bothered to shave after the

110

death of members of his family. His clothing was soiled, well worn, and wrinkled. He had a shabby appearance. Twice Nana Carlyle had fetched cool tea to him, and both times he had let it sit untouched. His face had become gaunt and his hands had a noticeable tremble.

When the carriage arrived, John only briefly glanced up. He thought it was probably Charles Mumford coming to have a chat. What good did that do? No matter how pleasant and encouraging the young doctor appeared to be, John could not rally or react with interest. The loss he felt created a hollow feeling throughout his being. He tried not to think about his dear ones, and, in so doing, he managed to make his mind a blank most of the time. He just sat and stared at nothing.

"Daddy!" came the voice as if it were riding the wind.

How often he had heard or thought he had heard a child's voice calling to him! Yet when he had looked, there was no one. He even imagined he had heard his Kate speak his name. Again he believed it was only his imagination, nothing more.

"Daddy! Where are you?"

A teary film covered his eyes as he peered between the grape leaves. Then realization came and he stood up. "Nellie?" He put his hands to the arbor frame to support himself.

Nellie came running around the side of the house. She slowed only for a moment as she beheld the sight of her dissipated-appearing father. With accelerated speed, she dashed to him. Arms about him, she hugged and kissed him.

"Oh, Daddy, Daddy, why didn't you send for me to come home sooner?" she asked, clinging to him.

"There's disease, my precious Nellie," John uttered, holding her as close to him as he could. "I didn't want to lose you, too."

"The disease is gone. Cousin Joseph Ornby received a report in Boston."

"It's gone?" John looked with disbelief. "My life is gone. All that I loved—"

"Not *all*, Daddy. *I'm* here. Don't you still love me?"

"Of course, I do, little Nell! Of course, I do." He lifted her in his arms and kissed her cheeks. "Come, let me show you where they are buried. I've planted flowers on the graves. And next spring I'll transplant a lilac bush. Your mother was so fond of lilacs."

Nellie held her father's hand as he led her to the cemetery.

Adam had gone to the house in the carriage and had the luggage removed. Then he saw Nana Carlyle, introduced himself, and explained his mission. Nana recognized Nellie's things and welcomed him into the house.

"How is John doing?" Adam asked, as Nana showed him to the room on the first floor that would be his.

"This room was not contaminated," Nana explained. "It will be safe for you. Dr. Mumford has assured us that—now that the house has been completely well aired —all of the germs are gone. As to your question, well, I don't believe he is doing well. It has been a terrible loss for him. He is such a loving, sensitive man—and he was so very devoted to Mrs. Collier. Why, I've never seen man and wife so close. What a pity it is!"

"The disease never touched you or the manservant?" Adam asked.

"We took prescribed precautions," Nana replied. "Dr. Mumford told us what to do. We tried to get the children to comply with his instructions, but they would not. Somehow, I believe, they were destined to go with their mother. I don't know why, that is just a feeling I get. But how does one console a man like Mr. Collier? I don't know."

Adam could see the cemetery from the window of his assigned room. He watched as the little girl and her father stood at the gravestones. It touched his heart to witness the sadness as both girl and man wept. Still, he believed it was not the time for him to intrude.

After changing his clothing, Adam went to the kitchen, where Nana was helping the cook prepare dinner. "Can you tell me where I can find Dr. Mumford?"

"I can tell you where his office is," Nana mentioned, "but whether he's there or not is another matter. You don't know your way around Greenfield, do you?"

"Not well," Adam replied.

"Then it would be best for you to take the road out front of the house—it's called Rebecca Lane now," Nana related, "and go up beyond the orchard to Old Indian Road. It's right at the end of the fence. One or two of the dogs will probably follow you. They're friendly enough, so you need have no worry. Then when you reach the square, you'll find Dr. Mumford's office near the school. You can't miss it."

"I'm certain I won't," Adam responded. "Will you be so kind as to tell Nellie and her father that I've gone for a little stroll to get the kinks out of my legs from sitting so long, traveling?"

"Certainly, Mr. Truff."

"Adam."

"Yes, Mr. Adam."

Adam laughed and went to the front door. Soon he was striding happily down the road. He couldn't explain the change that had come over him. He could only surmise that it somehow was a result of his conversation with Nellie. And especially the fact that she had mentioned Schuyler Callahan's name. He feared the next few days at Greenfield might be unpleasant. He would merely brace himself for whatever eventuality came his way. He had endured far worse situations.

# Chapter Eleven

There was an obvious small-town attitude about Greenfield. Heavy sadness hung in the air. Adam was looked upon as a stranger as he strode through the street. When he stopped to ask directions to Dr. Mumford's office, he was met by the glum expression of a woman who had lost four children to the cholera epidemic.

"We all shoulda left Greenfield, that's what we shoulda done," the woman muttered. "But I reckon you can't run away from memories, can you?"

Adam agreed with her and went in the direction she pointed.

Dr. Charles Mumford had taken over an old house on Main Street, the lower floor of which he had converted into his work area. He lived on the second floor.

Adam pushed the front door open to confront the curious eyes of a freckle-faced boy of ten. "The doc's in."

"Thank you," Adam returned. "I'll wait."

"You don't look sick," the boy commented. "Me, I've got a cut toe. I wrapped it up with an old rag, but Ma, she said I had to have the doc look at it, and bring a note back from him sayin' that I did. Pshaw! If I lived through the epidemic, I can live through a little ol' cut on my toe."

"Yes, I should imagine you're quite right."

"I took care of myself," the boy continued. "That's what Doc Mumford said saved me. I play hooky a lot from school, so I reckon I never became contaminated by the other children. Which goes to show that playing hooky ain't so bad after all." He chuckled.

"So it would seem."

A woman came from the inner office and motioned for the boy to go in. The kid winked at Adam before he left.

Ten minutes later the boy was back, hobbling for effect. "It's your turn, mister."

Adam knocked on the door before he slowly pushed it open.

"Yes, come in," Charles Mumford said without looking up from the paper on which he was writing. "Whay may I do for you?"

"I'm not ill, but I would like to talk to you about John Collier."

At the sound of the unfamiliar voice, Charles glanced up. "Oh? I don't believe I know you."

Adam introduced himself and explained his mission to Greenfield.

"We had fifty-seven deaths in all here," Charles explained. "There are still several people recovering from the disease, but it's gone far beyond the contagion stage. I'm certain there is no danger for Nellie—not now. Even when John returned, apparently the worst part was over. He tried to get himself infected. It didn't happen. Mentally and emotionally he's in a bad state. I wish Dr. Ornby could come up from Boston. There are so many persons here who are in a similarly depressed state. Why shouldn't they be? Many of them lost everyone. It was just fortunate that Nellie was in Boston when the epidemic broke out. She's a pretty little thing, isn't she?"

"Yes, quite pretty," Adam admitted. "Do you think it would be wise for me to try to persuade John Collier to

115

return to Boston with me, so that Dr. Ornby could work with him?"

"It would be wise," Charles replied, "but not very probable, knowing John's condition. I suspect Nellie will find a way to cheer him—once she herself becomes adjusted."

"Do you know the status of the Collier Furniture Company?" Adam asked, curiously watching the young doctor.

"I can't really tell you. I doubt if very much is happening there with John in the state he is," Charles commented. "His foreman died of the cholera. I understand the second foreman is trying to keep the place going, since so many men depend on it for their livelihood. But I don't think business can be very good."

"How much later do you have to work this evening?" Adam questioned.

"There weren't any other people waiting when you came in, were there?"

"No."

"If there's none when I finish with you," Charles said, "I'll close the door for the day. People know where they can find me. I've one or two patients I should stop by to see. None of them is urgent. I can do it tomorrow if there's something needed."

"Is there a Mrs. Mumford?"

"There's several," Charles returned whimsically. "My mother, two aunts, three cousins, and my sister-in-law. You see, the Mumfords go back in Greenfield about as far as the Phenwicks do . . . but not quite."

"I was only curious about your private life because I didn't want to interfere with family plans you might have when you finish working," Adam said.

"You won't be interfering at all," Charles stated as he went to the door to have a look into the outer office. "No one. Excuse me and I'll throw the bolt on the front door."

Adam waited in the comfortably cluttered office. His

eyes went from the diploma from the Boston Medical School to the bouquet of wild daisies in a water glass on the big notched desk. Two small oil paintings were on the wall, both still lifes. As he continued to scrutinize the office, Adam became aware that there was a certain order to the disorder.

Charles had removed his white smock. He stretched as he came back into the room, then went immediately to open a window.

"Mariah Zitter was in a short while ago," Charles remarked. "The hottest day of the year and the hottest hour of the day, Mariah would complain about a draft. Well, I had to pull the window down for her, and forgot to put it back up." He adjusted the window as he stood in his shirtsleeves. "I reckon I should put on a vest, but you'll have to excuse me, Mr. Truff. Since you're not here as a patient, I don't have to act like a doctor, do I?"

"Quite so."

Charles moved around in front of the desk and leaned against it, practically close enough that a slight movement of his leg would have touched Adam. Sitting with his arms folded, he looked down at the man. "You know, I've heard about you. I didn't recognize the name at first, but it came to me just as I was throwing the bolt on the door."

"You've heard of me in Boston?"

The doctor smiled. "Yes. Not only from the Phenwicks. I had a professor or two who at least knew of you. You're quite a hero in Boston, Mr. Truff."

"Adam, if you don't mind."

"Adam? Yes, of course." Charles leaned forward. "There was a Calvin Hamilton, as I recall and my good friend, Pace Forbes, both of whom spoke highly of you —and actually claimed that they had been your friends."

"Are you trying to tell me something, Charles?" Adam questioned, an eyebrow arched.

Charles rose and moved around behind the desk. He

did not look at Adam. His back tightened. "Yes, I believe I am." He slowly turned around.

"Something that you know about me?"

"And about myself, Adam."

Adam's face brightened as he rose and went to Charles. He extended his hand. "Friendships don't just happen. However, I suspect that, if we work at it, we might get along. At the moment, Charles, I desire to go to Collier Furniture Company while it is still daylight."

"It'll be daylight for several hours."

"Nonetheless, I wish to find the assistant foreman there, if possible. One of my missions to Greenfield is to help John Collier get back on his feet, both in a personal way, and in his business."

"I would be pleased to go with you to the furniture company. We can get to know each other better coming and going." Charles pulled into a lightweight coat. "We'll go out the back door."

Adam surveyed the young doctor as he fussed about with the details of closing the office. Then the two men went out to the stable. Adam helped fix the horse to the buggy.

Within three days after Nellie arrived in Greenfield, John Collier began showing signs of improvement. Because his daughter objected to the scratchiness of his beard, John shaved. That alone made a difference in his appearance.

Charles Mumford called at Phenwick House everyday. Often John asked the doctor to remain for supper. As likely as not, Charles would sit through the hot summer evenings in conversation with John and Adam. He had prescribed small does of laudanum to help John sleep. After John had taken the drug and he appeared to react to the effects of it, he would excuse himself and, with effort, go to his room. If Adam was willing, the doctor would linger to engage him in further conversation, preferably to hear tales he had to tell about the war.

Nellie interrupted their conversation one night, but she perceptively realized that she was inhibiting them with her presence. After that, when she overheard the mumble of their conversation, she discreetly returned to her room or went to look in on her father.

"John has shown great improvement since you and Nellie have been here," Charles commented toward the end of the second week. "Oh, he still gets terribly despondent and emotional, but that is to be expected. Of course the laudanum helps. I'm certain it is during the time when he goes alone to his bed that he most misses Kate. I know if I had lost someone I loved like that, it would doubtless affect me the same way."

"*Someone?*" Adam questioned. "Is there no one, Charles?"

It was one of the few times Adam had seen the doctor frown. Then he smiled. "I don't have time—my patients occupy so much of my—"

"Charles—we're no longer strangers," Adam said.

"No, so we're not."

"Even if you were to give me a whole bottle of laudanum," Adam stated lightly, "I'm certain it wouldn't put me to sleep tonight. In which case, if you can spare the time, why don't we take a stroll down along the beach?"

"I wouldn't be so certain about the effects of the laudanum," Charles responded. "However, for the sake of argument and convenience, I'll agree with you. As to the walk, I'm certain that will be most stimulating."

The two young men left the house dressed only in their shirtsleeves, and bareheaded. They walked down the path beyond the cemetery, and eventually north along the rocky shore.

A soft breeze played at the curtain to the window of John Collier's room—the room in which he had spent so

119

many wonderful years with his beloved Katie. Although the laudanum had made him groggy, it did not put him under as it usually did. Depressed, John broke down crying. It was the first time in nearly a week that he had had such a severe reaction. Moving unsteadily, he went into the sitting room and poured himself a glass of brandy. There he saw a tintype of Kate, and another of her and the children with him.

Downing one glass of brandy, he poured another. As he did, he misplaced the decanter and it fell to the floor with a shattering crash. He ignored the broken glass as he drank the second brandy. Tears had come and he was holding the pictures to his breast when Nellie entered the room.

"Daddy, what is it?" she questioned.

"Oh, Nellie, my little Nell, why aren't you asleep?" he cried.

"I heard a crash." She stooped to pick up the pieces. "What have you been doing in here?"

"Let me hold you, Nellie, please let me hold you."

Nellie went to her father.

"I'm so lonely—so very lonely without your mother," John sobbed. "I know you've had a great loss, too, my dearest Nellie. The end is such a final thing when husband and wife are separated."

"It isn't the end, Father," Nellie encouraged. "I do believe that Mother is not far away at all. In fact, I *know* she isn't."

"Don't speak that way, Nell, you don't understand."

"If only I could make you comprehend what I know," Nellie returned.

"I need more brandy. You know where it is kept. Don't bother putting it into the decanter," John said, slurring his words.

Obediently Nellie went for the brandy. While she was gone, John staggered back into his room, the floorboards creaking beneath his footsteps. He got the container of laudanum and lurched back to the sitting room. Before Nellie returned, he got two glasses and put a substantial amount of the drug into each. When his daughter returned, he quickly took the bottle and poured the brandy before Nellie was able to detect that the glasses had been laced with the laudanum.

"Are you going to drink both, Father?" Nellie questioned. She stifled a yawn. "It might not be wise."

"One for me, and one for you, my precious. I want us to have a drink together," John said, handing her the glass. "Drink it all. Here's to my deepest, most sincere love for you, Nellie—oh, my dearest!" He drank, emptying the glass. He poured another. "You're not drinking, Nellie. Please drink with me. Do you want me to believe that you don't love me?"

Nellie had a premonition, but she was also emotionally affected by her father's words. She sipped the brandy. It was bitter, but she forced herself to consume half of the glass.

John leaned against the small round table as he went to embrace her. "Nellie, you must realize how much I love you, how I want you to be with me always."

Nellie's stomach was churning. "I think I'm going to be sick."

"No, no. Make it stay down. Breathe deeply and control yourself."

"It burns my stomach, Daddy," Nellie whimpered as a dizzying reaction came over her.

"Drink the rest of it, darling Nellie."

"No, Daddy, I can't. I can't."

John staggered back to the chair and sat heavily in it. "Then go! Leave me the way your mother did!"

Nellie went to him. "Don't say such a thing, Daddy! Don't ever!" Her vision had become affected.

"Go to your room and leave me in peace!" John ordered, now apparently drunk.

"Daddy, I do love you! I love you so very much. I

121

loved you before, in a different way. That's why I came to be your daughter this time. How can I make you understand?" Nellie was crying as a heavy feeling began to come over her.

"I . . . don't . . . under . . . stand." John slouched over in the chair.

Nellie stroked his head, but her hand was beginning to get numb. "Oh, no!"

John had his head on the table. He was breathing heavily, irregularly.

"I've got to get Adam!" exclaimed Nellie as she staggered from the room. Her vision was clouded and she bumped into objects without really realizing what she was doing.

In the hallway, she headed for the stairs. As she reached the banister, she lost her balance. She managed to catch hold of the railing as she fell, supporting herself only enough to break the fall. Back onto her feet, she tried to navigate the steps, but her equilibrium was completely off. She tripped again and landed sprawled unconscious on the bottom step.

John reacted to the sound. He lifted his head. "Nell? Nellie?" He started to rise, then his attention went to the brandy bottle. With great effort, he managed to pour another glassful of the liquor. As he drained the glass, he made a sweeping movement of his hand, knocking the candle from the holder in front of him. He lost consciousness and dropped his head with a thud to the table.

Charles and Adam had walked a short distance up the shore. While they enjoyed each other's company, both men had begun to feel the signs of fatigue. They had turned back and were about to climb the path that led by the cemetery when Charles perceived the first aroma of smoke. By the time they reached the clearing above the path, both men could see the orange flames dancing grotesquely in the upstairs window of Phenwick House.

Adam ran ahead. Charles was closely behind him.

Nana had been awakened by the smell of smoke. She ran to arouse Paxton, whose room was close to hers.

Adam found Nellie and carried her unconscious body from the house. By then Charles had arrived and the two climbed the stairs. To their knowledge, John was the only one on the second floor. He had apparently reacted to the fire and had been able to make his way to the door before he collapsed.

Charles helped Adam hoist John's body onto his shoulder, then followed behind as Adam carried the man down the stairs.

"You look after Nellie and her father," Adam instructed. "I want to go back into the house."

Before Charles could object, Adam was gone. He went immediately into the parlor. Smoke was seeping through the ceiling. On impulse, he went to the painting of Augusta, took it down, and carried it out of the house. In the meantime, Nana and Paxton were gathering what items of value that they could, until the fire burned through the second floor and into the first.

Adam returned to the house and gathered four other paintings, including the one of Daniel Phenwick the first. He was able to get a few other things before he no longer dared enter.

By then the fire company had been alerted and the horse-drawn engine came speeding down the road, the bell frantically ringing. Townspeople, alarmed by the fire bell, had followed it.

Paxton had managed to get the horses from the stable, along with the carriage. The animals were distraught, reacting violently to the fire. Nana took charge, directing the firemen as best she could. Adam assisted where he could, but the blaze was well under way. The men would be lucky to contain it before it destroyed the adjoining barn.

"Adam!" Charles called when he caught a glimpse of the man. "Adam!"

Recognizing Charles's voice, Adam left the activity and went in search of him. By then the area was teeming with people, mostly the curious, who got in the way of the firemen.

"What is it, Charles?"

"We need a carriage—any carriage! I've got to get them to the infirmary."

"Is it that urgent?" Adam questioned.

"John has taken an overdose of laudanum, mixed with brandy," Charles stated. "And if I'm not mistaken, he has given some to Nellie."

"You're not suggesting—?"

"I'm suggesting nothing," Charles replied. "I only know I've got to get them both to suitable facilities before they die!"

Adam ran around to the side of the flaming building. He told one of the curiosity seekers that Dr. Mumford had need of his carriage, that it was an emergency. A few minutes later, Adam was back with the carriage and helped Charles load the unconscious bodies. Adam drove while the doctor remained inside with the victims.

Dawn had grayed the sky and faint tinges of pink had begun to appear before Charles ceased working over the bodies of John and Nellie. He had gotten assistance at the infirmary and all-out effort was made to save the two. Finally, exhausted and weary, Charles left his patients in individual rooms and trudged to the office where Adam was waiting.

"They're both still alive," Charles said weakly as he leaned against the doorjamb. "Nellie is over the worst of it, but I'm not that certain about John."

Adam went to the doctor and caught him in a stout embrace about the shoulders. "You come over here and sit down. I can't imagine how you've managed to continue on your feet."

Charles leaned heavily against Adam and permitted

himself to be guided. After he was seated, Adam went to get a wet cloth, which he applied to his friend's head, washing his face and moistening his hair. Charles had grown limp, and his head rolled beneath Adam's touch.

"I'll get someone to bring a cot in here," Adam said. "You're in no fit condition to go home."

"Whatever you say, Adam," Charles moaned. "I'm too exhausted to resist."

A short while later, an orderly brought in a cot. Adam got Charles to his feet and helped him partially undress before he led him to the cot. A lightweight sheet was spread over the doctor.

"Adam—?"

"Yes?"

"Will you sit with me a while longer ... please?"

"Certainly." Adam drew a chair up to the cot.

"How do you manage to keep going?"

Adam again applied the damp cloth to Charles's forehead. "I napped while you were working with Nellie and John. Besides, I require little sleep. Whether you realize it or not, I got close to four hours' sleep while you were busy."

"How could you sleep at such a time?" Charles questioned.

Adam chuckled. "With all I've been through, I can sleep standing up. My old Indian friend, Jamatu, has taught me many secrets about revitalizing myself. I'll tell you about them sometime." He wiped the hair from Charles's forehead. "Is there anything I can get you? Something to help you sleep, maybe?"

"No. I don't need anything," Charles replied. "Just stay nearby until I doze off. That will be sufficient for me."

Adam sat in the chair in a sprawling position. His fingers were clasped together at his chin as he watched the young doctor. Was this another reason why he had been drawn to Greenfield?

"Adam?"

"Yes, I'm still here."

"John Collier obviously tried to poison Nellie and himself," Charles uttered, so groggy that his words were barely audible.

"Obviously," Adam returned. Charles breathed heavily in sleep. Adam rose and went to the door. He extinguished the lamp before he looked back and repeated, "Obviously."

## Chapter Twelve

Nellie was obviously beyond the crisis period two days later when she suddenly blinked open her eyes and smiled up at Charles. "I feel quite hungry."

Charles sighed with relief. Desire for nourishment was always a favorable sign that the patient was well on the way to recovery. But he could tell that she was still weak, and advised her to remain in bed for another day or two.

"My father—?" Nellie asked.

"He is doing as well as can be expected," Charles assured her.

"Poor Daddy. He wanted to kill us both, didn't he?"

Charles made a straight line of his lips and shook his head. "One day I would like to return to Boston to do further study on mental conditions. Oh, I don't deny that your father had every right to be in a despondent state. I simply don't know how to adequately cope with such situations."

"I dreamed—"

"Excuse me, Nellie," Charles interrupted. "I have a patient prepared for an emergency treatment. I only stopped in for a few moments while he was being readied.

We'll talk later. You try to get more rest, and I'll order that food be brought to you."

Nellie perceived that Charles was telling the truth, but she also realized he appeared anxious to leave. It didn't matter. The important thing for her was to get nourishment.

A short while later Adam appeared carrying a tray of food. Smiling as he stood in the doorway, he said, "I was instructed to bring this to you." He stepped toward the bed. "So the sleeping beauty has awakened, has she? What magnificent prince kissed you awake?"

"I'm afraid there was no magnificent prince, Adam," Nellie replied, eagerly eyeing the food. "Of course, I might have been awakened by your approaching presence."

Adam chuckled uneasily.

Nellie stared at him, a change of expression. "Phenwick House has been burned, hasn't it?"

"Charles told you."

"Charles?" Nellie did not alter her gaze. "No, he didn't. No one told me. I just knew."

Adam set the tray on the bed and watched as she adjusted the napkin about her throat.

"My father started the fire, you know. Oh, he didn't do it on purpose—not really," Nellie commented after she had taken a bite of food and chewed it. "I realized I had been drugged with the brandy Daddy had given me."

"It was fortunate that Charles and I had gone for a walk up the beach," Adam said, "or I might have been asleep and not detected the fire in time."

Again Nellie stared at him curiously. "Draw up a chair. There is something I wish to confide in you, Adam."

Adam complied with her wishes. The chair was placed so they were in easy view of each other. He leaned back and waited.

128

"By the time I reached the infirmary," Nellie explained after swallowing another bit of food, "I had died."

"You had *what?*"

"Yes, of that I am certain," Nellie said. "I had stopped breathing, but Dr. Mumford was finally able to revive me."

"It must have been your imagination," Adam remarked.

"No. I know full well what happened. May I tell you about it?"

"If you wish."

"I became aware of what was happening when you carried me into the infirmary," Nellie related. "I saw you put my body on the pallet, only I was not in it. I had floated out of it and seemed to be hovering at the ceiling, looking down, watching what Dr. Mumford and the others were doing. Then I became aware of a tunnel of light. It was long and I moved very swiftly through it. I felt very good, happy, and I rather hoped Dr. Mumford would leave my body alone. It must have only been a few minutes or even seconds by earth time, but it seemed to be quite a long while, since so much happened."

"It sounds very much like a dream," Adam commented.

"I suppose it does. Anyway, when I reached the end of that long tunnel, I was met by a Being of Light—it was very, very bright. Words were not spoken, but I perceived thoughts coming from the Light."

"A Being of Light?" Adam altered his position.

"I was asked if I was ready to return to that place. I said I was. Then I remembered my father and my deep awareness that he needed me. The Being of Light seemed to understand my thoughts. I was told that I would have to go back." Nellie gazed at the blank wall. "Before I could return, however, I knew I had to meet

129

several—I have to call them *people*, because I don't know what else to call them. First, I saw the lavender-gray lady. She was surrounded by the scent of violets. She, strangely, called me 'Edward.' I told her I wasn't Edward, I was Nellie. And she said, 'This time you're Nellie.' I had the sensation that she kissed me. But my attention went from her as I became aware of the presence of my mother. She seemed so young and beautiful. I don't recall most of her actual words, but she did speak reassuringly. Then there were Elizabeth, George, and Rupert, all standing beside her. They looked very happy, and George, especially, asked me to stay. My mother shook her head and explained that I had to go back to look after Father, saying that he needed me now. But I received the impression that she called him Michael or Mickey, not John."

"That was quite a dream, Nellie."

"Let me finish. Before I knew what was happening, I was again in the presence of the lavender-gray lady. By then I recognized her from the painting of Augusta. She told me to thank you for saving her likeness."

"Her likeness?" Adam questioned.

"Her portrait, which was hanging in Phenwick House. You did save the painting, didn't you?" Nellie asked.

Adam had begun perspiring, as a prickly sensation came over him. "Yes, I did. But you couldn't have—"

"She told me. She said that Phenwick House must be rebuilt—but in a different location, nearer to the sea. I also saw Cousin Susannah. She frightened me when she came hurrying toward me, and appeared to merge with me. She called me 'Daddy' and I had a feeling of deep love from her—so I didn't remain frightened very long." Nellie stopped to take another bite. "Almost immediately thereafter, the Being of Light returned and I knew it was time for me to leave. I had to go back to my body. But I didn't really want to go. It was just my awareness that Daddy needed me that made me want to return."

Adam altered his position and wished he could escape.

"Almost immediately I was back in the infirmary," Nellie continued, "still hovering at the ceiling watching Dr. Mumford. I don't know what he did, but the next thing I knew I was back in my body. I felt so heavy and tired that I went to sleep."

Adam laughed. "You have quite an imagination, Nellie Collier."

"Was it all my imagination, Adam? I don't believe that is the case," she replied. She reached for his hand. "Dear Adam, I don't expect you to understand me; but I do want you to be my friend. You'll return to Greenfield."

· "I'm already in Greenfield."

"Yes, but you have a mission to go on for Cousin Stuart," Nellie said candidly. "It will take you to Savannah and Atlanta, and ultimately to Chattanooga, Tennessee. But you'll find the boy, then return him to Boston. You won't stay in Boston. You'll come back to Greenfield where, between travels, you will live out your life."

Adam rose and put the chair back where it had been. "This has all been very interesting, Nellie—confusing . . . perplexing. I wish to have a few words with your father before I leave."

"Yes, you must," Nellie commented. "You must see to his well-being until I am able to get out of bed. Thank you for listening to me, Adam. I always enjoy your company."

Adam kissed her before he left. Once in the hallway, he stopped. His head seemed to be spinning from Nellie's flow of fantastic narration. He knew he should disbelieve everything she said, but he could not. Something deep within his being seemed to confirm her

131

story. What was it? How could such a thing possibly be?

"Adam—" Charles called as his friend was about to approach John Collier's room.

"Charles?"

"Did you see Nellie?"

"Yes."

"She looks greatly improved, doesn't she?"

"She's full of some improbable tales."

"Improbable?"

Adam stared at his friend. "When Nellie was brought to the hospital—"

"She had stopped breathing. She was technically dead," Charles inserted. "For a while there, I wasn't certain I could bring her back. Yet I did things I had never done before, as if I were receiving instructions from some unseen force. And then there was that uncanny fragrance of violets."

Adam had grown pale. "Technically dead?"

"Are you all right, Adam? Let me help you to the bench."

"No. I'm quite fine. We will discuss this at length over supper, if you don't mind," Adam stated.

"I would be pleased."

They both spoke with their eyes before each went his own way.

Adam called daily at the hospital. He spent a minimal amount of time with Nellie, and as much time as he possibly could with John.

Adam was devoting several hours a day to the Collier Furniture Manufacturing Company, taking it upon himself to get it back into functioning order. He usually had many questions to ask John about the business, and accepted his suggestions to make improvements.

Physically John was recovering, but his continual severe state of depression was worrying to Charles Mumford. The doctor urged Adam to do his best to cheer the older man.

"I believe, Adam, if you were to stay on indefinitely in Greenfield," John stated during his second week in the infirmary, "that I might be able to rally some of my old strength and enthusiasm." Nellie had told him about her alleged "death experience," and John had been impressed. It had a reassuring effect upon him. "I need someone like you with me in my business. Moreover, since I presently doubt that I will ever marry again, I should like to have a friend like you close at hand in whom I can confide."

Adam put his hand on John's and patted it. "You know, of course, that I will always be your friend, John. I feel very close to you and to Nellie. But I am a wanderer, somewhat of a vagabond. I have a style of life that seems to require adventure. Furthermore, I have promised Stuart that I would go in search of his son, Alexander Augustus, who at the present time goes by the last name of Callahan. I've seen him. He's very much a Phenwick, practically a replica of Stuart. That venture alone is liable to take me several months. Then I might return to Greenfield and do what I can to help you."

"I need help long before that," John sighed. "I need incentive."

"Nellie will give you incentive," Adam assured him. "And you know Charles Mumford looks upon you as if you were—well, someone very special to him. You're far too young to be his father, but I'm certain he thinks of you with greater affection than he has for old Mr. Mumford."

"That's kind of you to say, Adam," John remarked. "I am dearly fond of Charles, too. But he is a physician, not a carpenter."

"Nor am I a carpenter, John."

"You could learn."

"I'll help you rebuild Phenwick House," Adam said,

133

"more in a supervisory capacity than as a laborer, and in time I might assist at the furniture factory. We'll have to see about that, won't we? But in the meantime, once you're back on your feet, I've got to return to Boston and go on the mission Stuart has hired me to do."

"Adam," the older man called as the other was nearing the door, "there is one other thing."

"Yes?"

"I know you are a private person," John explained. "And as such it would be wrong of me to expect you to live at Phenwick House with Nellie and me. There is a cottage on the northeast part of the Phenwick property that was built by the late Michael O'Plaggerty, a devoted friend of the Phenwicks. I would like you to have that cottage for your own. I owe that much to you— and more—for doing all you've done for me."

"I suspect you will have to live in the cottage for a while," Adam returned, "until you've been able to put up another house. But, when it's available, I'll be pleased to accept it. I've grown very fond of Greenfield. It would be a wonderful place to spend my declining years—that is, if I live long enough to have declining years."

"Where are you staying now?" John questioned. "I understand Phenwick House is in near ruins."

"The house is practically burned to the ground," Adam related. "Until such a time as I make other arrangements, Charles Mumford has been kind enough to permit me to stay with him. He has several spare rooms, so it's no inconvenience."

"Where then is Nellie staying?" John asked.

"Nana Carlyle made arrangements to rent a house as a temporary lodging," Adam said. "You see, it is imperative that you get out of the hospital as soon as possible and make arrangements for your child and your faithful servants."

"That would appear obvious, wouldn't it?" John returned. "Yes, I must stop being an invalid, mustn't I? I do have responsibilities."

Adam shook John's hand before he left the room.

# Chapter Thirteen

Stuart had received what was obviously distressing news. It came from his attorney in New York City, where he had vested interests. He had discussed the matter with his wife Ruth, who either didn't comprehend the seriousness of the matter, or simply didn't want to. She had her mind on other things: the children, the coming fall social season, a new wardrobe. Far from being vacuous, Ruth was quite intelligent, but she was of the opinion that she must be aware of social status for the sake of her husband and the children.

Stuart then turned to one person he had always gone to when problems pressed and there was no one else with whom he could discuss them. Nancy Phenwick was technically his step-grandmother, but since they were close to the same age, Stuart considered her basically a good friend.

"Will you have tea, Stuart?" Nancy asked as she welcomed him into the parlor.

"It's a very hot day," Stuart replied.

"Then something cool?"

"Nothing, thank you, Miss Nancy." Stuart crossed his legs. "How is Thad these days?"

"Greatly improved," Nancy said. "He seems to have

become a great deal stronger. The cough is all but gone. But you didn't come here to speak to me about Thad, did you?"

Stuart smiled. "Quite perceptive of you, dear Nancy. In which case, I'll get to the point. I received a letter from my attorney in New York, advising me that neither Captain Wellington nor Tim Duggan will prosecute Sam Dodsworth for murder."

"Sam Dodsworth?" Nancy blinked as if the action were the question.

"The man who allegedly killed Annie Duggan in New York," Stuart explained, "then later went on to torment both Leon and Ann Ornby Phenwick in Portland. The man is serving a ten-year sentence in Portland for what he did to Leo and Ann. I had hoped that at least Captain Wellington would have cooperated with me and pressed charges against Dodsworth for the murder of Annie Duggan."

"Why does he refuse?"

"It's a personal matter, Miss Nancy."

"May I be blunt and make a guess?"

Stuart shrugged and only barely nodded his head.

"It has to do with Mrs. Wellington and her—shall I say—her romantic interest in you, Stuart. Isn't that the case?"

"I had no idea Thelma Wellington had the feelings for me that she professes," Stuart explained. "I don't believe they were there at first, not when Roderick Wellington was a whole man. Returning a wounded soldier from the war, an imperfect masculine specimen, has left her with a man who can no longer function as a husband. She is still a youngish woman. I imagine it is terribly frustrating for her to live such an existence."

"I've lived a good many years since your grandfather died," Nancy commented sedately, "without a husband. I admit I grew quite attached to Brian Dabney; and I grieved bitterly when he was lost to the war. Still, I don't consider myself a frustrated woman."

"You have your sons. Thelma Wellington had no children," Stuart related. "The fact is, Wellington refuses to cooperate in any way with the prosecution of Sam Dodsworth. I fear Sam will one day be released and attempt to take revenge again on Leon, Ann, or their children. Or he may take his anger out on other members of the Phenwick family. I've about decided the only thing for me to do is to travel to New York and blatantly appeal to Wellington's mercy."

"And you felt you had to discuss this with me?"

"Ruth is involved with her own matters," Stuart said. "With both Danny and Ann Marie going away to school this fall, she has her hands full getting them ready."

"Stuart, may I ask you a candid question?"

"What is it?"

"Have you ever had an affair with Mrs. Wellington?"

Stuart reddened. "You know I fathered a child by Barbara Phenwick when she was married to Uncle Prentise. And after Marcia's death I did have needs—physical needs—that required fulfilling."

"You're evading the question."

Stuart stared at the floor. "Thelma Wellington presented me with several opportunities. I swear I did not take advantage of them. However, I will confess that after such overtures by the captain's wife, I, being a man with a lusty nature, did seek out professional ladies with whom I struck up liaisons."

"I see. I won't ask if that was while you were married to Ruth. That is none of my business."

Stuart rose and paced to the window. "I've not always lived a saintly life. Let us leave it at that."

Nancy moved to him. She put her hand to his shoulder. "I understand—I understand." She gazed out the window as a carriage pulled up in front. "Who do you suppose that is?"

Stuart did not reply until he saw the man alight. "It's Adam Truff. He's returned from Greenfield."

"Dear Adam! I know he will take tea. He always does," Nancy clucked as she went to inform the servants.

Adam explained the situation in Greenfield and the death toll caused by the epidemic. In the midst of his telling, Thad joined the three in the parlor and Adam repeated what he had first said.

"Phenwick House was burned to the ground?" asked Thad.

"There is still charred rubble," Adam said. "The barn was fortuitously saved."

"Oh, dear, those lovely portraits," Nancy exclaimed. "The original painting of Augusta was hanging there."

"I managed to get it out in time, as well as several others," Adam returned.

"Will John construct a new house?"

Adam explained about John's emotional-mental condition. "He spoke of having me help him erect a new structure, but he must devote much of his time to his furniture factory. I had promised Stuart that I would get Alexander Augustus, and that could well take a goodly period of time."

"Then I'll go to Greenfield," Thad declared. "There may not be time to put up a new house before winter, but I can work with John at the factory and make plans for a new Phenwick House."

"Thaddy, do you think you should?" Nancy asked, a slight pathetic whine in her voice.

"I believe it could do Thad a great deal of good," Stuart inserted.

Nancy did not like Stuart's response. She frowned.

Adam and Thad went off to discuss the situation in Greenfield.

"You mustn't try to cling to Thad forever, Miss Nancy," Stuart said kindly. "You must put the chicks from the nest eventually."

"But Thadius is—"

"Thad is a grown man," Stuart interrupted.

"But Paul is gone," Nancy said softly, "and John spends most of his time at Cambridge. I doubt he will ever come to live with me again. With Thaddy away in Greenfield, there would only be Daniel Louis left— and he's talking of going away to school—clear to New Hampshire at Dartmouth. My chicks are spreading out. It wouldn't be so bad if they would marry and settle close by, but California—Greenfield—Dartmouth—oh, my goodness, Stuart, it's all I can do to keep from crying."

Stuart embraced Nancy as they stood by the window. "My dear Grandmother—"

"I'm *not* your grandmother," Nancy scolded. "I merely was married to your grandfather when I was a very young girl, and he was well up in his years."

"Shall I call you step-grandmother?"

"Don't be impudent, Stuart."

"What I started to say before you interrupted me, Miss Nancy," he continued, "is that it is my feeling that you should consider marrying again."

"What!"

"My words were plain enough."

"I promised Mr. Phenwick—"

"No matter what you promised during a time of emotional stress," Stuart said, "I knew my grandfather well, and I'm certain he would not have wanted you to live a lonely existence."

"But I'm no longer a girl," Nancy stated. "I've matured. My old beauty is gone."

"There is many a man who is no longer a boy, Miss Nancy," Stuart commented. "They've matured, too. I imagine there are many lonely widowers who would be delighted to have your companionship, and—knowing you—your love and devotion."

"Stuart, what a silly thing to discuss!"

"Is it? Ruth and I are planning to have several parties this fall at Edward House," Stuart explained. "It's time we were entertaining and becoming socially prominent again. You will be expected to attend, and don't be surprised if you meet several eligible gentlemen of wealth, position, who are seeking a lady such as yourself."

"Oh, Stuart." Nancy giggled.

Stuart embraced her again, kissed her on the cheek and laughed with her.

During the time Adam was preparing to make the trip south, he spent many hours with Thad, discussing the situation in Greenfield. Together they came up with several house plans, which they meticulously drew. Adam suggested that John Collier be presented with a choice of plans and that he be encouraged to choose.

Thad would have liked Adam to stay at their house, but he had already made arrangements to spend his time in Boston at Triumph House with Millijoy.

"What is your relationship with Millijoy Phenwick?" Thad questioned one evening in early September while he and Adam were casually lounging in Thad's room.

"Strictly platonic," Adam assured him. "She's been a very good friend. Besides, she's originally from Savannah and has already given me several contacts to make."

"I thought you knew the whereabouts of Alexander Augustus," Thad commented.

"I did know," Adam said. "But chances are, if word has gotten out that I'm seeking the boy, that he has been moved."

"Why shouldn't they want you to bring him to Boston?"

"Because, whether Stuart or Prentise fathered the child," Adam related, "the Callahans of Savannah have claimed the boy. I've not been able to figure out precisely why they've taken such an attitude, now that

141

Milton Callahan is no longer in the picture—but I have some suspicions."

"I would dearly love to go with you to Savannah, Adam, but I've made plans to leave next week for Greenfield."

"You'll be needed far more in Greenfield than you will be in Savannah," Adam related.

Adam left for Savannah the same day Thad departed for Greenfield. As they said their good-byes, Adam gave his friend a letter to carry to Dr. Charles Mumford, as well as notes to both Nellie and her father. The two young men parted with a warm embrace and a promise to see one another before long.

"You're determined to do this, then, are you, Thaddy?" Nancy questioned as she eyed his suitcases in the hallway.

"I once had a long conversation with John Collier," Thad explained. "I know he would be pleased if I would consider going into partnership with him. I've given it much thought, and it seems to me that is where I belong."

"But what of me?"

"Once we get the new Phenwick House constructed," Thad said, "you can come to Greenfield and stay with us—if you haven't made other plans before then."

"Has Stuart been talking to you?"

"Would a nephew discuss such things with an uncle?" Thad teased. "As a matter of fact, I've discussed the idea of you getting married again to all three of my brothers. We all agree it would be good for you. Only Paul had minor reservations about it."

"What were they?"

"Nothing of importance. Besides, Paul is in California."

"I'm too old and set in my ways to marry again," Nancy complained.

"You're forty-one," Thad returned. "And that isn't old. And, in fact, it's too young to be set in one's ways."

"If Brian—" she said wistfully.

"Brian Dabney was killed during the war. Oh, Mother, I want you to be happy—not lonely. And don't be foolish and reject a man who may be a year or two younger than you are. Look at Millijoy! She has had a bevy of men younger than she is."

"I don't want a bevy."

"I know. But I do believe you would enjoy being married again, Mother," Thad said. "Just keep an open mind. I'll pray for you and your new man."

Nancy giggled. "Oh, Thaddy, you're such a tease! I'll miss your teasing."

"Well, once you get Daniel Louis off to school," Thad suggested, "why don't you come up to Greenfield? There's a hotel. You could take a room and we could be close."

"I hadn't thought of that. Maybe I'll just—oh, dear, then there's Stuart and Ruth's social season ..."

It was Thad's turn to laugh. "Obviously, Mother, you are coming into a very exciting time of your life."

"Who? Me?" Nancy blinked and swallowed the smile that seemed to be bubbling from within her.

# Chapter Fourteen

Thad was obviously at home in Greenfield. Something about the small town, remotely isolated from Portland, appealed to the young man. Long had he taken interest in stories about the Phenwicks, and especially about his great-grandmother Augusta. During the times he had visited in the past, he had immediately made many discoveries, both about the place and about himself. He had never known his grandfather, Danny, but he felt a deep compulsion to learn about him and understand what had made up his complex personality.

A row of cottages once had stood at the north of the Phenwick property. The largest of these was the one in which Tim and Molly O'Plaggerty had lived with their family. Later, when their youngest daughter, Margaret, had married Danny Phenwick, their house was refurbished. In time, the other houses along there became dilapidated and were torn down. Two remained standing besides the O'Plaggerty house. At one time John Collier had renovated those two, along with the O'Plaggerty place.

During the epidemic an entire family had been wiped out in one house. It had been superstitiously burnt to the ground. Because of the tragedy that took that one family, the renters of the O'Plaggerty house fled Greenfield in fear for their lives. The spacious, roomy O'Plaggerty establishment became the temporary home for John, Nellie, Nana Carlyle, and Alvin Paxton. There was sufficient room for Thad when he arrived.

Early on after his arrival, Thad set about helping John at the factory, and shortly thereafter arranged for a substantial loan of money from Stuart and his mother with which to make needed improvements. Furthermore, he invested his own money from the legacy left him by his wealthy father to make arrangements and to finance the rebuilding of Phenwick House.

The original house had been situated about five hundred yards inland from the forested coastline. With Nellie, Thad discovered what he believed would be an ideal location for the new building in a place that was densely populated with trees. However, once they were cleared away, the elegant new house would overlook an inlet of water and would be perched atop a knoll, not unlike Triumph House just north of Boston.

Nancy Phenwick had attended two of the lavish parties Stuart and Ruth had given at Edward House. While she enjoyed herself, they seemed so different from the formal balls that Patricia Phenwick had had, and had supervised when she was no longer strong enough to fully manage such affairs. Ruth, with all her charm and beauty, did not have the extravagance of taste or grandness of personality to instigate such things. Her parties were sedately nice, and all very proper for the proper Bostonian society; but Nancy felt something was missing.

Then, too, in their ardor to find a suitable man for Nancy, Stuart and Ruth had been a bit indiscriminate in their choice of guests. Those men who were affluent were generally stodgy penny-pinchers who wheezed and made other peculiar noises. Or they were staunch religionists with ultraconservative tastes. Or they were men who had a sickly history or shady reputations. After the second such party, Nancy decided that her relatives were inefficient matchmakers, try as they may.

To escape a third such party in mid-October, Nancy accepted Thad's invitation to visit Greenfield. Innately, Stuart realized why she had decided on the trip. He saw her to the train and sent her with his blessings.

Nancy visited three days at Falmouth House in Portland with Leo and Ann Phenwick. She enjoyed herself and promised to return if there were not adequate accommodations for her in Greenfield. Then Leo drove her to her destination.

Through Thad's encouragement and constant assistance, John Collier began to appear to be his old self again. Nellie did her best to take the place of the rest of their family. She was daughter and son, and tried to substitute in many of the household aspects of wife. Furthermore, the little girl worked as many hours a day as she possibly could at the furniture factory.

Thad had become good friends with Charles Mumford. Through the doctor, he met many of the townspeople. Of course he had the magic name of Phenwick, which made people eager to get on the best side of him.

Nellie was the first to see the carriage arrive from Portland. She ran to greet it. Fond of Leo Phenwick, Nellie sprang to his waiting arms, then she went to brightly greet Nancy.

Nancy and Leo surveyed the burnt ruins of Phenwick House. Little had been done to remove the charred remains. It was an ugly sight that Nancy decided to take on as her first project in Greenfield.

Leo stayed only a short while, long enough to greet the family, before he returned to Portland.

"There's room at the O'Plaggerty house for you," Nellie said to Nancy. "It isn't at all elegant, but it suffices for our needs for the present."

"I will make do wherever I am," Nancy returned. She smelled deeply of the country air and decided immediately that she would stay for an elongated visit. Greenfield presented challenge to her, and that was one thing she liked. The thought of rebuilding Phenwick House and being a vital part of it, excited her.

Fall was in the air, making the mornings crisp and nippy. The very blue sky along the coast was cloudless on that Sunday morning, when Nancy awakened early, put on a heavy coat, and prepared to scout about the construction site for the new house. Many of the trees had been removed, leaving several of the more stately and shapely ones to surround the building. She had seen to that while the others concentrated their energies at the factory.

"Where are you off to so early in the morning?" John Collier called from the door of his room on the second floor, as Nancy prepared to descend the stairs.

"To London to visit the Queen," she pertly replied. "It's a glorious day and I desire to walk before preparing for church."

John used the back of his hand to cover a yawn. "Do you particularly wish to prowl alone? Or would you like company?"

"It depends on how soon the company is ready to leave," Nancy replied.

"As soon as I get out of my nightshirt," John said, "and pull into some clothing."

"You'd better dress warmly. There's frost on the ground," Nancy advised. "I'll wait for you downstairs. But I'll wait no longer than five minutes."

"It won't take that long," John laughed and ducked back into his room.

Nancy had developed a round appearance over the years, but she was far from being plump. The soft beauty of her youth had faded, and a mature loveliness had taken its place. The touches of gray in her dark

147

hair gave distinction to her majestic character. She laughed with her eyes. And, being the mother of four boys, she had had to develop a gay sense of humor. Paul was her prankster. John was her scholar, but not without a light sense of whimsy. Daniel Louis was her sportsman who, she suspected, was destined to become a playboy of sorts. She discouraged such pursuits, but she wondered how much influence she actually would have over her youngest son. She thought of Thad as her adventurer, although she was not always certain about him. Thad worried her. Being the eldest, he was the one she tended to favor.

In those moments, as she waited for John Collier to dress, she wondered if she was doing right by her other sons, being away from Boston. Still, both John and Daniel Louis were living away at school. Then she thought of Paul. She had not heard from her next-to-youngest son in months. He wasn't the sort to correspond, but she imagined he would one day just show up in Boston for a visit. Again she quickly put the notion from her mind that she should return to the city in case Paul were to arrive.

"Where shall we walk?" John Collier questioned as he came bounding down the stairs. Both his mental and physical condition had greatly improved.

"I was planning to go to the site for the new house," Nancy explained. "I had the men working all day yesterday, and I want to see that they've cleared all the stumps."

"Then that is where we will go," John said lightly.

Only when they passed between the charred remains of the old Phenwick House and the cemetery did John become solemn. Nancy knew what he must be thinking. She did not intrude.

"I acted the fool, I know," John said as they neared the site that was being cleared, "in my time of grief."

"Not the fool, dearest John," Nancy corrected. "You

were deeply distressed and so emotionally upset you could not help your actions. I know how deeply you loved Kate. We all loved her."

"Thank you for saying that, Miss Nancy," John returned, and smiled although his eyes glistened with emotions. "While on her deathbed, Katie told me she thought I should marry again. At that time the thought completely repulsed me. Yet, now that I've come to terms with the fact that Katie is no longer in a physical existence, and I have conquered at least part of my distressing feelings, I realize that I am a man who needs the constant company of a woman."

"From what I've observed," Nancy inserted, "I believe you're right. My Peter told me once that he thought it would be far easier for a woman to live without a man than a man without a woman. Of course, he was a man. I still think of him, but only with loving, happy memories."

They walked to the edge of the cliff and stared out at the sea, glistening in morning sunlight. A chill wind arose and Nancy pulled her coat tighter about her. A lone seagull cried.

"Miss Nancy," John began after several minutes of silence, "do you honestly believe I should consider taking a second wife?"

"I suppose that would depend on whom you had in mind," she replied. "Just to marry for the sake of marrying wouldn't be a good idea—not at all. You could tie yourself to a shrewish woman who might not be capable of loving you. I would give careful thought to the matter, if I were you."

John smiled as he dug his hands deeply into his pockets. "I suppose you've given much thought to the matter of remarrying."

"There was a time when I was deeply, emotionally involved with Brian Dabney," Nancy said after a few moments of consideration. "I'm certain I would have married him had he returned from the war. But he didn't. Stuart and Ruth have vainly tried to match me up with some man. Those they've chosen have been too mature, too old in their thoughts and ways. I think I want a youthful man, one who is experienced, but not with one foot in the grave. Naturally, I'll be hard to please."

When the gull called again, John glanced up into Nancy's face. She was watching the bird as it circled and landed on the old quay. Then she turned her gaze to John.

"Nellie told me the other day that she believed I would marry again," John stated. "I laughed, since I thought it was ridiculous of her to say such a thing. But I've known only too well that her predictions have more often than not come true."

"Isn't that funny, Nellie told me practically the same thing."

"About me?" John asked.

"No, about me." Nancy chuckled. "That Nellie is quite a little girl, isn't she?"

"If you want the truth," John returned, "I think of her as quite a little adult. She is far too wise to be a child. Yet I have a fear about Nellie."

"A fear?"

"That she might devote too much of her time to me," John said. "When I came to the realization of that possibility, I became aware that not only should I consider another marriage for my own sake, but also for Nellie's. So many girls dedicate their lives to the welfare of a single parent to the neglect of their own true happiness. I might have selfishly accepted such devotion from either Nellie or Elizabeth, if it hadn't been for the epidemic. Now that Nellie is my only living child, I believe it would be wrong of me to jeopardize her future and happiness by permitting her to cling so tightly to me. Besides, I look forward to one day having grandchildren. I think you see what I mean."

"Precisely, John." Nancy walked back to where the foundation for the front of the house would be. She appeared to be examining the lines that had been stringed off. Then she called over her shoulder. "It's going to be a large house, isn't it? I don't dislike Millijoy Phenwick, but I would dearly love to see the new Phenwick House be far superior to her Triumph House."

"To build that sort of place would take a tremendous amount of money—far more than I have," John remarked as he moved to where she was standing. "Besides, such a house would require a mistress to see to the running of it. Nellie would assume the role of mistress of Phenwick House, if I permitted it."

Nancy stared up into his well-proportioned face. Ruggedly handsome, she thought.

"When I hear you speak of the new house," John commented, "I get the impression that you would like it to be *your* house."

"That's silly. How could it possibly be?"

Another gust of wind blew up from the sea. John was staring deeply into her eyes. They both looked away at the same time, as if the intruding wind had appeared for a purpose.

John breathed deeply. "Autumn is in the air. Already the maples have begun to change color."

"Autumn, yes, but . . ." Nancy hesitated.

"But what, dear Miss Nancy?"

"What is that fragrantly sweet scent? It can't be violets this time of the year," she said without thinking.

"Now that you mentioned it, I know the fragrance to be that of violets," John remarked.

"*Violets?*" Goose bumps had sprung out all over Nancy.

At the same moment John remembered the significance attached to the scent of violets by the Phenwicks.

He, too, got a prickly sensation. "I think it's far too cold for us to stand idly about. Perhaps we should head back to the house. There is church this morning, remember?"

Nancy did not move. "And I think—"

"Yes?"

"Perhaps it's daring of me to say this, but I think I would very much enjoy being the mistress of the new Phenwick House," she stated.

"I think—" John looked away, then back at Nancy, "I think that would be a beautiful idea."

"Then we must give it further thought, mustn't we?" Nancy said. "And you're quite right, it is far too cold to stand here lollygagging. And there is church before long."

"Miss Nancy, do you think I'm too old and mature in my thoughts and my ways?" John asked.

"Goodness no, you're still a very young man—"

"Well, younger than some."

"And I know you have an extremely loving personality," Nancy continued, aware she was speaking fast, but unable to slow down. "What you had with Kate was probably as beautiful as the life I had with Peter. There was so much giving and sharing, so many wonderful things, and—" She breathed deeply. "And I think we'd better get back to the house right away."

John caught her hand, detaining her from rushing off. "Miss Nancy, I still smell the violets. The scent used to make me sneeze."

"Nellie—Thad—"

"We'll go now." He smiled with understanding. "We don't want to miss the sermon on the evils of sin, do we?"

"Yes. I mean, yes, we must go."

Nancy permitted John to hold her hand as they walked back to the house.

"I dreamed of Mother last night," Nellie stated a few

days later, when she arrived to have breakfast with Nancy.

"I still dream of Peter after all these years," Nancy returned. "I suspect it means that the spirits of those we loved are still very near to us."

Nellie sat at the table and smiled enigmatically as she unfolded her napkin. "Yes, I suppose that is the case. Mother told me—and quite emphatically—that I should encourage a wedding next spring."

"A wedding?" Nancy looked up.

"I'm certain it wasn't meant to be mine. I'm far too young," Nellie responded. "Besides, I could never consider marriage—even if I were old enough—if Daddy were by himself. The only meaning I can derive from the dream is that Mother wanted me to encourage Daddy to marry again. When I awakened, I thought it was a silly idea. Now that I've had time to think about it, it almost seems a splendid notion, don't you think?"

Nancy avoided eye contact with the girl. "Yes. But, of course, it *was* only a dream, wasn't it?"

"Yes, Miss Nancy, but you know about *my* dreams," Nellie returned.

Thad entered and Nancy immediately turned her attention to her son. Nellie watched carefully. Then John arrived.

As John asked the table blessing, Nellie peeked through nearly closed eyes. Her father's hand had moved over the table until it nearly touched Nancy's plate. Nancy put her hand to the table and started moving it toward John's before it occurred to her that she might be being observed.

A wonderful feeling of happiness came over Nellie, and she knew precisely what was going to happen.

Stuart received word the following March that a wedding was to be planned in Boston toward the end of April. John and Nancy wanted to clear the date with him. It was to be a simple service, but a gala reception was to be planned at Edward House that would last the entire day.

Ruth was pleased. She immediately began making plans. Stuart wrote back and confirmed the date. Then he set about working out the details.

John Phenwick was overjoyed at the thought of his mother marrying again. He had received letters from both Nancy and Thad. In turn, John wrote to Paul in San Francisco and, surprisingly, he received a message by return mail. Paul, too, was delighted for his mother's decision. He, of course, would not attempt to return to Boston for the ceremonies.

Only Daniel Louis took a negative view of the situation. John and Stuart had long talks with him. He remained stubborn, but in the end he admitted that his mother's happiness was important. He would do nothing to stand in the way of that which was destined to be.

Adam Truff arrived back in Boston with young Alexander Augustus in time for the wedding. Stuart welcomed him and his son with open arms. Alexander Augustus was confused by all that had happened. But he was a bright-appearing, handsome lad, and the excitement of the celebration took some of the uneasiness momentarily away from him.

Nellie was to be the maid of honor.

Production at the furniture factory was closed down for three weeks so that all those who could possibly get away could attend the happy occasion. Even Dr. Charles Mumford took a vacation from his practice to go to Boston.

"You realize what this will do, don't you, Nellie?" Thad questioned the day before the wedding.

Nellie stared at his frowned expression. "What is it?"

"We'll be brother and sister," he said.

"Only stepbrother and sister," Nellie corrected. "I think it will be wonderful. I've begun to think of you as an older brother anyway, since you've been at Green-field. Now it will be real."

Thad lightly shook his head and turned away. "We'll talk later."

Nellie squinted as she watched the handsome young man stride away. As she did, a picture flashed into her mind. It was of a wedding. Only the bride and groom were *not* Nancy and John. Why had that thought come to her? Then she became aware that Thad obviously had more than a brotherly attitude toward her.

Nellie smiled and knew without knowing how she knew.

# PART II

# Chapter Fifteen

1875

The white three-story house stood majestically on the cliff overlooking the inlet bay. A new quay had been constructed below, alongside of which was a small boat shed. Stone stairs led to the beach, and the grounds surrounding the new Phenwick House had been elegantly landscaped. From the first crocus bud of spring to the last chrysanthemum of autumn before the freeze got it, the yard was a mass of colorful flowers.

Mrs. Nancy Phenwick Collier had imported a French gardener to supervise the plantings. She was convinced, despite her marriage to John, that she was still a designated Phenwick woman; hence she always used the name along with Collier. At the gardener's suggestion, she had purchased several marble statues for the garden, which were very much in the Greco-Roman style of heroic art. Tall marble columns supported a wisteria arbor and an ornate Italian water fountain splashed jubilantly on the lawn in good months.

After returning Alexander Augustus to Stuart in Boston, Adam Truff decided to take the cottage offered him by John Collier. He artistically refurbished it, added onto it, and made it into a miniature mansion, with landscaping planned and executed by the French gardener. Then he settled into devoting much of his time to Collier Furniture. Itchy feet made him an ideal person to periodically go on the road in quest of more business.

The interior of the new Phenwick House was spacious. John had constructed most of the furniture from his own designs. Nancy had purchased artwork for the house, and colorfully thick carpeting. She was an independently wealthy person due to the fortune left to her by Peter Phenwick and the expert management of her funds by Stuart. She felt she had the right to have an extravagant home. The days devoted to raising her sons had been spent in concern for them. She made a good home for them and cared for them as best she could. Her world had changed. In the five years she had been married to John Collier, she had emerged a grand lady, in a way patterning herself after the late Patricia Phenwick, whom she had greatly admired. Still, she was a devoted, loving wife, and she kept in regular contact with her sons and others of the Phenwick family. She even made effort to communicate with John's family in Illinois. Only his sister Nellie, for whom his daughter had been named, had written in response to Nancy's query.

Above all else, Nancy prided herself in the job she had done that had transformed Nellie into the most beautiful young lady that side of Boston. The girl, who had natural loveliness, had blossomed into a gorgeous creature. Nancy had personally seen to her education and manners. Seamstresses and designers created daringly exotic apparel for both Nellie and Nancy. They were considered to be queen and princess in the limited society of Greenfield, and were second only to Ann Phenwick among the social elite in Portland, where they often traveled.

With the spring thaw came the suitors from as far away as Boston and Portland to vie for the attention and perhaps affection of Nellie Collier. While the beautiful young lady took an interest, albeit often remote, in her father's business, she found herself more and more occupied by the attention of attractive and generally wealthy young men. Phenwick House boasted twelve guest rooms, and there were other rooms where sleeping accommodations could be arranged. A household staff of seven was employed, all of whom lived in.

John Collier's love for Nancy had grown over the years. Occasionally he would have remembered thoughts about Kate, but the love he had had for her was something entirely different from that which he had for Nancy. He could not analyze the difference, but he was well aware that it existed. He was proud of Nancy and the love that he had for her. And he took equal pride in his appreciation of the beauty Nellie had become. His life, too, had changed. He had a new confidence that success alone can bring.

While Thad deeply admired the new Phenwick House, he had become attached to the home that had once belonged to the O'Plaggertys. When the new structure had been completed, he made arrangements to buy the old house, and there he lived. Pleased over his mother's newfound happiness, nonetheless Thad preferred solitude and privacy. He worked long hours at the furniture factory and was considered an equal partner with John. During times when Adam was not on the road, Thad would spend many hours in conversation with him. He often wished that he had the outgoing personality that Adam possessed. Still, he was not envious of the man per se.

Thad had watched Nellie grow up. Even he was amazed to behold the beauty she had become. On one hand he was pleased with the way she had developed, but on the other hand he felt resentful of the fact that her attractiveness magnetized so many admirers to her. He often discussed Nellie with Adam. Adam and Charles Mumford spent many hours together. Thad found his thoughts during moments of solitude had become obsessed with speculations about Nellie.

"What is it, Thaddy?" his mother asked one day while he was visiting at Phenwick House.

"What is *what?*"

"That strange expression I see in your face," Nancy replied.

"I was unaware that my expression was singular," Thad said.

"It is, and it has been for some time now," Nancy remarked, going to him and catching his cheeks between the palms of her hands. "My precious Thadius, whatever is worrying you?"

Thad pulled away from her touch. "Nothing. I'm not worried."

"Well, then, some peculiar emotion is twisting your countenance."

Thad poured himself a glass of brandy. "I've been thinking recently about an old friend of mine. Kit Snyder."

"Kit? Is that a man's name, or a woman's?"

"A man's." Thad laughed. "He was a sailor I met while at sea. Kit tried to persuade me to spend my life at sea. It was good enough for him, why not for me?"

"You wouldn't."

"I *didn't* is more to the point, Mother. Which doesn't mean I won't," Thad stated. "You see, I told Kit if I wasn't married by the time I reached thirty, I would seriously consider becoming a seaman."

"And you will turn thirty the first day of September of this year, won't you?" Nancy said.

Thad nodded his head.

"That gives you three months in which to find a wife, doesn't it?" Nancy sounded only half-serious because she did not believe that her son would become a seaman under any circumstance.

"If I've not done it in thirty years," he returned, "how can I possibly do it in three months?"

"As you know, we are planning an extravagant birthday party for Nellie the twelfth of next month," Nancy related. "Naturally there will be many guests coming from Portland. And I've invited all the Phenwicks of Boston and their friends. I'll make a point of inviting certain attractive young ladies especially for you. I'll write immediately to Ann in Portland—she has friends. You may not be married by your thirtieth birthday, but we'll hope that you become seriously interested in the right young lady by then."

"The right young lady," Thad sneered. He was ready to leave.

"Thadius! What in the world has come over you?"

"Nothing. Absolutely nothing! I want to see if Adam has returned."

"Thadius—?"

The young man had walked out of the sitting room, leaving his mother in a temporary quandary. His boots clattered on the marble floor of the large entrance hall. Because of the situation of the house, it was difficult to tell which was the front and which was the back entrance. The one facing the south was usually considered the main doorway; but the driveway curved around at the north door, which was nearest to the road, and people usually entered that way. Thad was headed in a northerly direction. His handsome face was fixed in a scowl as he moved, and he appeared oblivious of the surroundings.

Nana Carlyle entered from the hallway. She was decked out in her fancy starched uniform, which went with her title of housekeeper. "Mr. Phenwick?"

Thad paused briefly and glanced at the woman. "Good

163

afternoon, Nana. And I mean that as a farewell greeting."

"Excuse me, sir," Nana said, moving closer to him.

"I have business," Thad said bluntly. "Excuse *me*."

"It's Miss Nellie, sir," Nana explained. "She saw you arrive and sent me with word that she wishes to see you before you leave."

"Nellie?" A change of mood quickly came over him. "Where is she?"

"In her sitting room on the second floor."

Thad altered his intended course and went directly to the stairs. He started to take the steps two at a time until he realized Nana was watching him. Slowing, he tried to appear nonchalant as he climbed to the second floor.

Nellie's hair had become auburn, with a light tint on top where it had been slightly bleached by the sun. Her face had become somewhat longer than it had been in her childhood and she possessed what Nancy preferred to call an aristocratic beauty. With milk-soft skin and cheeks the color of pale roses, even if she had been in rags, Thad was certain she would still be an elegant beauty. She was standing before a gilt-framed mirror, straightening the bodice of her lavender gown trimmed with purple velvet ribbons. A touch of white lace was at her throat and about her sleeves. Catching Thad's reflection in the glass, she continued with what she was doing until it was accomplished.

"You weren't going to stop for a short visit?" she asked. Her voice had a satin lilt to it. "I feel neglected."

"I have things on my mind," Thad replied, feeling a bit self-conscious.

"Yes, I know." She turned to him and smiled. A moment later she was reaching to take his hands and kiss him on the cheek. "Why do you make yourself a stranger?"

164

"Don't you know the answer to that, too?" he asked impetuously.

She dropped his hands and glided toward the French doors that overlooked the second-floor veranda. "I might."

"I can't get over how you've changed," Thad commented, stepping hesitantly toward her. "I mean, since I first came to Greenfield."

"I've grown up."

"Yes, I can see that."

"You didn't expect me to remain a little girl forever, did you?"

"No, of course not. But you once seemed so innocent and unaffected," he observed. "Now you've obviously— well—"

"I'm still innocent in many ways, dearest Thad," she stated.

"My mother is responsible for the change in you."

"Is she? In ways, I suppose she is. She taught me to become a lady." Nellie turned back to him. "I haven't seen Adam recently either—nor Dr. Mumford. You three are my closest friends, yet you seem to avoid me."

"Adam and Charles—well, I can't speak for them," Thad said. "I've been very busy looking out for my interests in Collier Furniture."

"Yes, I know." She moved to a bench and sat adjusting her skirts. Then she opened a small fan and fluttered it before her face. "Why do I keep *getting* the name Christopher?"

"Christopher? I don't know the name."

"But I get that name around you."

"Christopher?" Thad pondered the name.

"The last name is like *spider*."

Thad thought a minute before he laughed. "I was speaking a short while ago with Mother. I did mention the name of Kit Snyder."

"That's it. Kit is sometimes a nickname for Chris-

165

topher," Nellie explained. "Just a moment." She put her hand to the side of her face, the tips of her long fingers to her temple. "Kit is no longer alive. He was killed during a brawl at a seaport along the northern coast of Africa. But you made him a promise, didn't you?"

"Kit dead? Yes, I did—mostly in jest at the time."

"But that promise has been reconsidered of late, hasn't it?"

"You already seem to know all the answers, Nellie. Why do you ask me?" Thad questioned.

"I don't want to leave you out of the conversation." She threw her head back and laughed merrily. "You don't find that humorous, do you?"

"I'm afraid I don't," Thad replied. He shifted his weight from foot to foot.

"Perhaps we can go for a ride sometime," Nellie suggested. "Then we can talk when you're not so anxious to leave. Would you like that?"

Thad was confused. "Yes, I think I would."

"Good, then you decide when it's convenient and I'll make time for it," Nellie stated. "Now don't let me keep you from whatever is so urgent you must do."

Thad felt awkward. "I don't— He caught himself. "Yes, I had better go. I will call again soon."

Nellie stood at the door to the veranda after Thad left. Her uncanny precognitive sense told her too much. She knew what was troubling him, but at that point she was not prepared to deal with the reality of it.

That warm June afternoon, Nellie dressed in simple but attractive attire and went out for an evening stroll. Toby, the red Irish setter, who considered himself her dog, accompanied her. As she went past the cemetery, she stopped a moment and stared at the stones she knew to mark the graves of her mother and her siblings. She turned her attention from the graveyard to the old barn that stood next to where the original Phenwick House had been. The charred remains had long since been removed, and a summerhouse had been constructed on the site. The new structure, of course, was much smaller, and a lovely garden was planted around it.

Toby ran to the summerhouse and sniffed around. A cellar door was beside it, leading to what had been the basement of the old house. Original plans had been for the basement to be filled in with dirt, but Nellie had had a premonition about it and had insisted it remain as it was. John Collier complied with her wishes.

When Nellie discovered that Toby's attention was attracted to a squirrel hole, she called him away and they went down the lane that led to Adam's cottage.

Over the years Nellie had developed an emotional attraction to Adam. She tried to tell herself that she was not in love with him, but that was the only logical explanation for the feelings she had for him. Adam had always appeared romantically disinterested in the girl. He was a good friend and that was all he cared to be. Still, Nellie could not get him from her mind. It was strange, she thought, that, feeling as she did about him, she was unable to pick up any of his inner thoughts. Or perhaps she did, and did not want to believe what she perceived.

Toby ran ahead down the lane. Nellie sauntered, deep in thought. The Irish setter was out of sight. It didn't matter. He could find his way back.

Stopping at the stable, Nellie patted the roan mare. She was due to foal within two months and Nellie was convinced that the animal would give birth to twins. The mare, who was called Esmeralda, nuzzled Nellie.

"It won't be long now, Esmeralda," Nellie said reassuringly. "These things take time. Just be patient. If you have twin daughters, I'll name them for my cousins, Elena and Isabelle." She put her hand to the horse's belly. "But I have a feeling that boys' names will be more appropriate."

A sharp yelping noise came from the grove of trees behind the stable. Nellie recognized the sound and knew it to be a cry of distress. Lifting her skirts, she went in the direction of the noise.

The porcupine had scampered into the underbrush, but his quills were protruding from Toby's mouth. The dog was furiously trying to use his paws to remove the spikes, and at the same time was howling and leaping about from the pain.

When Nellie caught him, she managed to remove three of the larger quills before he dashed away from her. She followed him through the thickets and the limited area of small woods. Toby emerged near the wall that surrounded Adam's cottage. Nellie reached him before he could go through the gate.

"Now, please hold still, Toby," she pleaded, "or we'll never get those terrible things out."

As Nellie again tried to pull the quills, she was aware of a shadow that crossed her face.

"Here, let me help you with that," Adam said. He was both barefoot and shirtless. "I'll try to hold the dog while you yank."

Adam straddled Toby and held his head as firmly as he could, but the animal had strength. "Come on into the cottage," he suggested. "We'll have to tie him. And I have pliers we can use."

They managed to get the dog inside and bound his legs. With the dog thus constrained, Nellie was able to hold him down while Adam removed the quills. Prying open the animal's mouth, he examined the interior. Fortunately there were only two quills in his tongue. Once the projections were all out, Toby was untied and permitted to go outside.

"He'll be all right now," Adam assured her. "The great danger was that he might have gotten the quills in his throat."

"You know a lot about animals, don't you, Adam?"

Nellie questioned, trying not to obviously admire the physical attractiveness of the man.

"A very important thing my Indian friend, Jamatu, taught me," Adam explained, "was to learn how to handle animals. Jamatu could train wild animals and make pets of them. The first thing you must do is to learn to keep from having a sense of fear around them. Animals, particularly wild animals, seem to respond negatively to fear. I suppose people are the same way. May I fix you a cup of tea?"

"It's a bit warm for tea," Nellie commented.

"Something cool then?" Adam exuded great charm. "You must forgive my appearance. I was relaxing when I heard Toby's yelps."

"Something cool would be nice."

"I'll just put on a blouse—"

"No. Don't bother. You appear to be comfortable," Nellie said.

Adam laughed and went to fix the drinks. Nellie watched as he left the room. She could not help thinking of the Grecian statues of male figures that Nancy had imported for the garden. His skin was bronzed from exposure to the sun. Shortly after he took over the cottage, he warned intruders not to enter if the gate was locked during the day hours. That meant he was sunbathing without clothing.

A short while later Adam returned with the cool berry juice. "I took you at your word and did not put on a blouse. Won't you come in the parlor and sit for awhile?"

"Thank you."

"I love this cottage," Adam said after he had seated himself opposite Nellie. "It perfectly suits my needs."

"Your needs are simple."

"That's another thing I learned from Jamatu," he explained.

"Where is Jamatu now?"

"Wandering about, I suppose," Adam replied. "He likes to travel through the wilderness, live a very earthy existence. He'll show up one day, stay a few days and go off again. That's his way. I learned much from him."

The parlor was neatly and simply furnished. A small bronze figurine of an Indian was on a pedestal in the corner and a bust of Socrates stood on a table behind the settee. A blue glass vase held a bouquet of wild glorianas. Three pictures were on the walls: two were landscapes, the third was the portrait of Daniel Phenwick the first, which Adam had saved from the house at the time of the fire. The likeness of Augusta was hanging in Phenwick House; but because Adam seemed so taken with the portrait of Danny, John had insisted that Adam have it in his house.

"Doesn't it bother you living alone, Adam?" Nellie asked after gazing about the room.

"I'm perfectly comfortable here," he replied. "I have my books and, to be perfectly frank, I enjoy solitude. I have spent so much time traveling around, staying in hotels and wherever else I could get lodging—many times on a blanket in the woods—that I delight in my home."

"But to be by yourself so much of the time—?" Nellie questioned.

"You're wondering why I have never married," Adam said. "It is a personal matter. I have my reasons. I don't believe all people were meant to marry and raise families. Such a way of life may be right for the majority of the people, but not for everyone."

Nellie had other questions. Instead of asking them, she stared out the window and the answers came to her mind. Adam was watching her and he perceived what she was doing. Only the scratching of Toby on the door jarred Nellie back. She smiled embarrassedly.

"Where did you go?" Adam asked.

"Was I away? Yes, I suppose I was—mentally," Nellie

replied. "I suspect Toby has come to walk me back to Phenwick House."

"I suspect he has." Adam rose and went to the door. Toby came bounding in, all tongue and affection.

"There is one thing," Nellie said as she stood by the door, one hand reaching down to pet the dog.

"One thing?"

"Look behind Danny," Nellie said cryptically.

"I beg your pardon?"

"Don't ask me what it means, that was merely the thought I received." Nellie smiled sweetly, invitingly. "Miss Nancy is planning a large party for my eighteenth birthday, the twelfth of next month. People will be coming from Portland and Boston. If necessary, can you put two or three up here at the cottage?"

"I believe I can arrange that."

"Good." Nellie felt restless. "We'll leave now. Goodbye, Adam."

Adam walked her to the gate. After closing it behind her, he put the lock on. A few minutes later he was lying in the sun. "Look behind Danny?" he said aloud. Nellie was obviously having another premonition. He chuckled and turned over.

# Chapter Sixteen

Nellie's eighteenth birthday party was obviously the most lavish event that had occurred at the new Phenwick House in Greenfield. Relatives and friends came from great distances to participate in the week-long affair. It was Nancy's innovation, and she was the perfect hostess, flitting gaily among her acquaintances, living up to the reputation expected of a Phenwick woman.

Time had eased John Collier's unhappiness. His marriage to Nancy had been at first a convenience. In time he had grown to depend upon her, relying on her judgment both at home and at business. Although he still maintained thoughts of Kate, he realized the kind of love he had for Nancy, albeit beautiful, was different and, in some ways, even more satisfying. He had become successful in his business, particularly with the advent of his partnership with Thad Phenwick. Collier Furniture had done remarkably well, earning a reputation throughout most of New England as more and more furniture was exported from the small village of Greenfield.

Despite his protest, Adam Truff consented to be Nellie's escort at the party on the twelfth. That was also the day that Stuart and Ruth Phenwick arrived with their children from Boston. Accompanying them were Nancy's other sons, John and Daniel Louis. Leo and Ann Phenwick arrived from Portland, coinciding with the arrival of the relatives from Boston. Friends, people of society, who had become particularly fond of Nancy and the Phenwicks, also appeared. Naturally Nancy had made arrangements for many eligible young men to be present, selecting them from her acquaintances from both Portland and Boston. Much time had been spent going over the guest list, as she made certain she had things well planned and that people would be matched, at least in a friendly way, for the gala occasion.

Nancy had insisted that Dr. Charles Mumford be present at the party as often as his schedule would permit, especially for the greeting of relatives from the distance. Charles was handsomely attired and looked remarkably attractive on that occasion. Yet when the family arrived, he went immediately to embrace John Phenwick, his mentor at Cambridge, and the two soon fell into deep conversation, sometimes isolating themselves for long periods of time from the rest of the guests.

The erstwhile Michael Black, now known by his true identity of Leo Phenwick after recovering from his bout with amnesia, exuded a tremendous amount of charm. Lovely Ann, his wife, seemed to radiate happiness and contentment. She fawned over Nellie, often taking her aside and telling her little anecdotes about the Phenwicks. Ann also made a point of indicating certain young men who had arrived from Portland, from good families and wealth. She believed that at least one of these handsome youths would make an ideal prospective husband for her cousin.

Ruth and Ann quite often gathered with the other ladies in an attempt to make Nellie comprehend that she was expected at this time—although Nancy had never mentioned it—to scrutinize the young men in attendance with a possible thought of marriage.

"Marriage?" Nellie exclaimed, staring wide-eyed in her lovely white satin gown trimmed with pink roses and ribbons of a deeper rose pink velvet. She was doubtless the most beautiful young lady present. Were she not, no one would have mentioned it.

"Of course, child," Ruth exclaimed. "You're eighteen. That's quite a marriageable age, you know."

"But I—" Nellie hesitated. Her eyes moved to beyond the ladies and the edge of the veranda where the gentlemen were engaged in a game of croquet. Her attention went to Adam Truff, who had not only removed his coat, but had rolled up his blouse sleeves as well. He seemed to gleam in white attire from head to foot.

Ann followed Nellie's gaze, then looked back into her face. "You're in love with him, aren't you, Nellie?"

"In love?" Nellie blinked. "With Adam Truff?" She tried to laugh the absurdity of the matter off with a flippant attitude. "I find him most attractive. Doesn't every woman? I've not known of one yet who doesn't think that Adam is by far the epitome of what a handsome, gallant young man should be."

"Nellie ... Nellie ..." Ann said softly, putting her hand on the girl's. "Ruth knows Adam far better than I. Perhaps she cannot be as detached as I can be, but I think it is foolish for any woman to pursue a man who has lived as long as Adam Truff has without marrying. There must be a very strong reason for that. If that *is* the case, it would be foolhardy of you to even contemplate such thoughts, entertain such notions."

Ruth fluttered her fan and cast a longing glance at Adam. "What Ann says is quite true, dearest Nellie. I once had deep feelings for Adam Truff. I thought he was the man I loved. When I fell in love with Stuart, I realized that my husband had much more in a manly way to offer a woman than Adam Truff could ever have. Oh, Adam is a hero—a dashing figure and all of that—but it takes a certain sort of man to become a good husband. Although I love him dearly as a friend, I realize Adam does not have the ingredients for that. You're foolish to even contemplate him, dear Nellie."

Nellie rose from the chair in which she had been seated and stepped to the railing, where she cupped her hand about a red geranium blossom. Wistfully she gazed at Adam. Then she turned her attention to the lithe figure of Dr. Charles Mumford who, like Adam, was without his coat and had rolled his sleeves. When she viewed them together, she was reminded of two boys sharing a kind of mischief, she thought—children who had grown up physically, but when together, their boyish ways, the fun, the excitement of boyhood still seemed to be with them. Other young men, who were participating in the game or who were watching, appeared much more mature in their attitudes. She caught their sly looks of admiration and, she suspected, ambition.

Ultimately Nellie's attention turned to Thad Phenwick and his brother John, as they sat in a swing beneath the shade of a large elm tree at the far east side of the lawn. The brothers had had little opportunity to chat prior to that time. As they sat side by side, rocking gently back and forth, an awkward moment caught them. While extremely handsome in his own way, John had more the looks of a Phenwick, and Thad resembled their mother's side of the family, the Coxes. Thad had an amazing resemblance to Nancy; his coloring was darker than John's. John was doubtless a Phenwick, his features much different from those of his brother. John bore a striking likeness to his late father.

Upon meeting John and Stuart, one could see that they were closely related; but when Thad was with either his brother or his nephew, that similarity was not noticed.

John stretched a long leg forward and used the heel of his boot to rock the swing back and forth. "Are you doing well here, my dear brother?"

"I suppose I'm doing as well as can be expected under the circumstances. The furniture business is extremely good, and—" Thad looked down.

"What is it, Thad?"

"There are some personal matters," Thad replied. "Oh, don't mistake me, I enjoy the business very much, and John Collier and I have become great friends."

"But—?" John asked. "There is something bothering you, isn't there?"

"Yes. I think I'm in love."

John laughed heartily. "Oh, is that all it's about!"

"Don't make mock of my feelings, John," his brother sighed.

"You're a Phenwick man, the epitome of the Lothario, the great lover," John jested.

"Hogwash! You're a Phenwick man, Johnny. Are you all of those?"

"I try to be—on occasion," John boasted. "But I will be honest and say that I have not as yet lost my heart to anyone. I do spend much time at study. I figure that I will give myself another year or so, then I will seriously consider taking a wife. Until that time I'm going to enjoy myself and let the blossoms fall where they may." He laughed again.

"Life is different in Greenfield than it is in Boston and Cambridge," Thad commented softly. "There are a few young ladies of marriageable age here. But I haven't really noticed them. Nor have I had any desire to philander about."

"Philander? Do you think I'm a philanderer?"

"Aren't you, Johnny?"

"Not really. No. I talk a good game and I boast a lot, but it's all just that—wishful thinking, I suppose, or goodness knows what else it may be. The male pride, I should guess; or as Cousin Joseph Ornby would say, Sigmund Freud has called it *the male ego*. Whomever Sigmund Freud is, I don't know that." John cleared his throat. "Anyway, who is the young lady who has captured your love, Thad?"

"Isn't it obvious?" Thad questioned as he glanced over to the veranda, where Nellie was standing. At that moment another young lady had joined the others. She was a friend of Ann's from Portland.

John followed his brother's eyes, then looked back and studied Thad's face. "Surely it's not Ann Phenwick's friend from Portland, is it?"

"No."

John put his hand on his brother's leg and patted it. "So you've fallen in love with Nellie, have you?"

"I find her quite attractive. I suspect I've always had a kind of feeling for her ever since she was a young girl and first came to stay with us in Boston. You were away so much of the time then, you couldn't have known her very well. I was quite close and—"

John gripped his fingers into his brother's thigh, then patted gently. "You are serious about this, aren't you, Thaddy?"

"Quite serious."

"Does Nellie know of your feelings?"

"I'm not certain she does. I've tried to tell her in a subtle way."

"You mean you've beat about the bush?"

"I suppose that's the way *you* would put it, John." Thad sighed. "I'm inexperienced. Perhaps I should go back to Boston for a short duration and acquire a little experience in such matters."

"No, Thaddy, that would be very foolish. If you do love Nell, you simply should tell her so," John remarked. "The idea of you going off and becoming a humming-bird among the honeysuckle of Boston would be very foolish, in my opinion. I don't say a man shouldn't

177

have experience prior to marriage—of course he should somewhat—but I think for you—no, no, it would be wrong, very wrong."

"I've had experience!" Thad exclaimed.

"Dear Thaddy, can another brother love his brother as much as I do? I wonder. How often I worry about you, think of you, pray for you," John said. "If there's anything I can do to help you in this matter—perhaps if I were to speak with Nell—"

"No, Johnny, I'm the one who must do the talking, when I gain the courage."

At that moment a static silence fell over the entire Phenwick estate. New arrivals had appeared in an elegant landau carriage. Quite a stir had been created. Nancy was not the first to be aware of the newcomers. She wondered at the strange curiosity that buzzed among her guests. When she lifted her skirts and glided skaterlike over the marble floor of the entrance hall, she came face to face with the exquisitely gowned, faintly swarthy beauty of Millijoy Phenwick. Her red satin gown, trimmed with white ribbons and black lace, was the most extravagant and outlandishly fashionable dress at the gathering. She sparkled with diamonds and rubies. An exotic taste in jewelry was one of her weaknesses. By far she outglittered any other woman present. Every man's attention went to her.

"My dear Millijoy! How lovely you look!" Nancy exclaimed, bending forward over her large skirt to kiss Millijoy on each cheek. "I'm really so delighted that you could come—and young Tommy with you. This is a pleasant surprise." Nancy looked around. "Tommy is with you, isn't he?"

"He stopped to chat with someone along the way, I believe," Millijoy stated, tilting her head back slightly to get a view of all present, noting that people were edging toward where they were standing.

Nancy kissed her again, took her hand, patted it, and led her to the south side of the house where the croquet game and other activities were taking place.

"When I received your invitation, dear Nancy, I'll admit I was a little confused," Millijoy explained. "However, I did become quite fond of Nellie while she was in Boston, and I've thought often of her. It just seemed that I should take advantage of your kindness and hospitality and make the trip. Nellie will only be eighteen once, although she may choose to acknowledge that as her age for years to come." She laughed raucously and drew attention back to herself.

Nellie had witnessed Millijoy's grand entrance and was not quite certain how to react to her. She recognized the woman and, when she appeared in her near vicinity, Nellie had no other choice but to go to her and embrace her as Nancy had done. Nellie's embrace of Millijoy was followed by Ruth's and then Ann's. Soon the ladies who gathered on the veranda, the Phenwick women, sat and watched, giggled and tittered among themselves.

Stuart's son, Danny Phenwick, had become extremely handsome. At nineteen, he had his father's charm, his late mother's vivacious character and his own lust for living. He had developed from a shy adolescent into an aggressive, domineering, and often perplexing young man. His figure was lean yet remarkably well proportioned. He moved with ease and his bearing was such that, wherever he went, attention was attracted to him. Intense eyes were more lavender than blue, although at times they seemed to be quite iridescently blue. Long lashes accentuated those eyes, making his attractive face almost startling to behold.

Danny had spent much time with his sister Ann Marie, who was also quickly becoming an extraordinary beauty. She had many of her late mother's features, her beauty and elegance. There was no mistaking that she, too, was a Phenwick. In fact, attention was often called to her likeness to Augusta Phenwick in the portraits. Ann Marie had a strange quality that stemmed from insecurity: a feeling that comes from losing a parent when a child is quite small and is raised for a few years without a mother image to inspire her. Although she was fond of Ruth when her father married a second time, Ann Marie became envious of her half-brothers and -sister. That envy had somehow twisted her attitudes and basic perception toward certain things. She had become self-centered and arrogant.

Ann Marie was proud of her brother, and thought him to be the most handsome man that ever existed, even better-looking than her father.

Danny soon grew tired of the constant company of his sister, who had an irritating way of making snide remarks and unkind compliments about people. Because Ann Marie laughed and poked fun at the peculiarities of others, Danny found it trying to be with her, particularly at that party. He sought escape.

The youth with the large brown eyes and tan skin, black curly hair and thick, pouty lips was extremely curious about what was happening. The fact that he appeared to be different from most of those present made him stand toward the shadows and look on with a kind of fascinated interest; yet a feeling of not being accepted disturbed him. He was part Negro. Although he was very good looking, handsome and masculinely attractive, he possessed a kind of stigma that could not be denied, which caused other men to back away and ladies to whisper behind their fans. When Danny saw him, he went directly to where he was standing, hand extended, for they had been friends as well as first cousins.

"Tommy!" Danny exclaimed. "When did you arrive?"

"Weren't you aware of the commotion when Mother made her far-from-casual entrance?" Tommy asked, trying to control a contemptuous tone that wanted to come to his voice.

"Sorry, I didn't see her."

"You know Mother, everything has to be lavish and extravagant, far overdone," Tommy explained. "But she wouldn't be Mother if she were any other way, would she?"

"Not at all." Danny put his arm about Tommy and began introducing his cousin around to various people he had earlier met. There was always a shocked reaction whenever Danny explained that the other was his first cousin, the only son of his late uncle, Gordon. By that time people had all but forgotten about the notorious Gordon Phenwick and his unsavory reputation in Boston, his evangelical ravings and dabblings in witchcraft and black magic. Tommy had never seen his father. He was born after Gordon's death. Yet there was no mistaking, upon closer examination, that the lad had many of his father's characteristics, his temperament. There was also little mistaking that he was Millijoy's son. He possessed an extravagance in his personality, despite his inferiority feelings because of his racial heritage. In his own way, he had a flamboyant flare. Long fingers, which had for long hours caressed both organ and piano keyboards, were his most noticeable physical characteristic beyond his racial complexion.

Sometime later that day, Tommy had the occasion to be in the immediate company of Nellie. There was immediate recognition on the part of each. The girl began to feel uneasy in Tommy's company. His dark, deep brown eyes stared curiously into hers with an almost hypnotic quality. She tried to look away, tried to appear joyous and delighted in the celebration that was centered around her. Yet she could not ignore that penetrating stare and the insinuating smile that formed on Tommy's thick lips.

"You know, Nell," Tommy stated when no one else was near enough to hear him, "that you are destined to become a Phenwick woman?"

"Who told you that?"

"I know. I simply know," Tommy replied. "For you to become a Phenwick woman, you must marry a Phenwick man. Isn't that true?"

"*If* I am to become a Phenwick woman, I suppose that would be the only logical way for it to happen, wouldn't it?" Nellie replied. She laughed lightly, but she could not cover the uneasiness she felt in his presence.

"You do know what the logical match would be, don't you?" Tommy questioned, his voice tense and suggestive.

"I confess I don't know," Nellie answered, although she was aware of the direction his conversation was headed.

"Don't be naïve. We're distant cousins. Far too distant to cause any problems with producing children."

"I beg your pardon."

Tommy laughed. "You know what they say about close relatives marrying. Of course, brothers and sisters are impossible. First cousins are almost as bad. But we are at quite a distance to each other."

"Are you proposing marriage to me?" Nellie asked.

"I suppose I am, in a way."

"In that case, I will have to turn you down," Nellie declared, raising an eyebrow and getting an impish expression on her face. "In the first place, I don't know you at all, Tommy. We met as children long ago. I certainly have no great love for you. Nor, at the risk of hurting your feelings, do I feel any physical attraction for you or interest in you. So you see, it's pointless to bring up such matters, isn't it?"

Tommy glared, then a faint smile crossed his mouth. "You do know of my father, don't you?"

"I don't believe I do," she responded. "You must tell me about him sometime, but not now. There's Adam, and I have promised to entertain him at tea. Excuse me, won't you, Tommy? And I'm pleased that you're here."

Nellie sailed majestically into the crowd of people, leaving Tommy both bewildered and annoyed. He rationalized that such an early proposal to his cousin was ill timed, and perhaps a foolish gesture. He, also, was determined that he was going to marry a beautiful lady and that she would become an important Phenwick woman.

After dinner that evening as the guests were becoming a bit weary of the occasion, lodging arrangements were made for the guests. Some had to stay with strangers in town, others in the small Greenfield Hotel, while the intimate family and very close friends stayed at Phenwick House or with Thad at the old O'Plaggerty place or with Adam in the cottage.

As the evening wore on and most of the guests had dispersed to their designated quarters, Stuart remained at Phenwick House, and sat out in the garden beneath the statue of Aphrodite. He lazily gazed at the statue of Pan across the way. The shiny marble glistened in the moonlight. The scent of jasmine in the air mixed with honeysuckle and other aromas of summer.

After an extended period of meditation, Stuart rose and strode across the lawn toward the house. Something was troubling him. Deep thought filled his mind.

Leo Phenwick, tall and somewhat aesthetically built, appeared at the door. His footsteps made a crisp, clicking sound on the veranda. Upon recognizing Stuart, he called to him and the two met in a secluded area just off the veranda. Leo give his cousin a cigar and they both lit up.

"So far it's been a rather beautiful party, hasn't it?" Leo commented.

"Yes," Stuart agreed.

"And Nellie is quite lovely, isn't she? Lucky man who gets her," Leo commented. "Of course, I have a beauty of my own, just as you have, Cousin Stuart. Still, a man sometimes has curious speculations, hasn't he?"

"Yes, curious." Stuart frowned as he inhaled, then a relieved expression appeared to come over his face as he exhaled. "Leo, there is something troubling me, information I've recently received that is quite disconcerting. I've been pondering how to broach the matter. I suppose the best way is simply to come out with it."

"What is it?"

"Sam Dodsworth," Stuart replied, his voice husky with a hint of emotion.

"Sam Dodsworth?" Leo's face fell.

"He has been released from prison," Stuart said. "I received word of it just prior to leaving Boston. I only had time to alert the police in Boston."

"What are you trying to tell me?"

"As you know, Leo, I've been unable to get Captain Roderick Wellington to press murder charges against Dodsworth in New York. Nor will Tim Duggan. Hence, the man is free. And if he is vengeful or seeks revenge for his years of incarceration, there could be a problem."

"I don't quite see what you're driving at."

"Think a minute. Basically *you* were the one who stood in Sam Dodsworth's way of success. You were the one with whom Annie Duggan fell in love. You are the one, I fear, who will be the principal recipient of his anger and reprisal."

Leo wiped a handkerchief across his perspiring brow. "Are you trying to warn me, Stuart?"

"You have children. Dodsworth knows both you and your Ann. He could well strike again at your family. I've contacted Wellington. I've pleaded with Thelma Wellington to try to persuade him. She has no force

184

over him at all. She's helpless, a captive." Stuart sighed. "Chances are, Dodsworth will first show up in Portland. Although I wouldn't be surprised if he didn't aim some of his retribution toward me and my family. I will have special guards assigned to me, just as I suggest you do around Falmouth House."

"Sam Dodsworth again? I thought when he was apprehended years ago that we had heard the end of him," Leo stated.

"It would have been that way had sufficient charges been pressed and he had been tried for murder in New York," Stuart explained. "But—well—I'll not go into Wellington again."

Nellie had overheard part of the conversation between Leo and Stuart, during a moment when she had separated herself from the others and had indulged in pensive silence. Fatigue had come over her and she was making a last round of visiting with the guests. Fortunately most of them had retired by then.

"Sam Dodsworth," Nellie whispered aloud. She moved from the hiding place into the garden where the trees were dense. From there her cousins appeared to be only small silhouettes against the lighted window of the house. Sitting on a bench, she leaned back to gaze up at a tiny patch of moonlit sky through the lacy design of leaves. As she did, she cleared her mind of present thoughts, of the party, and the people, even of Adam and Tommy. The breeze was cool, but far from cold. The tiny bit of sky was like a crystal ball to her. When she focused her attention upon it, a face came into her mind. She was certain it was the face of Sam Dodsworth. A shudder of fear went through her as she witnessed the malevolent appearance in his features. Moreover, as she contemplated the man, or projected her mind into the future, as it were, she saw that she was destined to encounter the man in person. That terrifying thought roused her back to the moment at hand. She did not want to see what her relationship with the man would be. But she knew by the reaction that had come over her that it would be something terrible and that she would do well to be wary of Sam Dodsworth.

# Chapter Seventeen

"A week is obviously too long for any party to last," Nancy exclaimed at the end of the sixth day. Many of the guests had gone, but there were still family members who had remained at Greenfield.

Millijoy stayed on, as did Stuart and Ruth, while John and Daniel Louis had returned to Boston along with friends of the family. Millijoy had made arrangements to take a cottage in Cape Ann with Tommy for two weeks after the celebration in Greenfield. When she saw the reception that Tommy got, particularly from Nellie, Millijoy decided that she was not the designated Phenwick woman that her son would marry. Hence, she became quite different and almost inverse. Her elegant appearance and flamboyant behavior did not diminish, but she no longer took the family members into her confidence. She looked on Nancy with disdain, believing that the present matriarch of the Phenwick family had been in some way instrumental in turning Nellie against the prospect of her Tommy.

Nellie, too, had grown weary of the party scene. It had been enjoyable the first few days, and it became far more interesting when the majority of the people had gone. Too much was too much! The picnics had been enjoyable, down by the shore or in the woods. Nellie had delighted in the dancing and the frivolity of party gaiety. Every young, unattached man had made concerted effort to impress her with his charm, his heritage, and, most of all, his physical appearance. She had been amused by the exchanges of wit and scholarly dialogue. In a way she had been a little saddened over the attitudes she had sensed, the reality behind the expressions of cordiality and the kind words directed toward her. Psychically she knew when she was being told the truth, able to discern some contrivance of story that might have been given to her. It bothered her that people were deceptive, that young men with domineering parents were so ambitious that they could be so obliquitous. She was obviously a good catch. Many of the young men, who had come from prominent families in both Portland and Boston, had done their best to impress her.

Perhaps the biggest imprint made on her was a negative one. That had come on the last day, when Adam had told her in strictest confidence that she did not have a chance with him, that she was foolish wasting her time and emotions thinking about him. If Nellie persisted in so doing, Adam warned, he would be forced to move away from Greenfield.

"But why, Adam, why?" Nellie asked.

"Because you are depriving yourself of happiness," Adam explained. "There have been a multitude of eligible young men here at your party, fine, handsome, attractive, from well-to-do families, politically prominent and representatives of wealth. Surely you could have had your pick of any of them. I've told you time and time again that I am not the marrying kind. Why won't you do yourself a favor and find someone else, turn your attention to him and discover love? Love that can be returned, not just the kind of love I have for you as a friend, as another human being, but the kind of love a man has for a woman because he is physically and emotionally attracted to her. Can't you see the importance of that? You will only be frustrated if you continue thinking of me as you do. Please, Nellie, for your sake, do this. Find someone else."

"I don't understand, Adam. I really don't understand."

"Nonsense, you *do* understand, Nellie. You're psychic. You know about such things. And if you can't see the impossibility of the situation with me, then it is simply because your emotions are not allowing your psychic perception to come through."

Adam was gone. He did not remain to persist in an impractical argument. Instead he went directly to the cottage, and from there to Dr. Charles Mumford's office.

Nellie's immediate impulse was to cry. Her eyes did become a little misty. Adam's words reechoed within her mind, touched at her heart. Yet she was able to reason that the handsome man had never encouraged her to be anything but his friend. He had, for that matter, never acted in any way other than that which was perfectly natural for him. She had misconstrued meaning through her desire to be loved by him. She had let his persistent image in her mind stand in the way of truly getting acquainted with the men who had been at her party. She felt foolish and a little annoyed at herself.

After watching the next-to-the-last carriage of guests leave, Nellie turned her attention to Leo and Ann Phenwick from Portland. They planned to remain on another night and leave early in the morning from the trip back to Portland.

Nancy appeared exhausted. She had been so busy for so many days, it seemed, that, with most of the visitors gone, she felt as if she were going to collapse. She believed she could easily live out the rest of the summer in a state of inertia. That was not possible for Nancy Phenwick Collier, who was lively and always busy with one thing or another. Perhaps it was because of her fatigue that Nancy did not recognize the hurt and disappointment that Nellie was experiencing.

Ann suspected something in Nellie's attitude, but she was not that close to her cousin that Nellie would confide in her. Nor did Ann feel she had the right to ask what the problem might be.

In a vacant mood of melancholia, Nellie sauntered from the house in the direction of the graveyard. Whenever sad or despondent, she took solace in moving among the gravestones or sitting in the chapel in a meditative state. How little time, she thought, one has to live in this life form—and how very long that form is left to decay beneath the ground. She was convinced, beyond the shadow of a doubt, that man was immortal and that his spirit continued far beyond this one little earthly experience.

After a brief visit to the cemetery, where she had placed a few gathered daisies on her mother's place, Nellie lifted her white cotton skirts with one hand and held the large, floppy straw hat with the other hand while she made her way to the summerhouse. A sturdy sea breeze had risen with a cooling force. It was pleasant.

The summerhouse was open on all sides, permitting a free flow of wind and air circulation. Yet it was protection, should a thunder shower suddenly appear. Because of the steady breeze, she tied her hat with the pink ribbon loosely beneath her chin. She sat and gathered her thoughts. On one hand, she wished that she had invited Ann to join her, that the two might get better acquainted and perhaps she might find a confidante with whom she could discuss troubling matters.

Her thoughts soon returned to Adam Truff and her emotional reactions to him. She tried to detach herself from the response she had to the man. That was almost

190

impossible. Yet, as she ruminated and perceived his inner self, she realized that he had only been trying to spare her unhappiness. The same unhappiness, perhaps, that she had seen in Ruth's face when she stared wistfully at Adam.

As afternoon grew toward evening, Nellie glanced up to see the unmistakable stately figure of Thadius Phenwick as he returned from the furniture factory. He had not taken undue time away from his work to celebrate Nellie's birthday, but had managed to devote his leisure hours to it and had made his presence felt. His walk betrayed signs of weariness, yet he seemed to brighten and his footsteps quickened as he beheld Nellie seated in the summerhouse.

Thad's blouse was open to his chest. He wore no coat. A straw hat shaded his head from the sun. He was dressed as he did for work. Still, his appearance was presentable.

"May I join you?" Thad asked as he stepped to the summerhouse. He had stooped to pull a long stem of wild oat and it was still at the side of his mouth. "If you'll forgive how I'm dressed, I would be pleased to sit and visit for a short while. It has been a warm day."

"Come sit by me, Thad," Nellie said, holding out her hand. "I've been in a pensive mood for several hours now—I suspect. I've lost all concept of time. I would enjoy sharing thoughts with you."

"What has put you in such a pensive mood, my dear Nellie."

"I suppose turning eighteen has," she replied, trying to sound lighthearted and not as distressed as she had felt.

"You turned eighteen nearly a week ago," Thad teased. "You're already on the way to being nineteen. I don't see what should be so distressing about that."

"Oh, I'm not concerned about my age, goodness no,"

191

she said, now giggling and reaching to touch his hand. "Thad, I have a premonition about you."

"About me?"

"It returned today, but I first had it years ago," Nellie related. "Even before I originally went to Boston, I knew that I was going there with a purpose and that I had to meet someone who would be very special to me."

"That was when you met Adam, wasn't it?" Thad inserted.

Nellie blinked and retained her smiling expression. "Yes. But I also met *you*, Thad."

"And others of the Bostonian Phenwicks," Thad added.

"True." She laughed. "I've been sitting here, ruminating about many things. And suddenly I had an awareness— as clear as crystal! Adam has never encouraged my interest in him as anything but a friend. Today, he told me point-blank, in so many words, that I was foolish to carry on about him as I do. Well, that sort of made something snap within me and my thoughts suddenly seemed to become strung in a logical string."

"I confess I don't quite follow what you're driving at, Nellie."

Nellie rose and went to brace herself against one of the supporting poles at the edge of the structure. "It is now all very clear to me." She dreamily put her head against the post.

"Nellie—" Thad squirmed.

"I've known for almost as long as I can remember," Nellie announced, "that I was destined to become a Phenwick woman. My mother was certain of that too. But how illogical I've been."

"Illogical?"

"How could I have possibly become a Phenwick woman if I were married to Adam Truff?" she questioned. "In that case, I would have been a Truff woman." She laughed. "I don't even like the sound of it."

"Now I am confused," Thad said, rising.

Nellie turned to him. She held out her hand for his. "Don't you see, dearest Thad? Aren't you beginning to get the slightest notion of what I'm going on about?"

Thad liked the feel of her hand in his. He glanced down as his fingers curled tighter about it. "The only thing I can think is that for you to become a Phenwick woman, you have to marry a Phenwick man."

"And when I went to Boston the first time," she asked, "who was it that I met?"

"Several people."

"But only one was really important. I obviously went to Boston to meet the man who would marry me and give me the title of Phenwick woman," she said, giggling as she spoke and wiggling with the welling excitement within her.

"Have you been listening to my prayers, pretty Nell?"

"What a case of blindness I have had!" She surveyed the area in all directions, then she faced Thad, her eyes staring deeply into his. "Thad—oh, Thad!"

Thad took her in his arms. When their faces were so close that even air could not get between, she put her arms tightly about him. Thad hesitated.

"It's all right, Thadius, no one is watching," she coaxed.

His lips, his embrace made that moment the most exciting that Nellie had ever known up until that moment. She responded to his touch, his kiss, his very nearness.

The breeze began to play a love symphony through the trees. Sense and feeling awareness became magnified. Suddenly Thadius became the most beautiful name in the whole English language.

Although her eyes were closed, Nellie perceived that she was being watched by her mother, her sister Elizabeth, her brothers George and Rupert; and there was Cousin Susannah and the lavender-gray lady she knew to be old Augusta, herself. The scent of violets was there, but only faintly and soon to be carried away with the breeze. She was certain that those who were watching her from spirit were well pleased.

"Oh, Nellie, dearest Nell, how very much I do love you!" Thad exclaimed "All these years that I've waited, the love that began the instant I first saw you has grown into such overwhelming proportions that my love for you has become an obsession."

Nellie kissed him again, then gently eased herself from his embrace. With full awareness of her timing, she moved to another supporting post. "Tommy asked me to marry him. He's a Phenwick, too, you know?"

"Of course you didn't accept his proposal," Thad said as he crossed to her. He caught her again in his arms. "Nellie, do you love me—even just a little bit?"

"I love you more than a little bit, Thadius." She had her back to him as his arms wanted to crush her to him. She turned enough within his hold to permit their lips to meet again.

"Why did you tell me about Tommy?" Thad asked a short while later. He was still holding Nellie in his arms.

"I had several other—well, hints of proposals," Nellie added. She smiled. "I'm just telling you that, Thad, to let you know there are others who have interest. And, now that I'm eighteen, I intend to accept a proposal—from—someone."

"You would? After I've told you how much I love you?" Thad looked hurt and indignant.

Nellie kissed him on the cheek. "My darling, Thadius, isn't it obvious what I'm trying to get you to do?"

Thad stared blankly. He blushed, then suddenly grinned a silly smile. "You've practically asked for me."

"I know. But I want to hear you say the words." Nellie kissed his brow.

"Oh, Nell, you know the words—" Thad was flustered.

Nellie quickly jerked herself free of his hands and, lifting her skirts, ran into the tall grass beside the summer-house. A moment later Thad was following her. Nellie fled in the direction of a large maple tree where the grass was dark green and lush appearing. Tiny flowers bloomed in among it.

Thad touched her. She turned back, and, as she did, she lost her balance. He caught her in time to break her fall, but they were both thrown to the grass, magically locked in each other's embrace. He kissed her again and again, gripping her as if she were captive in his arms.

"Nellie—?"

"Yes?"

"Will you marry me?"

"Yes, my dearest Thadius, yes, yes, *yes!*"

As they were kissing again, now so passionately that they were about to explode, Nellie opened her eyes and realized that the tiny flowers blooming all around them were violets.

"We must not rush into marriage," Thad commented a while later as they were seated with their backs against the maple tree trunk.

"Are your feet getting cold already?" she asked.

"No. But I do think we should have a period of engagement," Thad returned. "I would like my sister Joanna to be present when we wed, and hopefully Joshua and his family."

"Joanna and Joshua are only your half-brother and -sister."

"But the half that is mine," Thad joked, "I would like to have here. I doubt if there's any hope of getting Paul to return for such a silly thing as a wedding."

"It's not silly."

"I didn't mean it that way. Oh, dearest Nellie." He kissed her. "We must celebrate."

"We've celebrated for the past week."

"Your birthday, not our engagement," Thad corrected. "I know, I'll take a few days away from the factory and we can go somewhere."

"We're not married yet," Nellie said.

"I didn't mean away from everyone." Another kiss. "How would you like to go back to Portland with Leo and Ann when they go tomorrow? We could stay at Falmouth House, and my nephew and his wife would be there to chaperone us."

"Your nephew?"

"Leo, like Stuart, even though they're older, are both my nephews." He hugged her. "Say, yes, Nellie. We both could do with a vacation away from Phenwick House and Greenfield. It'll give us time together, time to get used to being in love. I've known you so long, yet I've only known you a few minutes."

"Thadius—" Nellie sighed, *"yes."*

Thad rolled over to kiss her as they left the tree trunk and went back to the grass.


The sky was still bright when Adam left Charles Mumford's house that evening. The two had shared a quiet supper and conversation. Charles was called to visit an ailing woman and, knowing her symptoms, her realized he might be a considerable length of time with her. He suggested that Adam go on home and they would meet again the next day.

There was a light still on the horizon when Adam reached the cottage. He lit a lantern. After removing his shoes and enough clothing to make himself comfortable, he sat in a large armchair. A yawn and a stretch. He was too tired to read. Putting his feet up on an ottoman, he rested his elbows on the chair arms and folded his hands beneath his chin. In that position, he observed the room, the furniture, the pictures. He saw Nellie's face as he had seen it earlier that day.

"Dear little Nellie, do try to understand," Adam said aloud.

He yawned again and had about reached the conclusion that he could very easily nap while sitting in that chair. The last thing he saw before closing his eyes was the portrait of Daniel Phenwick the first, which he had saved from the original Phenwick House the night of the fire.

Nellie's face was still in his mind's eye. Then her voice. But the words he heard her say were not those they had exchanged that day.

Then the words went through his mind were mixed with those of Charles Mumford. He recalled Charles telling one evening of locating several old family relics of the Mumfords, among which was a diary and letters of a great-great-aunt, Kate Mumford, in which she claimed to have given birth to a son by Danny Phenwick and called him Elias. Later Adam had gone through other papers of Kate Mumford and discovered a reference to the portrait of Danny that had hung in the library at Phenwick House. Adam was convinced it was the same portrait that now hung on his wall.

Before he opened his eyes, Adam heard Nellie's voice as it was set in his memory. *"Look behind Danny."*

Adam sat up and stared directly at the painting. Moments later he was on his feet and striding toward it, lantern in hand. Putting the portrait on the table, face down, he examined the back of it. It was thick-feeling, and the back side of the canvas had an unusual texture for what it was supposed to be.

Upon closer examination, Adam discovered that the painting had a false back to it. He got a knife and a pair of scissors, then carefully proceeded to delicately operate.

What he found was a crudely drawn map. The scratchy writing around it was practically illegible. Adam was able to discern four words. The first two were: *the treasure*. The second two were: *Ben Strothart*.

Adam had read enough of *The Mysteries of Rosea Hackleby*, and the *Phenwick Family History*, by Patricia Phenwick, to recognize the name of Ben Strothart as the buccaneer uncle of Augusta Phenwick. Further-more, he recalled that it was in search of Ben Strothart's buried treasure that Augusta had first come to the place that was presently known as Greenfield.

Excitedly Adam pulled back into his clothing and boots. Moments later he was hurrying down the lane to Phenwick House. Since he was considered a member of the family, he dashed into the building and went to find John Collier.

Both John and Nancy examined the ancient map. Then Nancy took a closer look at it.

"The ink on the back side was applied at another time," Nancy remarked, "than when the map was drawn. The letters are terribly difficult to decipher. I'll get a magnifying glass."

"What do you make of it?" John asked as Nancy left the room.

"If, as you say, Ben Strothart was a pirate," John commented, "it could well be a legitimate treasure map."

"With a stretch of the imagination," Adam stated after taking another look, "I might suspect that this is a diagram of the area around Bar Harbor and the islands just off the coast."

"So it would seem." John's eyes brightened. "Do you suppose that such a treasure actually exists?"

"There would be one way to find out," Adam returned. He had generated a great deal of excitement.

Nancy returned with the magnifying glass. "Maybe this will help clear things up." She took the paper and examined it. " *This treasure I leave to my beloved great nefew by adoption, Edward Munsk Phenwick. I nigh missed walking the plank for this one.'* " She looked up. "What do you make of that?"

"What do you make of it, Nan?" John asked.

"Edward Phenwick was Aunt Patricia's first husband," Nancy remembered. "And Cousin Susannah was their daughter." A stark expression suddenly came over her face. "Oh, dear—!"

"What is it, Nan?"

"Nellie."

"Nell?" John rose.

"The night before Cousin Susannah died at Edward House," Nancy explained, "the old woman told Thad that she believed Nellie was the reincarnation of her father."

"Yes, I recall," John commented. The tiny hairs were raised on the back of his neck.

"Joseph Ornby said he believed Cousin Susannah was responsible for the explosion of Nellie's psychic abilities because of saying that she thought Edward Phenwick—oh, dear, I can't put it in words. The very thought frightens me."

John comforted Nancy, gently leading her to a chair.

A short while later, after John had given his wife a drink of water, he turned again to Adam. "How did you happen to find this map?"

"It was behind the picture of old Daniel Phenwick," Adam replied. "Nellie told me to look behind it."

"Nellie?" Nancy questioned, rising slightly, then falling back into the chair. "Then—"

"Now, now, Nan," John said comfortingly, "we don't know anything of the kind for certain." He looked into the distance. "Yet it *would* explain many things, wouldn't it?"

"John . . . ?" Nancy reached for his hand.

Adam observed without commenting. He strode to the large French doors that overlooked the veranda and the yard beyond. The air smelled of the sea. He hesitated at the doors. "There is one way we can find out if the treasure is still there, John."

"Yes, of course," John replied before he kissed Nancy on the forehead. "We must look into the matter."

Adam went forward onto the veranda. At first he thought the young couple standing very close to each

199

other by the statue of Pan were Leo and Ann Phenwick. He was about to go back in when the lovers stepped from the shadow into moonlight and he could see that they were Thad and Nellie. He closed his eyes and sighed.

# Chapter Eighteen

Nancy was obviously perplexed. She reasoned it first had been brought about by the announcement that her eldest son had intentions of marrying Nellie, who was more than a foster daughter to Nancy, and secondly by the discovery of Ben Strothart's map and the quick decision that her husband and Adam Truff had made to investigate the matter. To add to her joy and confusion, that next day she received a letter from her son Paul in San Francisco, California, announcing that he had taken a wife.

To Nancy's orderly mind, it did not seem right that her third son should marry before sons one and two. Yet Paul Phenwick had always been the most physically oriented of her boys. She had guessed that he was sexually precocious even before he left Boston, and she often wondered if that had not been a determining factor in his leaving. Her son John was the scholar, who seemed to devote most of his time to study, although he assured his mother that he intended to marry one day when he was well established. Thadius had always been somewhat aesthetic, a dreamer and a wanderer. She wondered if his planned marriage to Nellie would change him much. Obviously her youngest son, Daniel Louis, was the playboy of the family. He enjoyed the social scene and had already gained a reputation for being the life of the party wherever he appeared.

Four sons, Nancy thought, so greatly diversified in their tastes and dispositions. She often wondered if they might have turned out differently if Peter had lived to see them raised into manhood. Peter. She had thought less and less of her first husband after marrying John Collier. The love she had had for Peter Phenwick was one thing, that which she had for John Collier was quite another: both were beautiful, each experience different but vital and almost magical in its own way. She, too, knew that the love John Collier had for her was not the same as he had had for Kate. How could it have possibly been? Still she was abundantly assured of his love. Now, wasn't it ironic that her eldest son should have chosen John's eldest (and only living) daughter to marry?

Nancy was glad that, after a long discussion the night before, it had been decided that the wedding would not take place until the first weekend in October. That would give her sufficient time, she rationalized, to rest up from Nellie's birthday party, supervise the summer canning and laying away of vegetables from the garden, select an autumn wardrobe, and make elaborate wedding plans. But she was still perplexed. Even if the treasure map were authentic and such a fortune existed, why did John Collier feel he had to drop everything and go in search of it? After all, thanks to Peter's foresight and Stuart's wisdom and investing, Nancy was a wealthy woman. Why did she and her husband need more money beyond that which was being made in increasing amounts in the furniture factory? She could only reason that John had a quiet desire for adventure that occasionally had to be satisfied. She would send her husband and Adam Truff off on an exploring expedition with her blessings.

Although the two carriages arrived in Portland during the heat of the morning, the trip had been relatively pleasant and happy. The four adults rode in one carriage while the children and their governess went in the second. By the time they reached their destination, both Leo and Ann were certain they were far better acquainted with their cousins than they had previously been.

"Of course there is plenty of room at Falmouth House," Ann exclaimed. "I'll give instructions for my old room to be prepared for Nellie. And Thad, you can take Freddie's old room."

"Freddie?" Nellie questioned as a picture of Ann's brother came to her mind. "It's funny, but I thought he was still living at Falmouth House. Of course, he isn't. He's gone to New Haven, Connecticut, hasn't he?"

"He's at Yale," Ann replied. She cocked her head and gazed at Nellie curiously. "How did you know that?"

Nellie smiled. "I just knew." Then she thought she had better set her cousin at ease. "I believe someone mentioned it at the party."

"I could always take a room on the third floor," Thad remarked playfully.

"What, and have an encounter with Clayton?" Leo asked.

Thad laughed. "If a ghost indeed stalks the third floor of that old house, I should like to see him."

The carriage had stopped before the rambling, old, ominous-appearing house. How dark and overgrown with shrubbery it appeared. Nellie stared up to the third floor window she could see from within the carriage. A thought came to her. "He built the house, didn't he? I mean, he designed it and supervised the construction of it."

"Why, dearest Nellie?" Thad asked.

"Why, Clayton Latshaw," Nellie said brightly. "This was his favorite, his masterpiece."

The others were staring at Nellie until Leo had presence of mind enough to open the door and suggested that they go into the house where it was certain to be cooler.

Nellie received peculiar psychic impressions while at Falmouth House. She felt quite at home occupying the room in which Ann had grown up. There was something so very familiar about it, and often she felt as if she were tuning in to vibrations from another era.

"These rooms were first occupied by Jane Phenwick—Jane Munsk Phenwick," Nellie explained to Ann when the latter had come to see that her cousin was settled in.

"Jane Munsk Phenwick?" Ann questioned. "Oh, that must have been old Great-grandmother Jane Ornby."

"Yes, it was," Nellie replied confidently. "She was my sister."

"I beg your pardon?" Ann gasped.

"What? Oh, I'm sorry." Nellie wore a vacant expression.

"Jane Ornby was your sister?"

"No." Nellie laughed uneasily. "What I meant to say is that she was the real sister of Edward Phenwick. They were both the youngest children of John and Lydia Munsk, whom Augusta Phenwick adopted at the time of the death of Lydia Munsk."

"How do you know all this?" Ann questioned.

Nellie blinked and shrugged. "I just seem to know it."

"I'm aware that Great-grandmother Jane Ornby had been adopted by Augusta," Ann related. "That is why Leo and I are not kin by blood, yet we are cousins."

"Yes, I know." Nellie glanced around the room.

"Why did you say Jane Ornby was your sister?"

"I believe I said Jane Munsk Phenwick was," Nellie corrected. "I don't know why I did mention that. It was just a sensation that came over me." She related the experience she had had with Susannah Phenwick upon first meeting her.

"Cousin Susannah believed you to be the reincarnation of her father, Edward Phenwick?" Ann stated.

"When she first mentioned it, I was so startled and frightened," Nellie replied, "being a child, I could not cope with it. I now wish I had had presence of mind enough to act differently. I should like to have gotten to know Cousin Susannah better."

"But I think it's fascinating," Ann commented. "I mean the very supposition that you might have been a Phenwick man in a previous existence, and now you're intending to become a Phenwick woman. It's really too bizarre to be practical, I mean this whole theory." She looked beyond Nellie. "I wonder who I was in the past."

Nellie had become pensively silent.

"You know, Nell, there's a portrait of Uncle Edward down in the library," Ann explained. "I had the pictures all down last summer when the walls were refinished, and I chanced upon an inscription on the reverse side of the painting. It very clearly is marked 'Edward Munsk Phenwick.' Also, I ran across an ink sketch of three young boys which Great-grandmother apparently had had framed. It is signed by Clayton Latshaw, as is the large portrait of Augusta. Come, I'll show them to you."

When Nellie stared up into the likeness of the late Edward Phenwick, she had a sensation of recognition. Although she made no affirmative comment about it, her inner feelings caused her to have an eerie reaction. Then, when Ann showed her the ink sketch of the three boys, Nellie's face brightened.

"Do you know them, Nellie?"

"That's my father, and that's my mother and that's—" She looked up and giggled. "Isn't that silly of me?"

"But these are obviously three boys," Ann said, pointing at the outlines of the nude children.

"I meant to say, this is Michael O'Plaggerty, Danny

Phenwick and—and Edward Phenwick," Nellie explained. "Michael was very disturbed that he had not been adopted into the Phenwick family as Edward had been. There was a very close feeling between all three boys. I think they should have been brothers." She stared particularly at the likeness of Edward. "I guess time has taken care of that. I believe they all three have had the opportunity to love each other in different ways during more recent times."

"Nellie . . . ?"

"I'll explain it to you one day, Cousin Ann," the younger woman said, "if I ever become positive about it."

That night, after Thad had kissed her good night and had retired to his own room, Nellie prepared for bed. But after she had braided her hair and examined herself in the mirror in the long nightgown, a feeling of restlessness came over her. Then a curious thought. Slipping into her dressing robe, she went to the door. The hallways were quiet. Only in the distance she could hear one of the small children sobbing and the soft voice of the nurse comforting it.

Taking a candle with her, Nellie left her room. She held the light high, to examine further down the hallway to her right where she knew Thad to be. Her first impulse was to call on him and see if he would care to join her. Yet, recalling how exhausted he had appeared when he had said good night, she thought it best to let him get his rest.

Her attention went to the stairs leading to the third floor. Almost a compulsive sensation came over her, directing her toward them. She held the candle steady in the holder as she methodically took each step, desperately trying not to make a sound that would awaken any of the others in the house.

Ann had always given instructions for the servants to keep the third-floor rooms spotlessly clean, but they were only used when an excess of company came to spend the night. Richard Phenwick, Leon and Ann's eldest child, often played in the rooms above and occasionally he would coerce his sister, Paula, to join him. But the children were always stoutly reprimanded for trespassing above.

After opening several doors, Nellie felt the vibrations of one particular room to be different than what she had experienced in the others. Curiously she entered and sat in a large rocking chair. The tiny flame caused only a bleak glow of light. The room was warm. She rose and opened two windows, which permitted cross ventilation.

Picture after picture filtered into her mind. She had the awesome sensation of realizing that she was peering directly into the past. At first it was disquieting; then she began to relax, and almost came to enjoy those scenes that seemed to be playing before her. Yet when she closed her eyes, the images continued, and she reached the conclusion that what she had been experiencing was actually within her. There was nothing of a dream quality about them. The images seemed to have a textured substance and a singular reality to them.

A gust of wind entered the room through the window and extinguished the candle. Nellie was only momentarily aware that the candlelight had gone out. And before she could open her eyes, the candlelight appeared to be replaced by another form of light.

"*Well, Eddie, so this is where you are,*" a voice came from a bright glow of light opposite the rocking chair. "*I've been wondering what had become of you.*"

"*Clayton?*" she heard herself say, but it was not her voice as she knew it. "*Clayton Latshaw? Is that you?*"

Nellie was aware that the sound came from within her, but she was of the impression that she was an observer listening in on a conversation, and that she was *not* actually participating in it.

"You went to Boston, didn't you? And you rarely came back to visit your sister."

"That was a long time ago, Clayton."

"Don't speak of time to me, Eddie. I seem to be caught in a kind of time gap and can't move forward or backward. You—ah—you've gone on. You've married, I hear, and have had children."

"Not only that, Clayton. Now my wife and both of my children have returned to spirit form."

"And you, Eddie?"

"Can't you see I've taken on a different suit of flesh?"

"Is that lump of female form in the rocking chair you, Eddie?"

"Your contemptuousness for the female was never well disguised, Clayton. But you see, if you really did love me as a boy, then you have no choice but to love me as a girl, have you? I chose to incarnate as I did because I had need to be near Danny and Mike again. Things were all so very unsolved, or perhaps I should say evolved. Now Danny has gone on again, but I've still things to work out with Mike. You should understand all of this, Clayton. You were the teacher and we were the pupils."

"Oh, I understand the principle, I simply haven't been able to bring myself to adjust to it yet. Some of us make very slow—I should say snaillike progress."

Perhaps Nellie can help you become free of whatever is holding you in suspended limbo, Clayton."

"Nellie?"

"The lump of female in the rocking chair—another aspect of me."

"Oh, dear, I'll never be able to sort this thing out! Eddie—? Oh, gracious, what little power I have is burning out. Eddie, we must talk again."

"Get to know Nellie."

Nellie opened her eyes. The room was dark. Had it been a dream? Whatever it had been, she was certain it had significant meaning to her. Cautiously she left the room on the third floor and went to the one to which she had been assigned on the second.

Although young Richard Phenwick had pleaded with his parents to allow him to go on the picnic, it had been decided that only adults were to be present, that Sunday afternoon. Richard pouted and sulked, but Ann was determined that her eldest son was to remain with his sister and brother and the governess. She realized that Nellie and Thad were very much in love and even Leo's and her presence could be an intrusion on the young lovers' solitude.

The baskets were carried to a secluded spot among the trees on the shore of Back Bay. Both Thad and Leo were clad in white, while Nellie and Ann wore cool, comfortable pastel-colored dresses. Blankets were spread on the grass and they lounged about. After dinner, Leo and Thad went a short distance down the shore, where they hired a boat and paddled it back to where the young ladies were waiting.

For nearly two hours the happy young couples drifted about in the boat. The air was cooler on the water. Both Nellie and Ann carried parasols to protect them from the sunlight. While Leo and Thad wore straw hats, parts of their faces and arms began to get quite red.

Later, after the boat was returned, Leo and Ann went for a stroll, leaving Thad and Nellie to be together in the shade.

Thad could not restrain demonstrations of his feelings, of his love. And Nellie could not help but respond to them. They became oblivious of all else but the joyous wonder of the moment.

The large, hulking man had watched them from the shore when they were in the boat. He had observed Nellie and Ann while they awaited the return of Thad and Leo. He had seen Leo and Ann go for a stroll, and he had positioned himself behind a clump of bushes from where he had a good view of the intimate moments between Nellie and Thad. He had had practice in waiting—long years of it. He was in no hurry to make his presence known. It was better, in his opinion, to wait and gather information, to be very sure of the situation, then strike where there would be a minimal amount of danger for him.

When Leo and Ann returned, the four sat and conversed lightheartedly before it was decided to return to Falmouth House. Since it was a short walk, the men carried the baskets and blankets while the ladies managed their parasols. It had been a delightful afternoon.

Later that evening Nellie went to help Ann put the children to bed. Thad joined Leo on the summer porch, where they smoked and sipped brandy.

"Frankly, dear Uncle," Leo said as he reclined on a wicker chair with his feet resting on an ottoman, "I think you would do well to pursuade John Collier to merge with Medallion."

"Merge with Medallion?" Thad questioned. "My dear nephew, what ever for?"

"Well, now that I've completely taken over the business from Cousin Crandall Ornby, and he and Benita have gone out west," Leo explained, "I could do with a man like you to help me. Besides, why shouldn't the furniture business be part of shipbuilding?"

"I'll mention it to John," Thad said.

"It's your mother you'll need to speak with," Leo replied.

"Mother?"

"Everyone knows what powerful creatures the Phenwick women are," Leo commented with an amused laugh. "And we all know how the Collier furniture business has improved since John married your mother."

Thad smiled and flicked ashes. "John Collier seems to be more and more putting the business on my shoulders. Besides, now that Adam has introduced him to the treasure map, I suspect he'll turn his attention exclusively in that direction."

The man hiding in the bushes pricked up his ears upon hearing the last sentence. Was that what he had been waiting to hear?

"Were you speaking of my father?" Nellie asked as she emerged from the house, holding her skirts and carrying a fan.

"We were," Thad returned. "And of Adam and the alleged treasure map."

Nellie said, "I have reasons to believe the treasure map is authentic and, that when it is found, the treasure will be of greater worth than any of us can imagine."

A large dog of mixed heritage preceded Ann from the house. The animal was white, black, and tan and appeared to be part German shepherd. She growled as she went to the railing.

"Oh, for goodness sake, Mandy," Ann scolded. "You go back upstairs and stay with the children. You're to watch them, not be down here with us."

The dog held her place at the railing and barked.

"This is no time to go chasing squirrels, Mandy," Leo warned. "You do as Ann tells you."

Mandy barked again.

"All right, that's enough of that, Mandy," Leo scolded, grabbing her by the back of the neck and forcibly leading her into the house.

Mandy wanted to go back to the railing, but Leo had the stronger will.

In the confusion of the moment, the man in the bushes managed to escape, went around the back of the house and along the fence. He had heard all he needed to hear.

"It wasn't a squirrel," Nellie said when Leo returned.

"I beg your pardon."

"Mandy wasn't barking at a squirrel. I believe there was someone in the bushes."

"Someone in the bushes?" Leo stretched up on his toes and scanned about the area. "Which bushes?"

"It doesn't matter," Nellie replied. "They're gone now."

Leo's attention was attracted to the wildly waving hands of the stableman. "No one could have got on the property with Red keeping guard. He's the best watch-dog we've ever had. Wonder what Otis is all excited about. Excuse me."

Leon crossed the yard to intercept the black stable-man. "What is it, Otis?"

"It's the red dog, Mr. Phenwick," Otis replied. "I done found him with his throat slit. He's been killed."

Leo started back to the summer porch, when Mandy let out a dreadful howl. Realizing that the sound came from the area in which the children were kept, he went in that direction.

# Chapter Nineteen

"I have never seen two people so obviously in love," Ann commented as the carriage with Thad and Nellie pulled away from Falmouth House.

"Sometimes I wonder if there isn't a Divine plan," Leo remarked, "that arranges such couplings. Or maybe they've had past lives together and in this they are just continuing with the love that they had previously known."

Ann took her husband's hand. "My darling, I suspect those are things we aren't destined to know as mortals."

Nellie sat close to Thad on the driver's seat. She was not too proud to appear unladylike as long as she was close to the man she loved. Because Thad had to hold the reins with both hands, Nellie put her hand to his arm or to his leg. She wanted to lean her head on his shoulder, but feared she would hinder his ability with the horse.

As the carriage neared Greenfield, an alarming sensation came over Nellie. At first she thought she must be experiencing a physical ailment, the pain was that sharp in the region of her stomach. But was it physical distress that was troubling her?

"I think it best," Nellie stated as they came to the Old

Indian Road, "that we should go by Dr. Mumford's office."

"What is it, dearest Nell?" Thad questioned.

"I'm certain it is nothing," Nellie replied. "I have a feeling of apprehension that seems to have settled in my stomach. Still, it could be a stomach condition that is causing the apprehension. I'll feel better if Dr. Mumford examines me."

Charles Mumford examined Nellie thoroughly. In his opinion she was in good physical condition, and he suggested that she doubtlessly was reacting to the jiggling about of the carriage ride from Portland. He gave her a mixture of herbs with which she was to make tea and drink a cup every hour for six hours. It was certain to cure her problem.

"I understand," Charles Mumford said after his professional advice had been given, "that with your father and Adam away, certain conditions have arisen at the factory that could be a problem."

"Adam and John away?" Thad questioned.

"They rather hurriedly decided to go up to Bar Harbor," Charles explained. "It has something to do with that treasure map Adam found. I confess they reminded me of two young boys, in their enthusiasm and wild speculation."

Nellie frowned. "Perhaps that is why I felt apprehensive."

Charles's smile wilted into a concerned expression. "Why should you be apprehensive about John and Adam going to Bar Harbor?"

"I don't know." Nellie reached for Thad's hand. "I think we had best get back to Phenwick House and speak with Nancy."

Thad and Charles exchanged perplexed glances before Nellie hurried out the door with the men behind her.

Activity at the Medallion Company in Portland was

buzzing along at a well-paced speed. Even with Leo's brief absence, things ran smoothly because he had arranged them that way. He was precise and efficient. The fact that he was Joshua's eldest son, his second child, guaranteed that he was destined to be a success in the shipping business. As a lad he had spent much time at the Medallion Enterprises in London, where his father reigned with his cousin Gregory. Leo was motivated to get Medallion Portland into excellent shape, to show a tremendous profit and then invite his father and brother, as well as Gregory, to come see what he had accomplished.

Leo's desk was piled high with work that morning. He had first thing taken a look about to see that all was moving smoothly along; then he went to tackle the paperwork that was waiting.

The messenger arrived at eleven-thirty. The clerk accepted the telegram and took it directly to Leo.

"Read it, will you, Eugene?" Leo ordered, his mind occupied with another matter.

"Yes, sir," the officious Eugene replied. "It's from Mr. Stuart Phenwick of Boston."

"Stuart?" Leo looked up.

" 'Leo: S. Dodsworth free from prison as you know—stop. Rumor confirmed that he seeks revenge—stop. Advise you take extra precaution and hire men to guard your home and family at all times—stop. Be in contact—stop. Stuart.' " Eugene rustled the paper to catch Leo's attention.

"Thank you, Eugene. Just leave the wire on the desk," Leo said.

"Is there anything I may do to help you, sir?" Eugene asked.

"No, I don't believe—yes, there is. Have a run over to the police station and inquire as to where I can find some men to hire as guards."

"Yes, sir."

"Eugene—"

"Yes, sir?"

"Not a word about this wire to anyone. Understand?"

"Yes, sir."

Leo was able to concentrate on his work until about two-thirty. The full impact of Stuart's message struck him. He recalled the full horror imposed upon both Ann and him by the notorious Sam Dodsworth. Now he realized how foolish his decision had been not to go to New York and face Captain and Mrs. Roderick Wellington, to explain that he had been suffering from amnesia when he had worked for them. In his present state of mind, he did not recall the actual shooting incident, during which Annie Duggan had been mortally wounded; yet, at the time, when he was suffering the loss of memory of his past, he had fully related the matter both to Stuart and Thadius Phenwick, stating emphatically that it was Sam Dodsworth who had pulled the trigger that discharged the fatal bullet. Stuart had believed him. But Stuart also was aware of the emotional involvement, particularly on the part of Thelma Wellington concerning Leo. He had tried to make Roderick and Thelma understand the situation, and especially the fact that, since recovering from the period of amnesia, Leo did not recall what had happened during that era.

Leo had become convinced it would do little good to go to New York, certain that both of the Wellingtons would appear as total strangers to him. Now he wondered. Sam Dodsworth was free after all those years of incarceration, vengeance simmering in his heart. The Civil War veteran had seemed on the verge of insanity prior to the nightmare he inflicted upon Leo, Ann, and her brother Freddie. What would he be like after being in prison?

At the police station, Leo interviewed several men who were available to work as guards. He hired six to patrol Falmouth House and keep watch over his wife and children until Sam Dodsworth was apprehended. Then he went to the home of Mr. and Mrs. Zebidiah Robbins, Ann's mother and foster father, to explain the situation to them. Sally fretted, and pleaded with her husband to hire guards also, to protect them. Zebidiah promised to take the matter under consideration.

Leo armed himself. When he went home, he warned his family about possible danger. Richard, his eldest, was the only one of his three children old enough to even partially comprehend the meaning of the word. The servants were alerted. By then they were all certain the death of the dog named Red had to do with Sam Dodsworth.

"They were like two boys," Nancy exclaimed as she served tea to Thad and Nellie. "I've never seen your father so excited. And Adam, well, he's always had somewhat of a boyish quality about him. They took the train to Bar Harbor, saying that they would make arrangement to hire a boat up there. If you ask me, well—you didn't, did you?" She laughed.

"You don't approve of the treasure hunt, do you, Mother?" questioned Thad.

"I disapprove only of childish behavior in grown men," Nancy replied. "After all, Adam is 'footloose and fancy free,' but not John. It's quite another matter with him. Still I know my husband, and I'm fully aware that he has a natural curiosity. Besides, he would be ever so pleased if he could find the treasure so that he wouldn't feel as if—" She caught herself.

Nellie glared. "Feel as if *what*, Miss Nancy?"

"Dearest Nellie, do try to understand," Nancy said. "John Collier is an industrious man, and I love him very much, but he was not born to wealth nor had he acquired a large amount of it prior to our marriage. Nor, for that matter, did your mother have a large legacy from her immediate family. Being related to the Phenwicks doesn't necessarily mean that they have the Phenwick affluence."

"What Mother is trying to explain—" Thad interjected.

"That Collier Furniture would have failed had it not been for the Phenwick money Miss Nancy put into it," Nellie stated. "That's it, isn't it?"

"Oh, I don't believe it would have failed," Nancy inserted. "I just am of the impression that it would not have flourished as well as it has without sufficient capital to see it over rough periods. Why are we bickering? I am John's wife. What I have is his. Furthermore, you will soon be a Phenwick, not only my foster daughter but my daughter-in-law. Can't you see how silly this conversation is? The important thing is that I love your father very much. And I love you, too, Nellie—now and always."

Nellie rose and went to hug Nancy. "Forgive me, Miss Nancy. I'm simply on edge today for some reason. Dr. Mumford seems to think it's because of the ride from Portland that I feel as I do. I just seem to have a restless uneasiness."

"Then you must drink some of the tea Charles gave you to take," Nancy commented, "and let it settle your system."

Thad and Nellie excused themselves and went for a stroll. Nancy remained at the veranda and watched as they disappeared down the path that led to the store.

During those days after the party, Nancy was bombarded with letters from her guests in which they expressed their gratitude for having been included at the happy celebration. Nellie, too, had received notes, but hers were still unopened.

The letter with the return address from Mr. and Mrs. Stuart Phenwick of Boston was taken for granted as another of the obligatory thank-you responses. Nancy recognized Ruth's handwriting as she breezed through the newsy part and the explanation of the rather mundane events during their return trip. Most of what Ruth had to say was predictable. However, the second page of the letter was in a different handwriting, which Nancy knew to be Stuart's. In it Stuart explained the situation concerning the release of Sam Dodsworth. It had occurred to Stuart that Nancy and those at Greenfield should be aware of the situation and, perhaps, Thad and Adam, or John, or some of the others, could ride occasionally to Portland to see that Leo and his family were all right.

Nancy reread the part of the letter written by Stuart. She detected urgency and deep concern. Yet she put it aside and let thoughts of it slip from her mind. She had already begun to make plans for the wedding in October, plans that she intended to suggest to Nellie. It would be another lavish event: the day that Nellie Collier became a Phenwick woman.

# Chapter Twenty

Obviously Nellie was required to devote more time to Collier Furniture during her father's absence than when he was in town. Although her mind was swimming with romantic thoughts, she was still able to put them in abeyance while she concentrated on business matters.

Nellie occupied her father's office, which was somewhat remote from the office assigned to Thad. Still, they encountered each other many times during the day. It was all they could do to appear outwardly indifferent to the other and absorbed in business matters. True, there was much that had to be tended to concerning production, sales, and exporting of the furniture. Moreover, the pressing issue of the moment was the plant personnel. Union organizers had infiltrated the men, causing agitation and a slowdown in production.

Thad had to fire three men, two because they were instigators of revolution among the workers, and one simply because he was incapable of doing the work. He had first discussed the matter with Nellie. Not trusting his sense of judgment and intuition, Thad suggested that Nellie interview and hire the new men to replace those discharged.

Four men showed up to apply for the positions. Only

one of these leaned toward union organization. He was immediately not considered, and Nellie hired the other three. Ironically, all three were strangers to Greenfield. Two were Polish immigrants and the third was second-generation American of Irish descent from Boston.

Nellie had a positive reaction to the Irish descendant and one of the Poles. The second Polish man appeared to know his trade and seemed strong enough to do the work of two men, but Nellie could not dismiss the somewhat distrustful feeling she had about him.

"Your name is Stanley Dubrowski?" Nellie asked.

"Didn't you read it on my papers?" Dubrowski asked. "You see my papers are in order, don't you?"

"Yes, of course," Nellie replied. She could not discern what made her feel uneasy. "Very well, you may begin tomorrow."

The large, burly Dubrowski had piercing eyes that often seemed to be staring through Nellie, especially when she chanced to move through the factory. Without turning to face him, she knew that Dubrowski was watching her. At first she considered his staring the normal reaction of a man toward a beautiful woman. And, since Dubrowski claimed to be unmarried and was known to live in a rooming house which allowed only single men, she believed that he simply felt masculine desire for her.

Yet Dubrowski usually wore a fierce expression, devoid of the whimsical smile a man usually gets when appraising a woman. He was always polite and appeared to get along passably well with the other workers. His talent as a carpenter was average, but sufficiently good to assure his employers that he had had experience with the craft. What was it, then, that disturbed Nellie about the man? And why did she more and more fell ill at ease in his presence?

During the absence of John Collier and Adam Truff from Greenfield, Dr. Charles Mumford regularly appeared at Phenwick House. His visits were social, not professional, and stemmed from loneliness, since Adam usually spent considerable time with the young doctor. Nancy welcomed his company, especially with John away and Thad and Nellie deeply occupied with each other in the evenings. Nancy soon gave Charles a standing invitation to take supper with them, then sit and visit with her while Thad and Nellie went off for a stroll or whatever else they did to become better acquainted.

Charles regularly purchased the Portland and the Boston papers, both of which usually arrived at least a week late in Greenfield. Like Adam, he wished to keep up with current news events. While Nancy was perfectly content with her life at Greenfield, she still had a natural curiosity about social happenings in Boston. Often she would read mention of her son, Daniel Louis, in the social column, being from a prominent family and gaining a reputation for himself among the elite of Boston. Occasionally her son John's name would appear in the paper, but it was generally with a professional connotation and his standing as a respected attorney. Since Charles graciously invited Nancy to share his papers, one evening a week was spent in perusing them privately and together.

Nancy would cut out items of interest to show Thad, especially if such notices mentioned the names of her sons or other members of the Phenwick family. Charles would call her attention to articles of interest and Nancy would snip away.

"I do believe I find it more enjoyable to go over the news this way," Nancy commented, "than to merely have you send the used newspapers to me. This way I simply make the time to sit down and read. I trust that we can continue to do this, Charles, even after John returns."

"We'll see, Miss Nancy, we'll see." Charles recrossed his legs and adjusted the paper, creasing it at the fold.

A while later Nancy distracted the doctor's attention by using the paper to swat at a fly. Her face reddened when he glanced up at her.

To make her feel less uncomfortable, Charles chose an item that had attracted his interest to read aloud: "'Members of the Polish immigrant's family finally located him, listed among the prisoners being held at the state prison.'"

"Goodness! What a terrible thing for a family to discover!" Nancy declared.

"It's worse than that, Miss Nancy," Charles commented, and read on. "'When the family finally got permission to see him, they discovered that he was dead and had been dead for several weeks. The prison authorities permitted the family to take the body of the deceased to be given a Christian burial, since his only crime apparently had been poverty.'"

"Poverty? Since when has poverty been a crime?"

"I suspect he was caught stealing something," Charles added. "It doesn't say so in this article, but I surmise that was the case. Anyway, the conclusion of all this is the family hasn't been able to discover their poor relative's papers or personal belongings, which allegedly included a pocket watch. That may or may not be the case, but I do believe there should be some kind of prison reform made to assure the individual prisoners of having their property kept safely intact for them."

Nancy thought a moment. "You say the man was a Polish immigrant?"

"Yes. They're coming over by the boatloads at every opportunity they get," Charles stated.

"Hmm. Yes, so I understand. First it was the Irish—" Nancy paused. "Why, Nellie hired two Polish carpenters recently at the factory. Before you know it, we'll have them swarming around Greenfield. And here I thought Greenfield was so isolated and immune to the invasion of immigrants."

"No place in America is immune to immigrants," Charles commented. "Besides, once they become American citizens, what difference will their backgrounds make?"

Nancy sucked air through her teeth. "May I see that article when you finish with that piece of the paper?"

"Certainly."

Nancy scanned an article covering a wedding at which both John and Daniel Louis were mentioned as guests. She cut that out to show Thad.

Charles handed her the page upon which the item had been written.

"Dubrowski?" Nancy said aloud. "Yes, that certainly is a Polish-sounding name. Poor man. I wonder what *did* happen to his identification papers."

"I should think we will be hearing something from John and Adam before long now," Charles commented after he had scanned the paper. He chose certain sections to take back with him, and would leave the rest of the newspaper with Nancy.

"Oh, I do hope so," Nancy returned. "I get terribly lonely for Mr. Collier. He is really a very dear man, you know."

"I've always had great respect and admiration for John," Charles returned. "And naturally Adam—that is —he has nothing but good to say about John."

"Adam—?" Nancy tilted her head. "Dear Adam."

"Do you know something?" Charles asked, "I believe Adam enjoys being an enigma, surrounded by mystery."

"As you enjoy being one?"

"I'm not a mystery, I shouldn't think."

"But, dear Charles, you *are* an enigma," Nancy said. "And I like you the way you are. I wouldn't want you any other way."

Charles Mumford had gone home long before Thad and Nellie returned to Phenwick House. Nancy, too, had retired for the night. The house was singularly quiet. Only the chorus of crickets outside and the occasional hooting of an owl kept it from being deathly quiet.

A light had been left burning in the entrance hallway, but no other lamps were lit. A strange sensation came over Nellie as she entered with Thad, clinging to his hand.

Thad yawned and stretched. "We walked far too far, and stayed up much too late, my dearest Nell. I'll see you immediately to your room and retreat to mine."

"I'm still very much wide awake," Nellie explained. "Oh, I wish we were already married. I'm certain I would sleep well beside you."

Thad kissed her. "My precious Nellie, October will be here before you know it. And once we're married, we'll have the whole rest of our lifetimes to be together."

Nellie touched the cheek where Thad had last kissed her. He had gone to his own room and she was alone. It was not until after she had changed into her sleeping attire that she again noticed the strange atmosphere that seemed to hover over Phenwick House.

Nellie's thoughts lingered with Thad and the ever-growing love she had for him. At such times she wondered why it had ever taken her so long to realize her true feelings for him. She rationalized that she took so long because she thought of him as a stepbrother after the marriage of her father and his mother. Whatever the reason, she was delighted that they had discovered their love for each other.

It was nearly an hour later before Nellie fell asleep. Before she finally drifted off, twice she thought she had heard peculiar sounds coming from other parts of the house. Then the breeze came up, and she permitted herself to think that whatever sounds she had heard had been caused by the wind.

Her dream was confusing. In it she found herself running down a long tunnel, at the end of which was a bright light. But the more she ran, the farther away the light seemed to get. Ultimately a figure stepped out from the side of the tunnel, blocking the light as he stood silhouetted in it. Try as she might, she could not slow her running until she came within inches of the figure. It was Thad and he was badly bleeding. He appeared to be in a shocked daze, oblivious of the blood that was oozing from his head.

Nellie tried to speak to him, but he did not recognize her, nor was he coherent when he tried to speak. As she hugged him, he tried to push her away. The more she resisted, the stronger he seemed to get. Then, as she took another look at his face, she realized it was not Thad after all, but her father. She screamed as she recognized the mutilated condition of John Collier's face. The scream awakened her.

Terrified in reaction to the dream, Nellie did not try to comprehend the meaning of it. She only knew that she had to escape from that room and into Thad's loving arms. The dressing robe was thrown about her shoulders with no effort made to put her arms into the sleeves.

Flying from her room, she dashed barefoot to Thad's chamber. Without knocking, she threw open the door and went to the bed. It was empty! Thad was not there!

As she caught her breath, Nellie could see by moonlight that the bedding had been messed, that he obviously had been in it. She went to the window, and moonlight brightened her face. Her mind was troubled, both from the nightmare and the discovery that Thad was gone. She could only believe that he had somehow become restless, couldn't sleep and had gotten up to go for a stroll.

The ambience of the large, sprawling mansion was terrifying. The atmosphere was heavy. Even the crickets had stopped making sound in the background.

Frantically, Nellie raced from the room. Her intention was to go to Nancy's room, but at the last moment, she decided against waking the older woman. She went directly to the servants' quarters. When the servants did not respond to her knocking, she entered their rooms and found them each in a deep sleep. Had they been drugged? She could rouse no one.

Back upstairs, Nellie went to Nancy's room. She, too, while comfortably in her bed, could not be wakened. Panic hit her and she wanted to scream. Aware that she must do everything in her power to maintain control, she went back to her own room. She could not rely on her psychic powers if she were in an agitated emotional state. The thing she rationalized that she must do was to gain control over her emotions and see if she could not perceive what was behind the mystery.

Locking the door of her room behind her, Nellie threw the dressing robe aside. Lying down would be the ideal way to attempt to pull herself together, but she could not bring herself to go to the bed. Instead she went to the window, resting her head against the window casing.

*Calm ... calm ... calm.*

No! Nellie turned with alarm and stared wildly back into the room. The startling premonition that she was not alone in the room came over her. For a fleeting moment she thought it might be Thad—or at least she wished that it were. Then, her perception rife, she knew only that whoever was there had a negative, malevolent intention.

As Nellie inched into the room, she passed the dresser and her hand connected with a hairbrush. It was hardly an effective weapon. She pitched it across the room. If some actual physical person were there, his attention would be attracted in that direction.

A silver candlestick was on the commode beside the bed. Nellie edged toward that. Connecting with it, she took the holder in one hand and the candle in the other. Thus equipped, she went in the direction she thought she had left her dressing robe.

A huge dark shadow moved at the far window.

Nellie gasped, then threw the candle toward the opposite side of the room. That was her mistake. If she had tossed it in the same general direction as she had thrown the hairbrush, her pursuer might have believed she was there.

Again she saw the figure lurch in the moonlight, a hideous monster moving almost apelike toward her. She raised the silver candle holder. A moment later thick fingers clutched at her shoulders. Instantly she brought the candle holder down with crashing force. The rough fingers slipped from her shoulders as the attacker reeled in stunned confusion.

Nellie carried the candle holder with her as she fled from the room. She had reached the foot of the main stairway before she heard movement coming from above. Anxiously she ran from the house. Gravel and tiny sticks outside on the ground caused her feet to become raw. Her first thought was to attempt to run to Adam's cottage. She wanted to call for Toby, but she did not dare make a sound for fear she would be heard.

Bracing herself behind a large maple tree trunk, she watched as the brutish man appeared at the doorway. After looking around for a few minutes, he returned to the house. That was fortunate, Nellie thought. Although she had concern for Nancy, she realized that she was powerless against the strength of the man who had invaded Phenwick House. She had to get help.

Stealthily, remaining in the shadow, Nellie moved down the path to the stable. She glanced to her left at the summerhouse. There was no place to hide there, unless she went below to the old basement. No. Besides, she had to get help.

The stable door banged as she neared it.

There was no time to get a saddle or put it on a horse. Three of the animals were in the pen. The best she could do was to put a bridle on one and ride bareback. The bridles were hanging on the fence post.

Glancing back at the house, Nellie thought she saw a man's figure on the second-floor veranda. Had he heard the slamming of the stable door and come to investigate?

Nellie got the gate open and the bridle on the black mare. Then she slapped each of the other two horses and urged them to run out of the pen. As they did, she mounted the mare with great effort and, only by straddling it was she able to get the animal to move as she wished it to do.

The other two horses rode with her as if they were tied by invisible reins. Since she had seen no other horses tied near the house, her one hope was that the attacker had no means of following her. The work horses and carriage horses were kept in the barn a good distance from Phenwick House.

An inner voice seemed to be directing Nellie, and she managed to get the mare to go toward Dr. Charles Mumford's house.

Alarmed by the thundering of horses, Charles rose from his bed and went to the window. No more had he gone downstairs and had reached the front door, than Nellie was off the mare. She threw herself into his arms.

"Nellie!" he exclaimed. After hugging her, he pushed her aside and went to tie the horses. "Nellie," he called back to her, "what is it? What's wrong?"

Charles carried Nellie into the house after he had secured the horses. Then, as he dressed the cuts on her feet and other scratches about her arms and legs, he listened to her story.

"Here, take this," Charles ordered as he handed her a glass of water into which he had put several drops of liquid from a small bottle. "This will calm you and let you sleep."

"I can't sleep now," Nellie complained, "not until I get help to Phenwick House."

"I'll see to that, Nellie. You simply take this and plan on sleeping here on that chaise," Charles said soothingly. "I'll wait until you lose consciousness."

"Oh, Dr. Mumford, I'm so terribly worried about Miss Nancy and Thad," Nellie said, after drinking what Charles had given her.

"There is nothing you can do, Nellie. As soon as I'm certain you're comfortable, I'll go for the constable." Charles put his soft hand to her brow. "Are you certain Thad was not in his room?"

"Positive," Nellie said. And that was the last thing she remembered.

## Chapter Twenty-one

Four-thirty in the morning was obviously not the right time to get full cooperation from the men in Greenfield. Most were still drowsy when they were roused by the constable in the company of Dr. Mumford. The men who rallied to the call did so for Charles, not for the constable or for the assistance they might be giving the Phenwicks.

The new Phenwick House was an imposing sight that dwarfed all the other houses in Greenfield. There was envy and contempt for the house, especially from the poor people who labored long hours to make a meager living.

The morning sky had begun to brighten when the men and horses arrived at Phenwick House. Charles led the way with Constable Channing Boggs.

Toby barked a warning until he recognized Dr. Mumford, then he ran up to be petted.

"That's strange," Charles commented, "Nellie said Toby was nowhere around last night."

A servant appeared at the front door to inquire of the visitors. Upon recognizing the constable, he invited the gentlemen in while he went to fetch Miss Nancy.

Nancy was sleepy-eyed when she appeared at the

head of the steps, tying her robe about her. She squinted down. "Is that you, Charles?"

Charles went to her and quickly explained the situation. "Nellie is at my house. I don't believe there's reason to worry about her. But we must check Thad's room."

Nancy led the way. Charles opened the door and he and Channing Boggs entered practically at the same time.

Thad was lying in bed. The sound of the intruders apparently aroused him. He sat up, wiping his eyes and pushing hair back from his face. "What is the meaning of this intrusion?"

"Thadius?" Charles questioned.

"Ah, Charles!" Thad put his feet to the floor. As he rose, a sharp pain shot through his head, nearly causing him to fall backward. Regaining his balance, he stared into the startled expression of his mother.

"Where have you been, Thad?" Nancy questioned.

"I've been asleep," Thad replied. "What is this all about?"

Again Charles explained the situation as told to him by Nellie.

"She wouldn't contrive such a tale, would she?" Thad asked.

"Of course, she wouldn't!" exclaimed Nancy. "What possible reason could she have?"

"I believe she is on edge," Charles mentioned. "She's thinking of the wedding, and business and—I suppose many other things. Perhaps she's been under pressure. She probably dreamed the whole thing."

"I can see no other explanation for her behavior," Thad said. "I've had a perfectly good night's sleep right here in this bed."

"Well, I suspect," Charles said after dismissing the constable and the men, "that Nellie had a dream—to what extent we can't even begin to speculate. At whatever point she awakened, she called Toby. When the dog wouldn't come, she feared for him, afraid he might have met the fate of the dog in Portland. She went on about that. Obviously Toby is here, well and full of energy."

"She told me last night she wished she could sleep beside me," Thad related. "I naturally discouraged such a thing. Perhaps Nell has contrived a way to pursuade me to let her share my bed."

"Thadius!" exclaimed Nancy.

"I was only joking, Mother." But later that day Thad thought about it again and wondered if he had been.

Thad arrived by eight o'clock at Charles Mumford's house. There he awakened Nellie with a kiss.

"It did happen, Thad, just as I've told you," Nellie said sometime later. "I do confess that while it was all happening, I couldn't help think of Ann Phenwick and her description of what happened to her when she was pursued by whatever that man's name was."

"Sam Dodsworth?"

"Yes." Nellie laughed. "Ann said it was all part of the initiation to becoming a Phenwick woman."

"What was?"

"The peril, and being pursued."

Thad laughed. "Now do you think you qualify as a Phenwick woman?"

"Nellie thought a moment. Slowly she shook her head. "No, not yet."

Rarely did Millijoy Phenwick awaken before ten o'clock in the morning at Triumph House. Her usual custom included a leisurely bath in a large marble pool, then to receive a massage from a large Swedish woman named Helga, after which she had breakfast. However, on that very same morning, she had abruptly regained consciousness shortly after seven. As she lay among the satin sheets, she ruminated about her dreams. There had been several, and, as she could recall, there had been a recurring motif in them.

The servants were shocked to see Millijoy up and about at such an early hour, and were even more aghast to hear that she was abandoning her morning routine. Instead, she ordered the landau and driver while she took a light breakfast.

Equally surprised was Stuart Phenwick when the butler announced that Mrs. Gordon Phenwick was in the entrance hallway of Edward House wishing to see him. His sister-in-law had long been unpredictable, but never had he known her to put in an appearance at that hour of the day.

"I was awakened from a terrifying dream," Millijoy stated dramatically. "I believe it was prophetic."

"You'll excuse me, Millijoy, if I don't seem to comprehend your words," Stuart said, pulling his dressing robe up tighter about his chest. "Could you permit me a cup of coffee and the opportunity to wash the sleep from my face before you continue?"

"Of course, Stuart. Did you have a late night last night?"

"John Collier and Adam Truff arrived from—well, Bar Harbor last evening," Stuart explained, "in a state of excitement. I admit we stayed up later than usual in conversation."

"Adam? John?" Millijoy raised an eyebrow. "Are they here now?"

"Yes. Come with me into the dining room," Stuart invited. "Make yourself comfortable, and I'll return momentarily."

During his absence, Stuart donned a pair of trousers, a blouse, and shoes. He appeared far less sleepy-looking than he had been previously.

"Nellie Collier isn't the only one in the family who has premonitions and prophetic dreams," Millijoy stated. "I often—especially in recent years—have foreseen the

234

coming of events. That is why I came with such urgency this morning. And isn't it coincidental that both Adam and John Collier should be here?"

"Explain yourself," Stuart said.

Millijoy explained her dream, which was a kind of hodgepodge of symbols and abstractions.

"What does that mean to you? I make no sense of it at all," Stuart commented.

"Simply that Nellie Collier is in great danger," Millijoy stated.

"What in the name of blazes does that mishmash of nonsense have to do with Nellie?"

"It tells me that there is urgency and danger," Millijoy replied. "Then, when I awakened this morning, Nellie's name came to me—along with Thadius's. I can only conclude there is trouble for them."

Stuart laughed. "My dear Millijoy, I—"

"Don't laugh at me, Stuart! Don't ever laugh at me!" Millijoy reprimanded. "A third name came to me, and a fourth. The fourth was your name, Stuart."

Stuart controlled his laughter. "And the third name?"

"Sam Dodsworth," Millijoy bit out the syllables.

"Sam Dod—?" Stuart was immediately to his feet. Without excusing himself he dashed from the room. Millijoy could hear him calling Adam Truff and John Collier.

Millijoy's mission had been accomplished. She finished her cup of coffee and told the servant she would let herself out.

"Arrangements will have to wait for the searching expedition," Stuart stated as he watched John Collier dress. "I don't know how reliable Millijoy's sensitive abilities are, but I do know she mentioned the right names to distress me."

Adam joined the other two.

"You must take the first train to Portland," Stuart advised. "I thought Dodsworth would show up at Falmouth

House. Perhaps he did and it was there he learned about Nellie and Thad. Whatever the case may be, I suspect his revenge is aimed toward the entire Phenwick family, not merely Leo and Ann. Who knows what his deranged mind thinks?"

"I agree with Stuart," Adam said. "We should waste no time getting back to Greenfield. I, too, have had an uneasy feeling about Nellie—and Thad ... and—well, I won't speculate any further."

Stuart saw the two men to the train. As it pulled away from the station, he wondered if he shouldn't have gone along, too.

# Chapter Twenty-two

"You obviously don't believe me," exclaimed Nellie, her eyes flaming with rage.

Thad opened his arms to her. "Dearest Nell, I *do* believe you, simply because you have made the statement. I only question the lack of evidence to substantiate your explanation."

"It's the same thing as saying you don't believe me!" Nellie snapped. "Why would I make up such a terrible tale if it weren't true?"

"I don't know why," Thad said without thinking. "I mean—Oh, Nellie, please, let us drop the entire matter."

Nellie would not be placated so easily, it would take more than an apology and several kisses. "Dr. Mumford tried to find logical explanations, but he couldn't. He didn't believe me. Your mother desperately sought to discover answers. Yet when I showed her the hairbrush I had thrown across the room to distract my assailant —as well as the candle—she acted as if I had planted such evidence to support a concocted story."

Nellie fumed throughout the day. Fortunately she had much work to do, which kept her occupied and discouraged disturbing thoughts from bobbing up in her mind. During the afternoon, she had occasion to go out into the factory. Although she made a point to know the men by name, she rarely stopped to speak with any of them. She would nod when they spoke, but that was the only concession she would make.

An Irishman by the name of Clancy O'Malley tipped his hat and spoke with a soft brogue. "Sure now, 'tis a fine day, isn't it, Miss Collier?"

She smiled and nodded her head. Aware that Clancy O'Malley was single and had been heard to boast that he would one day have his own business, even if it meant marrying the boss's daughter, Nellie was prepared to defend herself against his charming ways. Hurriedly she walked on. Then she thought to herself that Clancy O'Malley looked no more Irish than—she hesitated— than Stanley Dubrowski looked Polish.

After leaving the shop area, Nellie wondered why she had made such a comparison. What did a typical Irishman look like anyway? Much less, how did a non-typical Irishman appear? She laughed at that question. But she glanced up and noticed both Clancy O'Malley and Stanley Dubrowski watching her. Clancy winked and cast her a broad smile. Dubrowski just seemed to glare.

"You've finished early today, haven't you, Nellie?" Nancy commented as the young lady returned to Phenwick House.

"I fear I didn't have enough sleep last night," Nellie replied. "I'm going to take a bit of a nap."

Nancy encouraged the rest. She had been reading through parts of the paper Charles Mumford had left the night before. It was Wednesday night. A traditional potluck supper was planned at the church. Nancy felt it her duty to attend, even if John was not there to go with her. She had meant to ask Nellie if she wished to attend. Probably not—not in those days when she and Thad were courting.

By late afternoon, Thad was beginning to feel the strain of the day. He worked overtime trying to get a project cleared away. Without watching the time, he had continued into the twilight hour. The days of summer were getting shorter. Here it was nearly the first of September, and darkness was coming earlier and earlier.

"Mr. Phenwick," a voice called from the shadowed side of the building as Thad left the factory and locked the door.

"Yes? Who is it?" Thad answered.

"You're working late tonight, aren't you, Mr. Phenwick?"

"Come closer so that I may see your face."

The hulking figure moved toward Thad. "I would like to show you something, Mr. Phenwick."

"Well, what is it?" Thad asked impatiently.

Even up close, the face was mostly shadow. It was familiar to Thad, but he could not place a name with it. The thick, meaty fingers reached to Thad's neck. "It's something I learned in prison, Mr. Phenwick."

Before Thad could speak, pressure was applied to his neck and he lost consciousness. He hands and feet were quickly bound after he was dragged behind a clump of bushes. It was than a matter of waiting until darkness completely invaded the sky.


"I can't imagine what's keeping Thaddy so late," Nancy had said before leaving for the church. Several of the servants accompanied her, since they were basically good, religious folks. She left word with Alvin Paxton to tell Thad where she had gone and suggest that he and Nellie join her at the church if they liked.

Paxton usually used the night of the potluck to go

into town to join some of his cronies at the local tavern. Only the stableman was left on the premises.

Charles Mumford had had to set a broken leg that afternoon. It took longer than he had anticipated. Then he spent time with the patient to record his reactions. The man seemed to be in severe pain, and Charles feared he might have to take drastic measures to give him comfort. The young doctor did not much care for the potluck suppers. Many of the young ladies in town found him attractive, hence they took every opportunity to force themselves on him. Church socials were ideal for such attacks.

Word was left on his door that a telegram had arrived for him. Charles realized that people did not send such messages unless they were important. He walked over to the hay and grain store, where the telegraph system was located. Climbing the back stairs, he rapped on the residence of the owner. A few minutes later he had the telegram.

CHARLES

SAM DODSWORTH IS OUT OF PRISON STOP WE BELIEVE HE MAY HAVE HEADED FOR GREENFIELD STOP BE ALERT FOR HIS PRESENCE STOP KEEP AN EYE ON PHENWICK HOUSE STOP WILL BE THERE TONIGHT

ADAM

Charles stared at the telegram as a sense of excited urgency began to come over him.

"The man who attacked Nellie last night!" Charles exclaimed. "Then it was true!" He should have gone to get the constable, but in his excitement, he harnessed a horse to the shay and headed for Phenwick House.

Frogs were vocalizing somewhere out in the night. Crickets were tuning up. Nellie awakened to a strange, eerie, ominous vibration that seemed to be vibrating at

240

her very bones. Her teeth even felt electric with a sense of dread anticipation. She sat up. How long had she been asleep? Why was the house so quiet?

She had changed into a lightweight gown for her nap. Because of that horrible sensation that had come over her, she merely slipped into a white peignoir and made a feeble effort at brushing her hair.

There were no matches in her room. A candle was useless.

Hurriedly she went into the hallway, then to Nancy's room. Her immediate desire was to find matches. She found none. From Nancy's room she went toward Thad's room. It was then that she realized no one else was in the house. Or, if there was someone, she perceived that it was someone who did not belong there.

Her impulse was to call out for Nana Carlyle or Paxton. Then she remembered it was Wednesday. Nana would have gone with Nancy to church. And she knew perfectly well what Paxton did on Wednesdays. But where was Thad? She could not believe that he would have gone with his mother, leaving Nellie behind.

At Thad's door she hesitated. Something was amiss. A vibration of fear came from within the room. If Thad was in there, something was wrong with him; if he was not, and she suspected that was the case, some alien person was in there. Almost as the thought of danger penetrated her consciousness and she had decided to run, the door swung open and the hulking shadow she had encountered the night before lunged out at her.

Nellie ran as she felt the large fingertips scrape against her back. Her eyes were fortunately accustomed to the darkness, but she guessed that so were her attacker's. The advantage she had was that she knew the house.

Gathering her wits as best she could, Nellie jerked open the door to Nancy's room. She knew there were three exits to the room. As she slammed the door, she tried to turn the key in the lock. The force against the other side of it was so great that she had to abandon the effort. With animal cunning, she stood directly next to the door, her back flat against the wall, the key in her hand. When the man entered, raging like a bull and thrusting himself toward the center of the room, Nellie crept out the open door and tried to lock it from the outside. She managed to turn the key.

Nellie's moment of triumph was shattered moments later when a tremendous thud barged against the door. She could hear wood splintering, cracking, giving way beneath the force of his mighty strength. Not waiting for the door to explode into tiny pieces, she ran down the hallway. She was halfway down the stairs when she heard the door shatter amid a whirlwind of profanity.

Three steps from the bottom, Nellie lost her footing and fell forward, crying out as she landed, bracing herself with flattened palms. Her knee stung and her wrist had a dull pain. Still she managed to pull herself upright and continue through the entrance hallway. If it were the same man she had encountered the night before, and she was convinced that it was, he would be onto her means of escape via the stable. Chances were that he had foreseen a repeated attempt of her maneuvers of the night before.

His feet were slapping against the marble steps of the stairway. His puffing and panting echoed throughout the hallway.

Nellie ran toward the kitchen. If only she could find a tiny closet in which to hide, or duck into a dark place until he went by. But she could think of no such places. She only knew that he was getting closer and closer. Taking a desperate measure, she got down in a crouching position in the middle of the hallway, where there seemed to be a pit of blackness. He came running, tripped over her and went flying, sprawling as he landed. His head hit against the wall and he moaned with pain.

Nellie ached. Spasms of pain came at her side where his foot had connected with her before he fell. The wind was knocked out of her. Still she was determined to outwit him if she could.

Managing to rise to her feet, she clutched her side and gasped frantically for breath. She started in the direction from which she had come. The throbbing in her side was so severe that she could hardly move. Only through sheer endurance, she made her way to the downstairs library, closed the door, and fell against it. Strength seemed to leave her and she felt her body wearily slide down the door until she was seated on the floor.

Then force was violently shoved against the door. Nellie tried to brace herself, tried to resist, but the pressure against the door was too great and she did not have the strength to attempt to get away.

Thick fingers wrapped around her wrist before she was jerked into a standing position. Moments later her hands were pulled behind her with a stout piece of cord. A match was struck and put to a candle. The pale, eerie light glistened in the perspiration on the man's face and she recognized him to be the man she knew as Stanley Dubrowski. Gasping for air, aching with pain, burning with desperation, Nellie rolled her head back and stared pathetically at her captor.

"What do you want of me?" Nellie managed to ask, gasping between each word.

"Revenge!" he roared. Then he chuckled salaciously. "But first, pleasure!"

"Why are you doing this? What have I done to you?"

"You are a Phenwick!" he declared. "And the Phenwicks put me in prison. If you're not dead by the time I finish with you, you'll wish that you were! And they—the almighty Phenwicks—will pay well just for the return of your lifeless carcass."

"Stanley Dubrowski?" she asked.

"Dubrowski died in prison. I stole his papers, if it's any concern of yours," he explained. "If you're curious to know who I am, I'll tell you. I'm Sam Dodsworth!"

Before Nellie could react to the name or recall from where she had heard it, Dodsworth had a dirty bandana twisted to make a gag to fit her mouth. It was all she could do to keep from retching from the nasty taste of it. Moments later her feet were bound and she was hoisted onto the large man's shoulder.

"I'll not take care of you here, Nellie Collier," Dodsworth stated. "I intend to take my time with the lovely torture I've been planning for my Phenwick victim all those years that I sat there rotting in prison. And if I like the sensation of torture, I may make a practice of it with other Phenwicks." He laughed maniacally as he carried her through the entrance hallway and out into the night air.

Nellie could hear the sound of approaching horse's hooves and the wheels of a vehicle. There was no way she could make a noise. Dodsworth had also heard. He drew into the shadows and waited to see the shay arrive at the entrance.

Charles Mumford only lightly wrapped the harness around the hitching post and quickly dashed into the house.

"Well, well," Dodsworth commented as he carried Nellie to the carriage and put her inside. Then, gently, quietly, he led the horse down the lane toward the cottage.

Charles searched the downstairs rooms of the house and went into the basement where the servants' quarters were. Finding no one, he was about to retreat when he heard a scratching sound, followed by whining. Moments later he located a closed door, the key in the lock. Toby leaped from the closet, nearly knocking Charles over with the power of his gratitude.

"Where's Nellie?" Charles asked, knowing the closeness the animal had to the young lady.

Toby reacted to Nellie's name enthusiastically. Then it seemed to occur to him that there was danger. He ran toward the stairway and looked back to see if Charles was following.

Upstairs and outside, Charles was shocked to see his horse and shay were gone. Toby kept dashing ahead and coming back for him. They both went to the stable. The horses were gone.

Toby was ready to go, but Charles was distracted by the sound of the drunken stableman. In an unintelligible conversation, the doctor learned that the horses had been used to take the household staff and Mrs. Collier to the church.

Since Charles could get no more out of the incoherent man, he went to join Toby, who was headed in the direction of Adam's cottage.

Upon reaching the dead end of the lane at Adam's cottage, Sam jumped down from the shay and lifted Nellie out. Roughly he hoisted her to his back and carried her around the cottage wall and down the steps that led to the shore. He obviously had been there before, and knew his way.

Nellie tried to resist, wiggling as best she could and attempting to kick at her assailant. Her efforts were fruitless.

After carrying her up the beach about two hundred yards, where large boulders obstructed the way, Sam eased her from his shoulder and put her down in the sand. He tore the bandana gag from her face and put his wretched, scabby, unshaven mouth to hers. His kiss was even more disgusting than the dirty bandana had been. Yet, when she endured the first assault, she opened her lips and tried to catch his lower lip between her

245

teeth. He mistook the meaning of her gesture and fell into her trap. She bit with all her might until she was certain she had drawn blood on both sides of his lip.

Sam swore as a tornado of anger and blind rage went through him. Moments later he had snatched the peignoir from her, and had ripped it into several pieces before he was finished.

"Why are you doing this?" Nellie asked.

"I told you, for revenge!" Sam declared, stepping back to view her in the dim moonlight. "They're looking for me in Portland. But I followed you and your friend, who is now just as he was last night under my power, here."

"Thad? Where is Thad?"

"In safekeeping," Sam grunted. "Which is more than I can say for you." His hand went to her body, clutched and twisted her nightgown.

Nellie kicked. He was close enough so that she managed to connect in a vital place. Writhing with pain, he fell back. She ran. But Sam quickly had gathered his senses and tackled her, rolling her into the sand before she could escape.

Leo had given John Collier and Adam Truff fast horses in Portland. He offered to join them, but John thought it best for Leo to remain with his family.

The lathered horses were exhausted from the run from Portland and were grateful when they were finally tied in front of Phenwick House. Both men ran into the house, each calling Nellie, Thad, and Nancy. When they did not respond, John called for the servants. He remembered it was Wednesday night.

"Our one hope is that Nellie and Thad went with Nancy to the potluck at the church," John stated, gasping for breath.

"Out to the stable!" Adam ordered.

The men dashed from the house. They discovered the drunken stableman, from whom they could get nothing.

"What'll we do now?" John asked. "Ride to the church?"

"I suspect we have no other choice," Adam replied.

As they reached the stable gate, Toby came barking up, jumping on Adam as if trying to express urgency.

"What is it, Toby?" Adam questioned.

Toby started to run up the lane, then dashed back to Adam.

"He wants us to follow him," Adam said. "He may be dumb around porcupines, but otherwise he seems to have a certain amount of intelligence."

"Maybe you should go with the dog," John suggested, "while I go to the church."

"No. We'll stay together," Adam declared. "Let's follow Toby."

Charles had reached the abandoned shay near the wall to Adam's cottage. Uncertain what he should do, he was relieved to see Toby coming toward him.

When Adam and John arrived, Charles quickly explained all that had happened, and how he had not received the telegram early enough to do anything to protect Nellie.

"Since Toby was locked in the closet," Charles speculated, "I'm certain he was put there for a purpose. Obviously Sam Dodsworth carried Nellie from here."

Adam held the reins for Toby to smell. The dog quickly picked up the scent and found Sam's footprints. The men followed the dog down to the beach. Adam was in the lead, Charles in the middle and John brought up the rear.

"What do you hope to gain by all this?" Nellie questioned, trying her best to resist the weight of the man above her.

"Pleasure!" Sam was crouching above her, preparing to kiss her again. She spat. He slapped her face with such force that he nearly knocked her unconscious. His swearing was mixed with licentious laughter. "And I'll *take* my pleasure, too."

A rock struck Sam Dodsworth on the shoulder. He looked up in the direction from which it had come. Seeing the silhouettes of the three men, he got to his feet and pulled the pistol from his belt. He might hit one of them, but the other two would charge him before he reloaded. Frantically he leapt up on a boulder. Toby was behind him, barking.

Saturated with fear of the prison guard dogs, Sam reacted irrationally. He had seen dogs connect their teeth about men's wrists and wrench weapons from them. Jumping to another boulder, he realized the only way he could elude Toby was by going toward the water. Yet he knew that dogs, especially those raised around water, were good swimmers.

Adam was within ten feet of Sam. "You're outnumbered, Dodsworth, give up!"

"I'll not go back to prison!" Sam shouted, half-running as he waded out into the surf. "I'd rather die than return to that hellhole!"

"Why have you done this?" John called. "What did you want of us?"

"Revenge!" Sam yelled at the top of his lungs. "Revenge!" His shriek was punctuated by the sharp report of a gunshot.

"Can you see him, Adam?" John asked, coming up beside him.

"He fell into the water," Adam replied. "I believe he killed himself."

"We must be certain," John said.

Toby had gone out into the water. John waded toward him. Soon the dog returned to his master, Sam's gun in his mouth.

248

In the meantime Charles Mumford had removed his coat and blouse and used them to dress Nellie. Sleeves had to be rolled, but the blouse was some protection to all but her legs. The coat was wrapped around her.

"We've got to get her up to the cottage immediately," Charles advised.

"I'll carry her," Adam volunteered. "You lead the way."

As John was about to join the others, he saw the lifeless bundle of flesh that had been Sam Dodsworth being washed up to shore. A single look told him that Sam was dead.

"Nellie, Nellie," John sobbed as he reached the cottage. Adam caught him to restrain him from going into the bedroom where Charles was examining the girl. "I must go to her."

"Charles will take care of her," Adam said with authority. He held John, bracing his weeping emotional body. "Nellie will be all right. I know she will, John. She was perfectly conscious. But she has been bruised and shaken up."

"No treasure in all the world is worth the life of my daughter," John stated.

Nellie was clad in Adam's burgundy-colored dressing robe. The taste of brandy still burned in her mouth and flamed in her stomach. After John and Adam had each kissed her, she stood limply in the dim lamplight. "I've obviously been through hell."

John held her hand and kissed it. "Forgive me, Nellie, forgive me."

"Oh, Daddy, there's nothing to forgive," Nellie returned. "Right now, all I want is Thad. I need his kind of love and embrace now."

"Thad?" Adam questioned. "Where *is* Thad?"

Fear plunged through Nellie. "He wouldn't have gone to the potluck without me."

"And he wasn't at Phenwick House," Charles inserted, buttoning back into his blouse.

"We must find him!" Nellie exclaimed, dashing from the others and going toward the front of the house. Toby was waiting outside for her.

# Chapter Twenty-three

Nellie was obviously having a premonition. "We must leave the shay here," she instructed. "We must walk back to the house."

Charles tied the horse, then went to join the others as they walked up the lane.

Toby took the lead, then ran back to Nellie.

"Go find, Thadius," Nellie said. "Get Thad!"

Toby barked, bouncing enthusiastically as if he understood. Moments later he was racing up the lane toward the stable.

Thad was not in the stable. A quick search had been made. There were few hiding places.

Toby looked disappointed. But, not to be defeated, he started out again, going toward Phenwick House. The others followed him.

As he reached the cemetery, Toby stopped, held his forefoot in the air and pointed his nose in three directions. He started to go toward the graveyard, then stopped and reversed his aim. A few cautious steps, then an acceleration of speed as he ran to the summerhouse.

By the time the others had reached the skeletonlike structure, Toby was scratching noisily at the cellar door that led to the basement of the former Phenwick House.

Adam was the first to reach the entrance. He raised the door. Charles had carried a lantern from the shay. He held it for Adam to look below. The two men were soon descending the stairs as Nellie held to her father. Toby, too, had gone below.

Thad had been tied with heavy ropes. Most of his sojourn in the old basement had been spent unconscious. When he had come to, he had difficulty realizing where he was or remembering how he got there. Though he appeared basically unharmed, Charles insisted that he examine him thoroughly as soon as they got back to the house.

When word had been called up to Nellie and John that they had found Thad and that he was all right, Nellie wanted to go back to the house, wash, and change into her own clothing. She was certain that Adam and Charles would see to Thad's welfare.

Nellie had changed into a white and lavender gown and had picked pink rose blossoms for her hair. She looked fresh and none the worse for the terror of the experience she had endured.

Adam was waiting outside her room when she appeared. His smile was reassuring. "Thad will be with you shortly, Nellie."

"Is Dr. Mumford still with him?"

"No. John and Charles went to get the shay and horse," Adam replied. "Thad is freshening up for you."

"For me?" Nellie smiled. "Thad *is* for me, isn't he?"

"I thought that was pretty much decided already," Adam stated, laughing through his words. He opened his arms to her.

Nellie went to him. "Oh, Adam, how wonderful you are! I do love you dearly."

"And I love you, too, in a very special way, little Nell," Adam assured her. "I have known many Phenwick women: Joanna, Olivia, Harriet, Nancy, Marcia, Kate, Ilene, Millijoy—ah, Millijoy—Barbara, Ruth, Ophelia—shall I go on? Dorothy, Ann—and now Nellie. I guess I've simply been destined to associate with many Phenwick women."

"I'm not a Phenwick woman yet."

"Oh, but you are, precious Nellie." He laughed. "Sometimes I feel as if I have been delegated by Augusta herself to keep an earthly eye on her chosen women. I pray that you will be the finest of all the Phenwick women."

"And I pray that you—"

"Yes?"

"Will find happiness, Adam, and whatever else you may desire," Nellie said. "I *will* be a significant Phenwick woman—not for Augusta—but for you, Adam."

Adam had led Nellie down the stairs. It was in the entrance hallway that they were joined by Thad. The handsome young man looked radiant, clad in white. If he had suffered from his experience earlier that evening, it did not show.

After a brief exchange of conversation, Adam excused himself.

"Shall we go out into the garden?" Thad asked, his hand wrapped about her arm.

"I think that would be the discreet place for us to be," Nellie replied. "There are stars tonight."

Thad stopped for a moment to pluck a pink rosebud, which he presented to her. During that time, the sound of Nancy and the servants arriving back at the house filtered to where they were. Thad reacted and urged Nellie to hurry out into the darkness.

John and Charles had returned, coinciding with the arrival of the others. John had decided it would be best to explain the entire situation to his wife in private. He took her aside to their room on the second floor.

"Oh, John, it's so nice to have you home," Nancy exclaimed. "But let me tell you about the potluck and all that happened this evening."

"No, my dearest, let me tell *you* about all that happened this evening," John said.

Toby's appreciation of the Greco-Roman statues was not from an artistic interest. Yet he regularly visited them, sniffing around and leaving his impression. From Aphrodite, the dog romped to where Nellie and Thad were standing at the wisteria arbor that overlooked the sea below.

After the young couple acknowledged his presence, Toby curled up on the marble nearby, panted, and, with a look of satisfaction, took a short nap.

"I will always remain close to my father," Nellie said. "My love for him is one thing; my love for you is quite another matter. I can hardly wait for October to get here."

"Nor can I." Thad kissed her. "Unless she decides to go live with any one of my brothers, I'll always stay close to Mother, too. From now on the Phenwicks of Greenfield are going to be important, I'll see to that. The inspiration of your love will propel me to heights of success in all aspects of life."

"Mr. and Mrs. Thadius Phenwick," Nellie sighed. "I have a premonition."

"Another one?"

"That we will be tremendously happy: the Thadius Phenwicks of Greenfield." She laughed and took the initiative to instigate the next sharing kiss. "I love you so very much."

A shadow fell across Adam as he stood on the veranda. The smoke of his thinly shaped cigar circled about his head. All he could see was the white of Thad's clothing and the faint impression of Nellie in the moonlight. The shadow moved closer to him. He threw the cigar butt out onto the lawn.

"Is all well with the young lovers?" the doctor asked.

"Yes, I believe it is," Adam replied. He breathed deeply, and his lungs seemed to fill with the scent of violets. Not mentioning the aroma he perceived, he smiled. "Yes, everything is obviously good."